Alone in the Wind

Judy Bruce

MERRIAM PRESS

FICTION 1

BENNINGTON, VERMONT

2015

First published in 2015 by the Merriam Press

First Edition

ISBN 9781576382950
Library of Congress Control Number: 2015953864
Merriam Press #F1-P

This work was designed, produced, and published in
the United States of America by the

Merriam Press
133 Elm Street Suite 3R
Bennington VT 05201

E-mail: ray@merriam-press.com
Web site: merriam-press.com

My Danny

Other books by Judy Bruce

Death Steppe
Voices in the Wind

Chapter I

MY guts churned as I exited the back door, forcing me to halt in the middle of our brick patio. I'd felt this queasy sense of danger before, so I knew to heed it. I returned to the house, and then emerged a few minutes later with my Glock 42 subcompact shoved into the waistband of my jeans. I checked the battery level of my smart phone as I walked across the plush lawn then stepped onto the curly gray-green buffalo grass that covered the crunchy-dry soil.

At my Uncle Bill's barn a block away, all seemed peaceful. I led my husband Brian's tall palomino, Rohan, to the adjacent pasture and let him loose. My hardy, black quarter horse bobbed his head in anticipation as I drew near to saddle him. Out in the wild country, nobody owned weak-ankled, skittish horses. Before we exited the barn, I took his head in my hands and stared at him until he became still.

"Danger, Gondor. Danger."

I stared at him for a few more moments then I swung myself up onto the saddle, hoping he sensed this was an unusual, possibly perilous outing.

"Danger, Megan," I murmured.

Riding across the jagged ground of western Nebraska, we skirted south of the bluff Big Leo toward the house of the man who tried to kill me.

Yet, the Eldritch house had been vacated last year. The last member of the family, Lew, sold all his family's land, including the house and his small herd of heifers, to my uncle and me. We were pleased to help our friend start a new life as a carpenter. Bill's cowhands cleared out all the furniture in readiness for the demolition of the decrepit home-stead next week. Compelled to check for any squatters on the property, I let Gondor pick his way through the harsh, rocky ground as I guided him northeast.

To the south, Rohan charged through the smooth pasture in contented oblivion, his gold coat shimmering in the sunlight. Once we cleared the rugged, uneven soil, I spurred Gondor to a gallop. Soon, the gray house, long weather-stripped of its white paint, came into view. When we were fifty yards away, I slowed Gondor to a halt. His muscles rippled in anticipation of a longer ride. I stroked his neck until he became still.

"Danger," I said as I walked him forward, my queasiness increasing by the moment.

I checked to make sure my denim jacket covered my gun, which dug into my spine. The dilapidated wood frame house, complete with a rotted and partially collapsed front porch, looked shrunken with tragedy. As I approached the south side of the house, Gondor remained quiet, though the pounding of my heart reverberated through my chest.

Just then, I spotted the glimmer of a truck's chrome rear bumper in the dirt front yard. I yanked us to a halt. A man in a black hoodie and black jeans strode around the corner of the house, his head down.

"Hey!" I yelled. "What are you doing here?"

His head jerked up. "Who the hell are you?"

He looked to be early thirties, about six feet tall, with close-cropped dark hair and a full beard, also trimmed short.

"The owner of this property. You are trespassing."

"Yeah, right," he said as he put his hands on his hips.

In a flash, I swung my leg around, pushed off from the saddle, and landed on the ground. I whipped out my Glock and aimed it at his head, my finger on the trigger and safety.

"Holy shit!" he said. "Take it easy."

"Face down, on the ground. Now!"

ALONE IN THE WIND

"Fine, just cool your jets, princess." He slowly went to his knees but no further, and then returned his hands to his hips akimbo, mistakenly relaxed.

I really wanted to shoot this bastard. With my heart hammering against my chest, I walked behind him and kicked him in the back of his head with my boot heel. His chest smacked into the dirt. With his right arm, he reached to his back, but I stomped on his arm then pulled his gun from the back of his pants. He thrust his arm out to grab me, but I hopped back out of his reach. I tossed his gun behind Gondor.

"Bitch!"

"By law, I may not be entitled to kill you as long as you stay down, but I can maim you—" I swallowed the vulgarities I wanted to add.

I moved my aim to his leg as I tried not to let my hands shake. Sweat trickled down my back. If he tried to grab me, I would fire.

"Sweetheart, you don't have it in you."

"Oh, I bet she does," said a woman's voice.

I whipped my gun toward the front of the house. A woman in a tan Nebraska State Patrol uniform raised her hands.

"She killed a man summer before last, just west of here."

I lowered my gun. "Who is this jerk?"

"DEA," she said.

"I want to see ID. Hey, moron, why didn't you say so? I nearly put one through your skull."

Starting to rise, he froze when I raised my gun toward his head. The jerk respected me now. The State Patrol officer stepped forward and handed me her identification. She smiled at me. My blood pressure began to moderate. Up close, I could see she had freckles to go along with her fair skin and brown hair, tied back in a ponytail. I dropped my gun from eye level to my hip, but kept it pointed at the snake in the dirt.

"Rachel McNeill," she said.

"Thank you. Now will you get his?" I handed her ID back.

He took a black vinyl case from his back pocket and handed it to her. I allowed him to shift to a sitting position.

"He's legit," she said as she handed me the ID.

"Oh, I believe the DEA part," I said. "Now charm school, no way."

She laughed. He scowled. Now that I wouldn't be in a shootout, I was calming down and becoming curious, though I was angry that this idiot nearly forced me to shoot him.

"And you would be Megan Docket Culhane, senior partner at Docket Law Firm."

I nodded then flipped open the case and read out loud: "Reginald John Martin, the Third. Drug Enforcement Agency, Las Vegas, age thirty-three. So, Reggie, what are you doing on my property?"

I tossed the case back to him but made sure it landed in the dirt.

"It's RT," he snapped.

"Fine. I hope you're good at laundry."

He looked down at his shirt, which was a fancy sport shirt, one that's supposed to wick away sweat with a miracle fabric. His black jeans were covered, front and back, with the dirt ground fine by decades of Eldritch boots. He jumped to his feet.

"Give me my gun."

"Get it yourself," I said as I walked over to Gondor.

As I stood by Gondor, RT took a couple of steps toward me but my steed snorted, so he veered toward his gun. Gondor tried to watch him, but I blocked his view. I stroked the white splotch on his forehead shaped like Mozambique. His haunches rippled a moment before he kicked. RT howled and fell with thud.

ALONE IN THE WIND

"You idiot," I said, squelching a grin. "Tell me you didn't just walk behind my horse. You have to pat his rear so he knows where you are."

Officer McNeill laughed so hard she had to wipe her eyes. Chuckling, I tied Gondor to a tree so he could graze. I crept up the rickety front porch steps through the open front door and beheld the scene—creaking wood floors black with filth, dirty walls darkened by cigarette smoke. The railing for the stairway upstairs was loose at the bottom so that it rested on a lower step. I took a quick look around the three upstairs bedrooms. I decided not to inspect the bathroom—the stench of a clogged toilet and a cockroach scurrying across the chipped gray linoleum floor convinced me to go back downstairs. If I was forced to choose, I'd take the pungent manure fumes of the barn to the stink of this house. No wonder Lew abandoned the place a year ago.

DEA. State Patrol. I knew what it meant.

On the north said of the porch, the part that hadn't collapsed, RT was rubbing the outside of his lower left leg.

"It's just bruised," said Officer McNeill.

I nodded. It was time for a different approach. "I assume you two aren't just passing by. We have a problem in the area."

Officer McNeill nodded.

I looked at RT. "Are you undercover?"

"Yeah. I'm a photojournalist researching the Nebraska panhandle."

"Well, you've made it clear that you haven't done your homework. So you're going to need the backing of a few key people."

He huffed. "Like you?"

I ignored him and said, "Officer McNeill, why don't you come for supper and we'll talk about all of this. And bring Prince Charming. Do you know the red brick house on Harney Street?"

"Sure. We'll be there. And call me Rachel."

"What?" RT scowled.

"Oh, you prefer greasy fast food to grilled steaks?"

He snapped his mouth shut. Men were so predictable—sex, food, and beer.

"Six o'clock," I said as I picked my way down the stairs.

As I mounted my stallion and turned him homeward, I looked back at the house and grounds. I assumed the black Toyota Tundra pick up was his, paid for by U.S. taxpayers. In the copse across the street, a hint of metal shone—she was hiding her patrol car. This was serious.

As we worked our way south, the land to the east appeared in a state of repose; high grass, once eaten by free-roaming bison, stretched out in a lazy, verdant expanse. The wind rumbled over the grassland with an incessant rhythm, giving the land its pulse.

After I left Gondor in the barn, the wind intensified, roaring against me as I fought to make my way home. I ducked my head as I trudged forward against the bellowing wind. Was the wind's fury a response to the arrival of the invader? If it meant to warn me of new danger, it was too late. With every footstep I'd taken since I wandered out here as a kid, I made this wild land, this world mine. I meant to protect it.

Back at home, I paused to appreciate the cool breeze blowing through my family's stately, spacious, clean two-story red brick house in the Georgian Revival tradition. The sight of the Eldritch house always cast a heaviness over me. I shook myself out of my doldrums to make the necessary preparations for supper—none of which included cooking. Patty White Horse, my family's loyal friend and my former nanny, and now our housekeeper, began her cooking in earnest. I called Brian, my former Husker linebacker husband of two months, and told him of the plans. He was at his Docket Law Firm office today, though he also had an office in Sidney, a fifteen minute drive to the east. Then I called my Uncle Bill, the robust rancher with whom I shared the Docket land. Finally, I called my next door neighbor and friend, James Wilson, a member of our Harney Street gang. I grew up with his kids and had forged a tight bond to Mrs. Wilson, Beverly, whom I had loved like a mother.

While I was still in law school, Beverly died in a car accident that also killed Bob Eldritch, the patriarch of the family and father to both Lew, our friend, and his brother Salt, the lunatic who had tried to kill me and James two summers ago. I used a steep ditch dubbed Miss Gulch, a steak knife, and rock to kill him. The event brought me a strange sort of notoriety—my clientele now extended into counties even my father, the famous Frank Docket, hadn't forged ties to.

My last phone call went out to Mark "Gus" Gustafson, my law partner. He would miss the meal, but would be out later. As a means of securing my commitment, my father had made me a partner two years ago, even though I was fresh out of law school. Strangely enough, I was now the boss, the senior partner, though Gus was the experienced attorney I hired after my father died last year.

Before our guests arrived, I described in detail the interaction at the Eldritch house to my inner circle. However, when RT arrived, showered and in clean black clothes meant to make him look urban, he presented a more agreeable persona. Despite his nature, he didn't show any disrespect to Patty, who was three-fourths Oglala Lakota Sioux, or to James, who was African American. Rachel drove up in a red Subaru, now wearing civilian clothes, navy slacks and a silky crimson blouse. After meeting Brian, Bill, and Patty, she smiled at James.

"Mr. Wilson, how are you?"

Nobody needed to smack us over the head for us to figure out that Rachel must have been one of the investigating officers at the fatal accident in which James and Bob Eldritch were driving.

"Fine, fine, thank you, Officer McNeill."

The meal was comprised of small talk and big steaks. After supper, Gus arrived and we moved to the family room to digest, drink the traditional Docket bourbon, and stir up the nitty-gritty. RT was annoyed that I exposed his cover at the start, but I explained that he needed a few people who could confirm his story. Gus pointed out that he would want connections to people who could report suspicious activity directly to him. He and Rachel passed out their business cards to us. I asked about the extent of meth in the area.

"Oh, we're just beginning our investigation," he said.

I glanced at Rachel. She deferred to RT, but looked like she was ready to talk. So I looked at her when I asked, "Do you think the meth is coming in from Mexico or is it being made in the area?"

"Well—"

RT cut her off. "Oh, it could be either, but it's most likely being made in the area."

Rachel turned to him but said nothing.

He was lying.

"That's why I've been searching for a place somewhere in this area," he continued. "We don't know who the leader is, but we think he or she is somewhere around here."

My uncle, who had seemed deep in thought and less genial than normal, looked up at RT and said, "So that's why you're lookin' to hide out at the Eldritch ranch."

"Yes, sir. If that's possible."

Bill looked at me and I nodded.

"Well, I think we could delay demolition for a bit," he said. "The plumbing doesn't work, except in the kitchen and hall toilet. You'll need to shower elsewhere."

"You pay for utilities and rent," I said. "I'm sure you receive a government allowance. You won't be able to stay in the house until tomorrow, so that I have time to draw up a contract and disclaimer for any injury you might suffer in that pit. You won't have water and electricity until Monday."

RT shrugged. "I'm getting a gym membership in Sidney...I can shower there."

"And I see no reason for you to access the barn."

Something flashed in his expression then he quickly said, "Oh, that's fine. Don't need it."

"That will remain locked. Not that locks have stopped you before."

His color rose a bit and we stared at each other for a few moments. He would make a lousy poker player.

After they left, my brainy blond stud said, "Well, I didn't think he seemed that bad."

I loved my husband with every ounce of my being, but he was not a good judge of character. He needed to stick with his columns of figures and tax forms. Still, I didn't see the point in arguing—it would all play out. But for now, we collectively pondered the tragic news for our community.

Later that evening, I stood atop Rufus, the low hill just north of our house, as the stars began to prick the twilight. For me this land meant the pioneer games of childhood, the ridges and mounds of rock, the thunderstorms without rain, the eerie sounds of cries and whispers, the harsh majesty of earth undefiled, and the presence of wind, always the wind. Yet now a sense of disquietude began to spread through my body. I had entangled myself in something that made me shudder. I knew trouble was ahead and I went to meet it with a gun. What did that say about me? Where would it lead me?

Danger smelled like gunpowder and hay.

What? That didn't make any sense.

When I returned to the house, I finished my bourbon to fight off the chill of premonition.

Chapter 2

I was odd. The people who really knew me would agree. I sensed things other people didn't, like last summer when I knew from two blocks away that my father had a heart attack, or when I felt my twin's death. And I have a knack for finding trouble, so I've been told. But on this Saturday afternoon, a week after my encounter with RT and Rachel, I was simply enjoying a picnic lunch with Brian near the Raccoon Creek. I had been coming out to this scraggily, worthless area north of the Docket family house since my father brought me out here from Omaha when I was a toddler. We lounged under the cottonwoods that hugged the banks on both sides; the creek flowed southward through Docket land past Highway 51, a quarter mile to the west.

"No, better not," said Brian declining a second beer. "I plan to work through to supper in our study and turn off my phone."

"I hope you plan to take a break this evening," I said. "You're going to fry your brains."

He smiled, I loved that smile. When he laughed his brown highbrows arched upwards. With him, I knew what love meant. He was a gift I could keep forever. Truly, he was a wonderful hunk of man—tall, kind, brainy, and muscular, he spoke in a smooth baritone voice; when he softened it I wanted to rip off his shirt and meld into his heat. I leaned toward him and we kissed. Just as his hand touched my cheek, we heard it—the sound of metal hitting something hard. It wasn't close, but the ever-present wind brought it to us. We jerked and looked west.

"The highway," said Brian.

In a flash, I threw everything into the picnic basket. Brian grabbed it and I scooped up the blanket. We ran as hard as we could along the creek then scrambled up the ridge that blocked our view of the highway. Two cars were stopped in the road southbound and a northbound pickup was parked crosswise to block traffic. We picked our way over the rocky top of the crest, and then scooted down the slope, scattering rocks and kicking up dirt, toward a white commercial pickup that must have gone off the northbound lane and down the embankment. It was smashed up against one of the concrete supports for the bridge over the creek. The entire front end was scrunched up like an accordion.

I gasped. "God in heaven," I muttered as I dropped the blanket and slid down the bank behind Brian.

The people from the vehicles stopped on the highway were also making their way to the truck. I couldn't see anybody from the crashed pickup as the load of wood beams and metal fencing poles was smashed up against the back window. Troff Construction was printed on the side of the front door. Brian reached the passenger side door, which was buckled, then ran around the back of the truck.

I paused to look in the window, which was halfway down and shattered. A man was slumped over the steering wheel. No one was tending to him. He must be dead. It felt like a hand grasped my neck, for it was suddenly hard to breathe. I took a step back and gulped air as the ground seemed to move under me. I forced myself to stick my head back inside the window and look for details. His dark hair was matted against his head and the back of his tan jacket was streaked in blood. Lord above, so much blood—it made my stomach pitch and roil. The chemicals from the air bags stung my nostrils. The rear window was cracked and punctured on the passenger side. Blood covered the back of the passenger seat and the headrest. Something wasn't right, in fact, it was all wrong. Where was the passenger?

ALONE IN THE WIND

On the other side of the truck, people from the stopped traffic were gathering around Don Troff, who was sitting on the ground holding his left arm. His coat was free of blood, though I saw that his hands were bloody. His older brother, Delmer Troff, who owned Troff Construction with Don, drew Don's shoulders back so that his brother lay on the ground. That was probably Delmer's truck stopped on the highway; he must have been following Don on their way to a worksite. Don kept muttering as Brian knelt next to the stout man. Both brothers had thick bellies with bald spots on the crowns of their heads that made them look like medieval monks. Delmer had thin arms and legs, and looked like the brother who spent his time behind a desk.

A siren sounded from the town to the south. Knowing it would be Police Chief Ray Dobbs, I quickly put in a call to Rachel. I then stepped over to Harold Gush, who stood beside the open door of the crunched pick up.

"Jake Breeley. He's dead." Harold shook his head and looked down.

"Did anyone touch him?" I asked.

"No, Brandon and me were the first ones down here."

"What did you see?"

"We were a good half mile away when we saw the truck go off the road. From the top of the hill, I saw Don look up at us then he shut this door and sat down on the ground. Brandon called the police and said we needed an ambulance."

"Did you hear a second door close?"

"No."

"Thank you. Now would you and your son try to keep people from walking on the tire tracks? I suppose you've seen enough blood for now."

He nodded then walked with his son up the hill. As Chief Dobbs descended the slope, he stepped right on the tracks. What a screw-up. I wished Rachel would get here. A siren alerted me to the approach of an ambulance, which looked like the one my uncle and I rode in after his house got hit by a tornado two years ago. Soon, two State Patrol cars parked on the highway. Brian walked up beside me.

"He's busted his arm, I think," said Brian. "He's saying that the driver, Jake, he calls him, just drove off the road for no reason."

"He's lying."

Brian looked puzzled, but didn't say anything. He walked back to the crushed truck. I skirted the approach of the town bully, Chief Dobbs, a thin, short man, with a bow-legged walk, to meet Rachel as she came down the hill.

From a distance I called out, "Officer McNeill." Up close, I said, "Rachel, keep an open mind. I'm sure you'll spot the lie. And I recommend you send Dobbs on an errand…he's already walked on the vehicle's tire tracks."

"Oh, brother." Rachel turned and introduced me to Troopers Merritt and Waters, big men with crew cuts and thick necks.

I backed away as the three officers took over the scene. Dobbs was charged with clearing people away. I was soon joined by Brian and town Deputy Bo Schnitzel, Dobb's opposite in every way. Bo was a lanky, mild-mannered, thin-faced man of thirty-five years. He was good at calming the rowdies at the Cowpoke, our local tavern. His slow-talking manner made some people think he was slow-witted—I knew better. We discussed what I had seen and Brian had heard. Bo nodded.

After a brief interview by Rachel, Don Troff was taken away by the ambulance. Jake remained in the vehicle. Officer Waters interviewed witnesses while Officer Merritt poked around the cargo bed behind the passenger seat. Rachel began taking photographs of the interior of the cab. They had figured it out.

"Someone will need to tell Joy," said Bo.

"Oh, Lord," I muttered, sincerely hoping for divine help.

Brian left to find Bill, while Bo and I sat in the grass. Onlookers were forced to leave the scene as the final area photographs were taken and measurements were made. A tow truck idled on the road above us. In time, Rachel came to talk to us. I introduced Bo to her.

"Megan," she began, "I have taken into consideration your opinion...though I'm not at liberty to divulge mine."

"Don't you think it's interesting that the truck is set in reverse?"

Rachel stared at me. She walked a few steps away and made a call on her cell phone. Officer Merritt walked down the hill to the truck.

"And that passenger door is so buckled, I bet it doesn't even open," I said. "Don is a bit thick to get through a cracked, half-open window. And I'm sure you'll be getting a blood test on Mr. Troff. For someone who didn't seem to have a head injury, he was babbling a great deal."

"Yes, Ms. Docket...er, Culhane. Thank you," said Rachel.

My name legally changed to Culhane when I married, but nearly everyone still referred to me as Megan Docket. I hadn't even changed the name on my office door or ordered new office stationery with the name change.

"My pleasure, Officer McNeill." She was pissed I had spotted a bit of key evidence she missed.

"Officer, I think we ought to be telling his wife before someone else does," said Bo. "I'd be willing to go, if Megan went with me."

I swallowed hard. Joy was a friend; her younger sister had been a classmate of mine. I nodded in agreement, though I would've preferred a root canal.

The Breeley house was located on Hickory Street, a couple of blocks south of my office. The home was a modest, white A-frame with a front porch and a single car lane and garage. Jake's silver Jeep Laredo was parked in the driveway. White tulips were sprouting in front of two yews in the mulched triangle next to the porch. When Joy opened the door to us, her smile indicated she had not been told the news. Double shit. I wished I was making love to Brian on our blanket near the creek or even riding Gondor across a field, any field. I wished I was anywhere but here, sitting on her sofa, telling a friend that her husband was dead, but that I suspected Don Troff had been driving and had pulled Jake over to the driver seat.

Joy cried for a bit, brushed her brown bangs off her face, then began to think. "So, Don is at fault and I need to sue him."

"Well, you will want to assert a claim. Most accidents are settled out of court."

"Megan, will you help me? You make the claim. I don't want to talk to anyone. My God, I've got to tell the girls." She broke into a new round of sobs. I promised to help her then handed her more tissues while my intestines knotted up.

After Bo drove me home, I didn't even go inside the house, I walked straight out to the hills behind our house. I crested Rufus then traversed the pathways through the Seven Dwarfs, a series of five rocky-topped mounds. I sat down at the base of one of the dwarfs and felt the warm sun on my face and reflected. Jake Breeley dead. Poor Joy. Fortunately, she had parents, a sister, and two brothers to help her get through it. Jake was a decent guy, but his younger brothers were numskulls and former classmates of mine. Jake had claimed the heart of Joy Jefferson when he and Joy were high school seniors. He was smart enough to propose before he lost Joy to college, where she should have gone.

Most of my classmates had left town for jobs or college, to return only for Thanksgiving or Christmas. Brian and I were exceptions; then again, we benefitted from our names and connections—Brian as a former Husker with family in nearby Sidney, me as the daughter and protégé of the Frank Docket, Esquire. Swamped with business, I possessed success I never could have achieved as a nobody from Omaha. A half hour ago, I landed my first fatality case. I would've chosen to go my whole life without one. Yes, the size of my contingency fee would be substantial, perhaps the largest of my life; yes, I wanted to keep the case to make sure it was handled properly so Joy and her girls received appropriate compensation; yes, the monetary value of a man's life was often difficult to prove, but money was the only means we possessed to try and make the family "whole." Last year my father and my brother died— I can't say that life insurance benefits and the helm of a law firm made me feel complete.

As I wandered northward, I knew most people would look at this land and see nothing but scraggily wasteland. We owned acres of fertile pastureland, but these rugged miles to the north of our house possessed no value—except as the playground of my youth and the place where I still wondered at its eerie, forceful nature.

I heard voices in the wind.

Those close to me knew it. Growing up, I heard the voices of a woman and a young boy. Sure, I thought I was nuts at times. Then, one night I felt as if I was having a heart attack. In time, I discovered the truth—the young man was my disabled twin brother who died of the heart attack I felt; and the woman's voice was that of my mother, who was alive despite the lies I was told regarding her death. My father was a great attorney, but also the cold-hearted man who had torn apart the family and let me live in a lie to keep me from returning to my mother and discovering my brother. God had given me the strength to forgive; I salvaged a relationship with my mother, did my utmost to maintain the good name of my father, and kept the secrets of my family from the gossip of Cheyenne County.

I roused myself and went home. Patty, Bill, and James were waiting for me. They knew better than to go hunt for me out in the wild part of the Docket land, even though I hadn't ventured far. I sat down hard at the kitchen table as they studied me.

"You've had a powerful shocker," said James, "so I brought this over." He placed a bottle of his brandy on the kitchen table.

I nodded as Bill set four glasses on the table then poured us each a small portion.

"A dead man and a weeping widow," I said just before I downed a swig then felt the heat coarse through my chest and arms.

Bill poured me another portion. Brian joined us and drank his allotment.

"Brian told me what you figured out," said Bill. "But Don was never a liar."

"He just panicked," I said. In truth, I thought it was devious and cowardly to push the blame on his innocent passenger.

Bill was quiet for a few moments. "I don't get why the truck was in reverse."

"Well, a driver wouldn't be trying to shift the car or do anything so mindless—especially not a dead one. No, it got knocked out of drive when Don dragged Jake from his seat to the driver's."

My uncle looked stricken, so I didn't add that it was a clumsy attempt at deceit. Had Don succeeded, he could have asserted an injury claim. It made me sick to think that he could have made money off his own deadly driving error.

After supper, I called Rachel and asked about Don's blood test.

"It was positive," she said, "but I can't tell you for what."

"You mean it's not just for booze? You mean to tell me it was meth?"

"I can't affirm that."

"But you're not denying it either."

She was silent.

"Well, you can tell me this. Who is the insurance company for Troff Construction?"

"State Farm."

"Ah, hell. I do a lot of work for them. But I'll be on the other side...Joy Breeley hired me this afternoon."

"RT is pissed," she said.

No shit. "He's put up a failing grade so far."

Chapter 3

MONDAY morning I rose early, as I usually did, went for a run, and was in the office before my dark, shoulder-length hair dried. I was wearing my favorite outfit—a charcoal gray wool pantsuit with enough silk in the fabric to give it a sheen to go along with my burgundy silk blouse. I composed a letter to State Farm advising them of my representation of Joy Breeley. At this point, all they would have was Don's statement that he was the passenger, so my letter would kick their investigation into hyper drive. I then worked on an irrevocable insurance trust for the Reinhardt family of Potter, a village to the north, and then perused the interrogatories I'd received on a tractor-trailer accident from Kimball, a town to the west.

At nine o'clock, I received a call from Beulah Shuster, one of my favorite people. Bear Lake Beulah, an eccentric spinster and a loyal Docket family friend, had brewed root beer on an island in the Minnesota-Manitoba border water region for over twenty years. At seventy-three, she had settled in as the face of Custer's, a local diner owned by her nephews, Dane and Blaine Shuster.

"This is the big day," Beulah said. "We're gonna try out Davey at the diner bussin' tables and washin' dishes. Do you think you and Brian could come by early for lunch?"

I hadn't seen Davey Shuster in several years. He was the younger of Blaine and Barb Shuster's two children. Davey had been attending special needs classes in Sidney for as long I could remember. Profoundly autistic, yet of normal intelligence, he was shy and socially awkward. I promised Beulah that we'd come then I did a quick bit of research on autism, which was a neurological disorder adversely affecting social skills and communication, both expressive and receptive. In short, the wiring in his brain was out of whack.

At eleven o'clock, Brian and I arrived at Custer's diner, a golden brick building with a limestone façade, on Elm Street, our main drag. Co-owner Dane Shuster, divorced a dozen years ago, lived in the converted offices on the second floor. As Beulah led us to our customary booth, Davey walked by the unoccupied tables with a gray tub, looking for dishes to collect. When I smiled at him, he dropped his chin into his chest in response. Tall and skinny, his sandy-brown hair was trimmed short. He possessed a youthful face for twenty-one years, one that rarely needed shaving, and a blank look that relaxed his face when he walked past empty booths.

"Shy is right," whispered Brian.

"He was in a vocational program in Sidney," said Beulah. "We thought we'd give him a try here. We told him he's only supposed to talk about the weather, but it might be awhile 'fore he talks at all."

We watched Davey walk back into the kitchen with the empty tub.

"We'll make sure you get lots of dishes to dirty. Say, terrible thing about Jake Breeley drivin' off the road like that. Died bloody from what I heard."

"Yes, he died bloody," I said. "But he wasn't the driver—Don was. He moved Jake to the driver seat before anybody could get to the scene."

Beulah's eyebrows arched and she rubbed her chin with her thin, veiny hand.

"Brian and I were at the scene soon after the crash. The evidence is a mile high."

"I don't doubt ya. Not a bit."

As I didn't ask that the information be kept in confidence, I predicted it would spread faster than a drought-year grass fire.

ALONE IN THE WIND

"By the way, have you seen a new guy around here? Brown hair, early thirties?"

"Yeah, been seein' him for a while now. Has breakfast with that State Patrol officer. Always makin' jokes about hicks and this bein' nowhere like he's Mr. New York."

"That's him," I said. "And he says he's a photojournalist, right?"

"Yeah, somethin' like that."

"He's DEA. But you don't need to tell anyone that. Just keep your eyes and ears open even wider than normal."

"Heh. Undercover cop. Drugs. That sounds bad."

"And you just blew his cover," said Brian.

"I nearly blew off his head when we first met. He's dangerous. I don't trust him."

Davey came out of the kitchen with his tub. I downed my coffee and placed the cup at the edge of the table. Brian did likewise.

"What about that State Patrol officer?" asked Beulah.

"Rachel McNeill. She's okay."

Davey stopped at our table. Beulah nodded to him.

"Okay to take?" asked Davey.

Beulah nodded to him.

"Yes, thank you, Davey," I said.

He took my cup and placed it in his tub, and then looked at Brian.

"Yes, thanks."

He took Brian's cup then moved along the rest of the booths, at the same, unhurried pace. He looped around the edge of the tables and headed back to the kitchen muttering.

"Yes, thank you, Davey. Yes, thank you, Davey."

We both looked to Beulah.

"He does that sometimes. Hears somethin' and just gets to repeatin' it."

Beulah shuffled away, but honored us with one of her Queen Elizabeth waves. We laughed, like always.

We finished our salads and sandwiches then talked about Brian's invitation to a Husker football convention at a resort in Colorado.

"It's a kick-off party for the upcoming season," he said.

"Do you know the exact date?" I asked.

"Hmmm. I think it starts the tenth or eleventh of August. I'll check. We'll have a blast."

It was now nearing the lunch hour and people were starting to fill up the tables and booths. Davey emerged from the kitchen with his tub, but stopped when he saw the new arrivals. He slowly backed up through the doors to the kitchen. Beulah shuffled over to our table.

"Guess that's it for today," she said.

When I returned to my office, I discovered Paul Ritter, a client and owner of the local hardware store, waiting for me. He apologized for dropping in without an appointment, so I told him it wasn't a problem and we went into my office. Across my cherry wood desk, I watched him fidget before he could come to the point. He cleared his throat and rubbed his palms together. His skinny legs began to bounce with nervousness.

"Sheila says she wants to drop the divorce," he finally said. "Kayla is not as happy as I thought she'd be. She says her mom's being 'weird' and 'moody' and those are her words. Now doesn't that seem strange to you? A teenager calling her mother moody?"

"It does," I said. "What do you think about dropping the divorce?"

"At first, I woulda been thrilled."

"But..."

"Now I'm not so sure. Not sure at all. I went to counseling, but she refused. So, I don't see what's gonna be different." He scratched the scraggily goatee on his chin, reminding me that not all men should grow facial hair.

"What do you want?"

"Well, I don't miss all the tension, all the fightin', and I don't really mind livin' in the back of the store. Kayla says it feels like we're camping. So last weekend I put up a tent and shoved her air mattress inside then I put out a couple of old duck decoys. She thought it was a hoot."

"I think you're a fun dad. And that means a lot to her."

"She still goes to counseling, but she says she likes talkin' to you better, 'cause you don't lecture her."

"Oh, I have. Maybe it just didn't seem like it."

"Even Sheila is pleased you got her talkin' again, and it takes a lot to please her."

"I haven't received notice from her attorney that the divorce decree has been withdrawn." I studied him and then my pen for a few moments. "Maybe if you hold off returning to her, you can find out if she's serious. It might even persuade her to go to counseling."

He intertwined his big-knuckled fingers and sighed. He dropped his chin into his chest as he pondered the situation. His brown hair was thinning on top. Slumping in the chair, his soft midsection pressed against the arms of the chair as his gut spilled over his belt. Neither he nor the frazzled Sheila with her frizzy hair, were prime candidates for the attention of others. He made me appreciate Brian.

"Oh, and can Kayla drop by this afternoon?" he asked.

"I have a three o'clock appointment, but Glenda can feed her if she has to wait."

Glenda was the firm's receptionist and my old second grade teacher, bored in her retirement. Last fall her hair style changed from lavender-gray poofy curls to a styled short cut in silver that made her look like Judi Dench. Her new mission in life was to make great coffee and provide homemade pastries for the firm's occupants—me, Gus, Brian, and Melanie, our paralegal—and to anyone who stepped into our office, a ranch style house that my father had converted into offices.

I looked across my desk at the soft, heartbroken man in front of me. Sometimes only a thin line existed between giving legal advice and playing psychologist. I resolved to do even more to help Kayla. Once Paul left, I alerted Glenda that Kayla would be by in the afternoon.

"Oh, that poor dear. I'll make sure I have a strawberry shake ready for her. She loves those, as you know. Shall I whip up a chocolate one for you, Megan?"

"Thank you, Glenda, shakes will be fine."

Perhaps I was in a grace period, but I wasn't soft. I'd keep working out to make sure I stayed that way. At my height, if I became obese, I'd look like a bowling ball. In the meantime, I'd continue to enjoy Glenda's sugar-laden delights once or twice a week. Glenda scurried away as I prepared to immerse myself in the Hadley bankruptcy case.

At three, Charles "Chuck" Hadley entered with a cream cheese pastry and a cup of coffee. Despite my questions, I could never determine how this man had gone into such debt. It was if the money evaporated. I sensed deceit permeated and befuddled his life.

After Chuck left, Kayla entered with Glenda close behind her carrying two shakes. Kayla, age thirteen, tucked her long blonde hair behind her ears and drank her shake. She seemed to have trouble with what she wanted to say; instead, she stopped drinking and began to bite her lips. When I wheeled my chair over to the window and started sipping my shake, she brought her chair over. We chatted about some of the middle school kids who were walking by on their way home from school. Kayla was trim, unlike her parents, yet she was also out of shape, a fact I discovered when she struggled to climb Big Leo, the bluff north of my home. I resolved to help her with her fitness; she'd get no help at home.

She stopped drinking and clenched the arm of her chair till her knuckles turned white.

"Emily Breeley is a friend of mine. We're not, like, close, but we hang out in the same group."

Oh, help, she'd be wanting gems of wisdom now.

"I don't know what to say to her."

I considered then said, "You don't need to say anything. She's in shock right now, so she may not say much. Just be there ready to listen if she wants to talk. It will mean a great deal to her. You could take her a shake or something."

"She likes chocolate, like you." Kayla smiled.

"Some of her friends will avoid her because they don't know what to say. Don't be one of them. She won't be expecting magic words from you. Just listen. Just be there."

Kayla nodded. "Do you think Glenda would make a couple of shakes for me tomorrow?"

"I know she would."

She started twisting her fingers through the belt loop of her jeans.

"How's your mom doing?"

Kayla shrugged, looked down at her sneakers, and then looked up at me as if she suddenly remembered I was from a broken home, too. "Sometimes I think she's nuts. It's like she doesn't make sense one day...then she's okay the next."

"These are tough times for her. What does she do to make herself feel better?"

"Mmm. Watches a lot of TV. That's really all she does. Never reads anymore. She doesn't even go visit her friends like she used to."

"Does she drink?" I asked, hoping the answer was no.

"There's some beer cans in the fridge my dad left, but she never drinks those."

I waited while she seemed to be lost in thought. In time, she turned and looked at the clock on the wall.

"I better go do my chores. I got a test tomorrow...so I gotta do that, too."

"I'll make sure Glenda has those shakes for you tomorrow. By the way, I'm the attorney for the family regarding the car accident."

"But I thought Mr. Breeley was driving...wasn't he?"

"Not in my opinion."

"But everybody is saying he was...oh...wait. Something wasn't right."

"Not from what I saw. We'll see what the State Patrol says. But the facts of the accident aren't what Emily will want to talk about."

"Okay," she said, as if I had all the answers.

She was a sweet girl, though wrong about me, but I was trying.

The next morning, I was on the docket for a trial in Sidney at the Cheyenne County Courthouse. That idiot Police Chief Ray Dobbs had given Carlos Hernandez a ticket for exceeding the speed limit by three mph on Elm Street. Carlos was the town mechanic and a family friend. He kept my white Acura SUV, "The Great White Shark" in good condition. And he was tired of the years of crap he had taken from Dobbs. So I found a case my father handled in which he challenged the accuracy of the police speed gun, then I subpoenaed the testing records for the radar gun, intending to challenge Dobbs.

At the trial, Judge Dean Shelton dismissed the speeding charge, citing the evidence of the gun's lack of testing and prior mechanical failures. The verdict's affect on Dobbs was colorful—his face turned tomato red, his crooked nose nearly glowed, and purple veins bulged in his neck above his collar. It was another loss to another Docket.

I caught up with Dobbs in the courthouse hallway. He turned to me, angry and humiliated, though his neck veins had receded.

"Chief, that was a victory I didn't want," I said. "I don't like it when people challenge authority. And I don't want people to think they can avoid responsibility and fight everything you do."

"Well, you're making them think they can now go speeding in town whenever they want."

"I'll make a deal with you. You buy the new radar gun you need, and then get it tested regularly as it should. You provide me with that documentation and I'll never challenge you again."

"What about Gustafson?"

"Gus won't take a case like it either. I'll even make sure Stan Spurlock is advised. But you get that new gun and get it soon."

As I drove back to Dexter, I gloated in my victory over that incompetent butthead. I would stay good to my word, but that didn't wipe the smile off my face.

At lunch, Brian and I were joined by Patty and James, each taking a long lunch to meet Davey. He kept making his rounds at his unvarying pace, maintaining a rigid, thorough routine when he cleared off a table, always collecting the flatware last and cleaning the left booth first. We tried to dirty as many dishes as possible, for he seemed pleased when he could be of service. At the end of the meal, I ventured a question.

"Davey, how warm will it get today?"

His face brightened. "The Weather Channel indicates a high of sixty-two degrees Fahrenheit with a southwest wind of fifteen to twenty miles per hour. Chance of rain tonight will be zero."

We smiled and nodded.

Brian asked, "What will be tonight's low?"

"Forty-five degrees will be our low tonight."

"Good sleeping weather," James said.

Davey seemed to ponder his opinion, then he picked up a plate, set it in his tub and left. As he completed his route we heard him say, "Good sleeping weather. Good sleeping weather."

Just then, RT and Rachel sat down at the table next to our booth. We exchanged greetings.

RT said, "I wonder if Forest Gump will bring us some water."

I felt a growl in my throat.

"Don't be a jerk," said Rachel to RT.

"Oh, he didn't hear it," he said. "But I still want some water."

Patty muttered, "Maybe you should have shot him."

Beulah stood at the counter, fuming.

"Good thing Beulah isn't toting a gun in her apron," murmured James.

While most of my table glanced over to Beulah, I noticed that RT had wrapped his feet around Rachel's ankles. She had been coming over to our house on occasion after her shift. She was disappointed our poker games didn't involve betting money. She was a good player, so it was a blessing for the rest of us. She even borrowed my copy of *Les Miserables*. I told her it was a great story, but she'd learn more about the ancient sewer systems of Paris than any person needed to know. Like geometry, Victor Hugo's detailing of the Parisian culverts had little application in daily life. Still, Rachel said it was a great way to pass the time on stakeouts she knew would be fruitless. Now that I discovered she was intimate with that snake, it made my insides roil with disgust.

Davey failed to emerge from the kitchen for the rest of our meal. No doubt, Beulah held him back. If RT hadn't been federal police, she probably would have kicked him out. Knowing Beulah, as soon as RT left, she'd make sure everyone in the diner knew the phony journalist had mocked Davey. She'd point out that he never carried a camera and the only stories he could tell were tall tales. That klutz just made a powerful enemy.

Chapter 4

FTER I left Custer's, I decided it was an ideal time to snoop around the old Eldritch property. Given that RT hadn't even been served when I left, I figured I would have at least a half hour to check our family property. Approaching the house this time didn't give me that heart-pounding feeling of peril I experienced the last time, but I still felt uneasy. First, I checked the barn. The lock was secure and no signs of anyone's presence, such as footprints or tire tracks, were visible. Though the paint had long ago worn off, Bill said the building was structurally sound; he thought he could use it after a few repairs and a new roof. The barn had two double-wide doors and an upper floor rear opening for, well, different reasons, I suppose. As a kid, I recalled cowhands dumping bales of hay into the back of a truck. But the lack of a rear main floor door was a fire hazard; I would insist one be installed and the barn painted as soon as it could be arranged.

RT must intend to use only the main front room of the house, for it contained his air mattress and an electric heater. For safety purposes, Bill and I decided not to turn on the gas, so the heater was necessary for the cool April nights, though it was still in the box. No bed linens or clothing were stored in the room or anywhere else in the stinky house. He sure wasn't sleeping here. He had swept the floors and made a minimal attempt to clean the kitchen. The refrigerator contained only Budweiser and Pepsi. It struck me that repairs to the barn would be a good way to keep tabs on RT. Back at my office, I called Bill to discuss plans for the barn. He said he could get Lew and maybe a couple of his hands working on it next week.

On Friday night, we attended a birthday party for Beulah at her brown brick house on Benson Street across from the law firm. The guests included some oldsters, but mostly we were an odd bunch, namely me, Brian, Bill, James, Patty, Marva Gush, our local Avon lady, Lew Eldritch, Gus, Glenda, Melanie, and an eclectic assortment of neighbors, who popped in and out for cake and punch. In the presence of so many people, Davey was nervous, stiff, and quiet; meanwhile, Lew was nervous, fidgety, and quiet. Beulah showed off her new retriever puppy I had given her. She named him Buddy, after the last dog she kept in her border waters shack. She also raved about my victory over Chief Dobbs in court.

Brian was tired, so we left early. We had parked in the law firm lot behind the building. Just as we reached the Shark, we heard tires screech then a crunch of metal against something solid. We glanced at each other.

"Not again," said Brian.

On the next block, we beheld the front end of an old blue Chevy pickup smashed up against a street light pole, steam hissing from the contorted engine. A short man climbed out of the truck and stared for a few moments at the damage. I put up my hand to keep Brian from calling out to the man. The man staggered away from the truck, looking around to see if anyone saw him. I backed Brian behind a yew just in time. The man's unsteadiness made me wonder if he hit his head or if he was drunk or both. He ran between two houses.

"Wasn't that Chief Dobbs?" asked Brian.

"And I bet the old drunk claims his truck was stolen," I said.

"Shouldn't we do something?"

"Yes, we leave and tell no one what we've seen."

I now held an ace in my hand—I'd find just the right time to play it.

A week later, as I discussed the advantages of a living will to Gordon and Lois Demkowski, our librarian, yelling came from the lobby. I excused myself and opened the door. Don Troff was unleashing a string of profanities and some garbled declaration that he was not a liar. I wasn't surprised he was upset, for the State Patrol finally charged him with motor vehicle homicide. Brian grabbed Don Troff by his hayseed shirt collar and backed him against the front wall. When he drew his fist back, Don cowered and whined something unintelligible. Brian let him go and Don slid to the floor. I winked at Brian, who I knew had no intention of hitting Don. I walked up to where Don sat on the floor. It was an unusual opportunity to talk down to someone, since my height only exceeded that of most fourth graders.

"Don, if you have a problem, you take it up with your attorney or your claims rep—she's conceded liability," I said. "Come back to this building again and I'll have you arrested for assault and trespassing. Now get out."

Brian and Gus helped him out the front doors. I worked at calming Glenda till Melanie took over so I could go back to my clients.

"Thanks, Gus. Maybe we should file a report."

"I'll call Bo," he said.

However, it was Chief Dobbs who showed up a few minutes later. Having finished with the Demkowskis, who had flattered me by dressing in their Sunday best for our appointment, I asked Glenda to show Dobbs to my office. I met him at the door then closed it behind him.

"Listen, Megan—" he started.

"No, you listen to me. You keep Don Troff away from here. Otherwise, I might recall seeing a drunk stumbling away from the truck he crashed on Sprague Street. Yes, I know you've told everyone that the truck was stolen, but I know the truth—I saw the truth."

His face reddened and he sputtered instead of speaking.

"Don't worry, I don't intend to tell anyone. Good day." I opened the door.

After staring at me for a few moments, he stomped out.

Several weeks passed. Brian and I began to make plans for the Husker football convention in August. Davey continued to give us daily weather reports, though he rarely spoke to anyone but me and my lunch gang. I checked in with Joy Breeley occasionally, but she seldom wanted to talk. Then one Friday afternoon in mid-May, she called. I offered to come see her on Saturday and she agreed. My mother was also coming from Omaha to visit for a few days.

At noon, I picked up Joy, and her daughters, Emily, age thirteen, and Chelsea, age nine. They were dark haired like their late father, and shy of me, but sweet. Chelsea often grasped her mother's arm as if she needed the reassurance of her mom's life and warmth. It always brought a lump to my throat, so I usually looked away. I was supposed to be the one strong enough to fix what I could—they did not want to see me cry.

They climbed into the Shark for a destination unknown to them. I picked up Kayla on the way, which made Emily brighten and actually speak. In planning our outing, I considered driving out to the creek, but the thought of marring the wild land with tire tracks repulsed me. So Brian hauled our basket and cooler out to the creek. We ate our sandwiches and drank our Bear Lake Beulah root beer in the shade of the cottonwoods along the Raccoon Creek.

While the girls splashed their feet in the creek, which ran low due to our drought, Joy and I discussed the deteriorating family finances. Joy worked part-time at the Sidney Walgreens, but she couldn't possibly support herself and her girls on her salary. The bills were piling up. Without Jake's wages, she was even more afraid of a medical emergency. As with most people without health insurance, she was one medical disaster away from bankruptcy and fore-closure. A trip to the dentist was out of the question. She was upset that neither girl would be able to continue dance classes at a studio in Sidney next fall. Grief and stress weighed heavily on her; she often dropped her chin into her chest, even while she spoke. The Cheyenne County bank set up a fund for her; the Dexter community and the people from the surrounding area made impressive contributions, especially since many people were in precarious financial straits due to the worsening drought. But that money would soon run out. Nothing she said surprised me; in fact, her complaints played right into my hopes and plans.

"Now, Joy," I said, "I'll do everything I can to help you, but I want to ask something from you."

She gave me a bewildered look, as if I missed the extent of her plight.

"You see, my paralegal, Melanie, is up to her eyeballs in work. She's taken on more responsibility and also helps Brian most days. My firm is busy and successful. I need to hire an assistant. I was hoping you would accept."

"But I don't know anything about law. And...um, what hours?"

"It would be full-time clerical work. You can start at eight or nine. And I can offer you full benefits—medical, dental, and I just added eye care."

"It sounds great, but I've always been home for my girls after school. I-I mean, I know I can't do that any-more—"

"They can come by after school. They can do their homework at the kitchen table and Glenda is always look-ing for someone to play cards with her. I bought her some cards games to play on her computer, but she prefers hu-mans."

"Mrs. Purvis, our second grade teacher?"

"The very same. She does so much baking for the firm that I have an account set up at Shaver's grocery for her."

"Gosh. Megan, you're not just doing this to be nice, are you? I don't want to be a burden...as good as it all sounds."

"Come by the office on Monday and take a few minutes to watch Melanie. You'll be convinced there's plenty to do. Just think about it for now. Let's get the girls and go see Big Leo."

"Who's he?"

"You'll make his acquaintance very soon."

We packed up the lunch and headed east to the bluff. I glanced back at Kayla and she gave me a big smile. We left the coolers in the shade of Rufus.

The bluff, the smaller of the two north of our house, was steep on three sides and more graduated on the east side, where I directed them. I showed them how to scale the bluff by keeping your body low and scampering up the side like a spider. Kayla made good progress and Emily tried to keep up with her. I had convinced Kayla to start running, even showing her how to warm up, stretch, and plan a route. It was already paying off for her as she beat everyone to the top. I stayed behind to help Chelsea and Joy.

At the top, everyone was sucking air and laughing at the dirty mess we'd become. Emily's eyes were burning a hole in the side of my head.

"You want to know where it happened," I said.

Emily nodded. I led them to the west side, pointing out Rufus, the first hill we climbed then narrated the scary run through the dark. Joy never protested the scary details; she seemed as enthralled as her daughters. I didn't dwell on my injuries, nor did I mention the shock of killing a man, the frightening nightmares, and the loss of sleep afterward. I certainly didn't mention that it bought my mother back into my life after twenty-three years of separation.

After we scooted down the bluff, we walked back to my house. As the girls climbed into the Shark, Joy took me aside.

"I thank you for your offer. I know I must accept it."

"You will get a settlement from the accident claim...it's just hard to know when. But I'll need to collect some information, when you're ready, so that I can submit a demand for settlement. But that will take time, especially given the extent of the claim. Now when we get back to your house, give me those unpaid bills. I'll see if I can convince the creditors to delay any action against you."

Once I showered, I went through Joy's bills. Most involved utilities, which I paid—I couldn't allow my future employee to be showering in cold water and dressing in the dark. The last thing they needed was more distress. I made partial payments on the two credit cards bills, hoping she hadn't concealed any bills from me. I called the manager at Shavers to set up a $1000 line of credit for her, to be paid by an anonymous benefactor.

Bill's entrance through the back door reminded me that my mother would be here soon. I was pleased she was coming, though the event always caused my stomach to stir with excitement. I downed several Rolaids from a bottle I kept in my study desk drawer.

My uncle and my mother were reminders of just how screwed up life can be. The lies entangled us so deeply that we never found a way out. We called my mother, Elizabeth "Liz" Simon, "Beth" in Dexter, and she was identified as my aunt. My parents' marriage fell apart before she found out she was pregnant. My father couldn't deal with the fact that my twin brother, Scott, was disabled with cerebral palsy. So he took me, the healthy, feisty one, with him to live here on the family homestead. My mother agreed to the split to keep my father from forcing my brother into an institution. They remained in Omaha, while I started a new life at age three. In time, they passed from my memory.

To make the situation even messier, my Uncle Bill had begun an affair with my mom after my parents separated. Then came the knowledge of the pregnancy, the exposure of the affair, and more discord. My brother and I were torn apart. Because of the lies and guilt, and the desire to keep me from returning to my mother, my father and uncle led me to believe my mother was dead. Through my own sleuthing, I discovered the truth.

Last summer, my father died guilty and apologetic, while my brother died without any memory of me. Yet, we were stuck in the lies. From the time we moved here in 1987, everyone had been told my mother was dead. Rather than expose my mother, father, and uncle to gossip and scorn, my mother became my Aunt Beth. Brian, Patty, James, and his kids, Derek and Vonny, my friends and childhood playmates, knew the truth, but they were completely trustworthy. They all thought I'd been dealt a rotten blow, and I agreed with their assessment. However, they looked to my acceptance of my mother and treated her with kindness.

Even though I thought of her as my mother, calling her Beth seemed natural as I never became accustomed to calling her mom. I looked forward to her visits, yet we seemed more like friends than mother and daughter. My uncle wanted to marry her, but he hadn't asked, for I urged patience. She had been tied down to the incessant and overwhelming needs of a severely handicapped son for twenty-three years; I considered it natural for her to want to enjoy her freedom. She had visited Italy last fall and Barbados in March with her sister, Sophie. My father had supported Scott financially and provided a death benefit to my mother. My uncle and I also received generous life insurance benefits. His assets, including the house, the law firm, the Shark, all his money and investments, passed to me. I shared ownership of Docket land equally with my rancher uncle.

So, while I enjoyed a comfortable life, I lived a lie—and she was approaching our front door. Her thick, black hair and olive-toned skin reflected her Lebanese heritage. Brian stood by me, his warm, meaty hand in mine. Moments later, I was in her embrace.

Chapter 5

MY mom was still staying with us when the date was set for the Stansky trial. It coincided with the Husker football convention in Colorado Springs. I tried to explain to Brian that I'd already received a postponement to make certain my expert orthopedist was available. I was stuck. Brian stomped off to the study and slammed the door shut.

"He'll get over it," said Bill, who'd been standing in the doorway to the kitchen.

"I don't know," I said, wondering how long he'd fume over this. He'd had a fit of petulance last year and it took my near death for him to apologize. "I'll give him awhile."

I wandered to the family room where my mother was watching a Cubs game and reading the newspaper. She admitted overhearing the conversation and urged forbearance. I remained patient for two innings then went down the hall to the study. He stood facing the window.

"If this convention had taken place on April tenth, would you have gone?" I asked.

"Of course not," he said.

"Because you had professional obligations. Now I have a trial, a damn important one that I can't postpone. What would I say to my client or Judge Shelton—sorry, I need to go for some playtime in Colorado?"

He didn't turn around; he intended to remain unreasonable. Shit.

"Are you saying that your work is more important than mine?"

"No," he said, turning his head slightly. "It's just that we've been planning this."

"I know and I'm disappointed. But it can't be helped. Maybe the case will settle before then."

But I didn't think it would, for the plaintiff was a crusty old shithead, too foolish to compromise. I'd made every effort on the part of State Farm to settle without avail.

He looked back to the window to pout.

Now I was getting angry. "Don't cancel. Go see your football buddies and adoring fans. You don't need me—you can enjoy your ego trip without me. Just go."

He whirled around. "You don't understand because you've never—"

"Worked hard at something? It's true, I didn't have adoring fans watching me study law, applauding every time I got a decent grade or when I passed the bar. Nope, I didn't have that...I didn't need that. Good grief, grow up. Just go to Colorado and don't give me any more crap about it."

Starting down the hall to the stairs, I realized I couldn't be sure if I'd be alone. So I looped around the stairs and walked past the dining room and kitchen where Bill and Mom helped Patty with the groceries. Well, damn. I couldn't even have an argument in my own house without an audience. I went out the back door to the one place I'd get privacy.

I was a reasonable person, why couldn't he be one, too? I passed through the Seven Dwarfs, heading straight north. I spotted James walking from the creek. I waved and walked on. He would never bother me, not out here. I wondered if he was listening for Beverly. Soon, the Beast loomed over me, yet, I lacked any desire to climb it. I gazed northward—I hadn't explored all of our new land. Someday soon, I would let Gondor take me there; but for now I turned westward toward Miss Gulch.

I sat down at the edge, dangling my legs above the dry river bed. My bloody battle with Salt Eldritch in the dark had taken place several yards to the north—a place I didn't desire to see today. Facing west, I felt the hot July sun baking my skin, so I rolled my short sleeves above my shoulders to avoid a stupid tan line on my arms. I wished I heard Beverly, for she often comforted me in her death; she had been more like a mother than anyone else while I grew from a toddler to a teen. Yet, I rarely heard her when my head was all knotted up. So I sat there in the sun and the ever-present wind, wondering if a year and half was too quick to marry a man five years older than me. By the time he came back from the convention, I would know.

During the next two weeks, he rarely spoke to me. We didn't make love once during that time, which shocked me physically and emotionally. I thought about kicking him out of our bedroom to the room across the hall, my dad's former bedroom, but I remained optimistic. If there had been a way to concede or even compromise, I would have done it. So, I worked and waited. My hope was that the separation would peel away at his stubbornness and end my punishment.

On a Sunday morning in early August, I watched him from my pillow as he zipped up his suitcase and headed for the door.

"I hope you have fun," I said.

"I plan to."

While I was at the office going over my trial notebook that afternoon, I received a text from him telling me he had arrived. "I'm here," was so brief and sharp it stung. His change of heart sure didn't happen during the drive.

Jury selection started at eight in the morning in the Cheyenne County courthouse in Sidney, with Judge Dean Shelton, an old family friend, presiding. By ten o'clock, the opening arguments had begun. My client, Ginny Creevey, sat next to me. Gus sat with me during the afternoon, ready to help me if needed. The prosecution paraded witnesses to the accident to establish liability on the part of defendant, which we conceded. Next, the plaintiff's wife, and three doctors proclaimed that Ed Stansky suffered a serious lower back injury that required surgery as a result of the negligent driving of the defendant.

However, during cross-examination, I was able to get all three physicians to admit to a prior back condition. I introduced into evidence a ream of medical records establishing the fact of a prior lumbar injury. Late in the afternoon, Dr. Morrison, my expert orthopedic physician from the Creighton med center in Omaha, detailed the extent of the plaintiff's injury and discussed the concurrent disk and spinal fusion surgeries undergone by Mr. Stansky. Dr. Morrison attributed sixty percent of the pre-surgery lumbar impairment to a pre-existing vertebral fracture and forty percent to the injury caused by the auto accident. Bam!

With the expert testimony and the concessions by the plaintiff's own doctors, we were kicking butt. I wondered if our pre-trial counter-offer was too high. The trial had proceeded more quickly than I anticipated. After Dr. Morrison's testimony, the court was adjourned for the day. The counsel for the plaintiff, Rich Dewey, would begin questioning Dr. Morrison the next morning. I had a slew of co-workers and witnesses who would attest to the physical limitations of the plaintiff before the accident. Yes, it was a shame that Mr. Stansky was essentially disabled, but the law made clear that my client was only responsible for the extent of the injury she caused in the accident. As I packed up my notebook and papers, I noticed the plaintiff and counsel stayed at their table.

Out in the hallway, I discussed the case with Gus then called State Farm to apprise them of the trial status. My mom grinned at me as she stood against the wall. Rich Dewey walked up to me once I concluded my phone call. They wanted to discuss settlement.

"I'm not so sure we want to do that," I said. "I think we have a good chance of a favorable result from this jury, especially after they hear my witnesses tomorrow. In fact, we are withdrawing our last offer. I'll see you in the morning."

State Farm hadn't withdrawn the offer, it was my tactic. When I started down the hall, Gus was so surprised that he had to rush to catch up to me.

"Damn, you're gutsy," he said.

Rich Dewey had to run to catch us. "We'll take your offer of $65,000."

I stopped. "The offer is now $55,000."

The attorney ran his hand across his mouth. "Damn it. I'll make them take sixty, if you'll offer it."

"I'll wait," I said.

Dewey ran back to the courtroom. I hid my smile till the attorney was out of sight. Hot damn! I just settled a court case for less than our last offer. The State Farm superintendant was thrilled. Gus shook my hand three times.

"Your dad would've loved this," said Gus. "In fact, he couldn't have done better."

That comment made me flush fuzzy warm.

I drove home feeling pretty good about myself. It all changed when I received a call from RT. I returned his call once I got home then met him in the driveway. It felt rude not to invite him in, but I didn't like him enough to be hospitable. In fact, I detested the guy; he raised my blood pressure. But here he was, in his customary gray wick-away sweat sport shirt and black pants. I asked about his progress and he confessed that he wasn't having much success. He hadn't even determined how Don Troff got his meth. It disappointed me that no local contact had been identified as a link to the meth in the area. Just when I began to wonder why he was taking up my time, he got to the point.

"So I have a couple of buddies who are Husker fans. They went out to that kick-off party in Colorado Springs. One of them even ran into your hubby. Wanna see a picture?"

"Fine," I said.

He held out his smartphone so I could see the photo. Despite the fact that I was standing on concrete in the August heat, it froze my blood. He sat on a patio chair in what looked to be the courtyard of the resort. In his left hand was a beer, on his right thigh sat a dark-haired woman.

RT was gloating, he had wanted to get back at me, but I wasn't going to make it easy.

"Well, here, turn it this way," I said, "I can't see with this sun."

Once again, he made the error of relaxing in my company. I took the phone out of his hand and as I maneuvered the phone for less sun glare, I deleted the photo. I was familiar with the brand of phone, so I did it in a flash. I turned off the phone and handed it back to him.

"Well, I guess I'll just need to get some answers, won't I? Thanks, see ya." I headed to the house. Just as I entered the garage, I heard him react.

"Damn, you!"

I leaned against the inside of the kitchen door. My breathing became so shallow I started to get dizzy. I sat down on a chair.

Did he cheat on me?

A sense of panic welled up in me from my kneecaps to my skull. My first inclination was to dash out to my wild backyard; however, I was still in my work clothes, which I had sweated through, and in two-inch heels. I scampered up the back steps to avoid being seen by my mother and Patty. I closed my bedroom door, even locking it. Then I plopped down on my bed. Could it be true? Or was it just a pose for a photo? Shit and double shit. I told him to have fun and he said, "I plan to." Was this his plan? He punished me for two weeks—was man-whoring the climax?

I needed to think. And I needed to avoid jumping to conclusions; surely, RT was still gloating. It all made my stomach roil rancid. I popped several Rolaids, though I really wanted bourbon. Patty knocked on the door, tried the knob, paused for a moment and then announced supper. I needed a plan. I would find out for myself by driving out to Colorado Springs tomorrow. But for tonight, well, damn. Okay, I wouldn't discuss the photo. I'd discuss only the trial until I determined what, if anything had happened. Innocent until proven guilty, I told myself. My husband deserved that much.

After working a couple of hours in the office, I returned home to change and load the Shark. Patty made me a lunch—she knew I loathed fast food. I was certain my stomach wasn't up to the challenge of a greasy burger and fries. I didn't tell Brian I was coming—if everything was fine then it would be a fun surprise; if things were otherwise, well, I was more likely to discover the truth. I traveled west into Wyoming so I could stay on the interstate, and then south so I could drive parallel to the Rockies. It would have been a beautiful drive if foreboding wasn't rising in my chest like the acid in my esophagus.

I arrived in the mid afternoon. At the front desk, I received my room card and the services of a bell hop, a red-headed, acne-faced teen. Outside room 413, I tipped the red-head and sent him on his way. I wanted to turn and run to avoid the situation, but I had to push forward. My hand paused for a moment before I inserted the card. I didn't knock; I just pushed the door open. Immediately, I knew there was no need to drag in my luggage, for the brown-haired bimbo was peering out the bedroom door wrapped in a white towel. Without a word, I walked up to her and pushed the door open. I waited only a moment before my husband, the love of my life, emerged from the bathroom in a towel secured around his waist.

"Whoa, shit!" he exclaimed.

He froze. I gasped. I turned, but paused long enough to look the slut in the eyes. Brian beat me to the door.

"Wait," he said.

"For what? Get out of my way."

He put his hand on the door knob. I did what I felt necessary and appropriate—my knee jerked upward much too fast for him to stop it. He fell to the ground gasping for air. After I dropped my card on the floor, I walked out the door, yanking my bag on wheels down to the elevator. I coolly went out through the entrance to my SUV. I drove about three blocks before pulling over to a side street to cry.

Chapter 6

AFTER drenching every Kleenex in my travel pack, I wanted to go anywhere other than home to face the sting of humiliation. I sat in my car feeling pain sharper than if I'd been knifed. Had I lost him? Did I even want him? I called Vonny Wilson, James and Beverly's daughter, deleted the three calls from Brian, and then set my GPS for her Denver apartment.

I sat on her bed while she changed from her work clothes. She emerged from the bathroom in jeans and a black cotton top. She had a way of looking elegant even when she dressed down. She worked at a brokerage firm, but her walls held her passion—books. Shelves covered her main room and overflowed into her bedroom. She read everything from Shakespeare to Tolkien to Persian poetry to Warren Buffet biographies. I often wished my friend from my earliest memory lived closer to Dexter, but there was no life for a beautiful black woman in rural Nebraska. She was where she needed to be.

I told her about Brian, RT, Rachel, and Davey. She wanted to meet Davey, didn't want to be in the same state as RT, and said I'd already done what Brian deserved.

"I just can't believe he did this to you," she said.

I just shook my head. My phone began to vibrate in my back pocket. I pulled it out and read a text message from Brian. I dropped the phone on the bed.

"He says we need to talk."

"Well, duh."

"I don't know. I gotta figure out what to do—I either divorce him or punish him."

"Or both. Do you still love him?"

I sighed. "Yeah. Though right now, the thought of him makes me sick."

My head was beginning to clear. I grabbed my phone, texted him, then read his response.

"He says he has to stay till three tomorrow afternoon. That will give me time."

"Time for what?"

"To move him out. That is an absolute must. But I dread the gossip and shame of it all."

"He will too. Dexter is your town. He'll be despised and you'll be pitied."

"Pitied." I groaned. "I suppose he'll move back with his dad."

"Patty will help you pack him up. It seems like she likes him, but she can't stand a cheating husband and she'll hate anyone that causes harm to you. My dad will be pissed, but he'll follow your lead. Damn, we need tell Derek. He really likes Brian...or at least he did."

"I'd love to find a way to keep it all under wraps while I punish that son of bitch."

I pondered my suddenly shitty life while Vonny ordered Chinese for us.

We wandered back to the living room.

"Oh, yeah. That RT knows or suspects. I bet he's having a good laugh over this. Then he'll blab it around town and rub it in my face. I need to get the goods on him and fast. Know anybody in the DEA?"

"No, but Damian's cousin Robert is FBI here in Denver. And DEA is backup for the FBI. Maybe he knows something. Let me call Damian."

Although Vonny's sofa was comfortable, it took me hours to get to sleep. When I did doze off, I saw that skanky bitch's face. The wide-eyed look I'd seen was gone—now she smiled like a whore as she wrapped her arms around Brian, who was now brazenly naked. They started laughing at me, the fool. I hated her hands on him. At times, I gasped for air with shame; other times I wept into Vonny's purple pillowcase. At one point, his laughter grew so loud it reverberated against the apartment walls and woke me in a sweat. My love, my torturer.

I left Vonny's apartment the next morning, promising to keep her informed and carrying a blue sticky note with a phone number for Robert Foxworthy. The drive home was long, but I gunned it to make sure I had plenty of time to pack up Brian's things. My mood changed from miserable to calculating. As Vonny guessed, Patty was distressed, but in full support of me. She helped me box up all of Brian's possessions. I invited my uncle to supper and asked him to bring his dolly. My mom had received her wish and saw me in court, but the events with Brian clearly troubled her—she either followed me around or sat in her bedroom fretting. I was too busy to deal with her now. James would already know—Vonny probably called him and Derek the minute I was out her door. I spoke with Derek briefly when I got home. James would wait until he was summoned for aid or company. I asked my mom to call and ask him to join us for supper.

When Bill came, I informed him of the situation. He stood dumfounded till I started hauling the boxes myself. Soon we had all of Brian's stuff in his stall of the garage, for I didn't want his expulsion to be obvious to anyone driving down the street. I covered his suits in plastic bags and hung them from hooks used for shovels and rakes. Then I changed the setting for the garage door opener so that his code no longer worked. I left the garage door open then locked the floor bolt from the garage to the kitchen so that he wouldn't be able to get in. We were quiet during supper. I ate little then went to my room, certain Patty would inform them of the details. James was so upset he didn't even stay for bourbon after the meal. I came down from my room to say goodnight to him and to floor-bolt the front door before closing all the first floor curtains.

Bill was still around when Brian came home. Brian got so angry he started pounding on the doors. Bill and Patty left for the night out the back door when Brian was in the garage. I had that door bolted to the floor before Brian could get around the house. Following my instructions, neither Bill nor Patty spoke to Brian when he accosted them.

Though I usually drank only a few sips, I put away a glass and half of bourbon that night. When I came down to load my glass and start the dishwasher, my mother was sitting in the kitchen waiting for me. I had spent most of the evening drafting a divorce decree.

"Are you sure you're doing the right thing?" asked my mother.

"Oh, yes. This is the plan and it's very straightforward—he's out till I decide what to do with our future. Please turn off the light when you come up. Goodnight, Mom."

I went to bed, though my sleep was slow in coming and fitful. I awoke before dawn, tired of the effort. I peeked out the front window and saw a foot in the backseat window of his red Jeep Cherokee—he'd spent the night there. I went for a run to clear my head for our confrontation. But it was hardly cleansing—each step pounded on the pavement like the hammer crashing down upon my heart, my mind, my ego, my love for a man that had been cruelly checked. I ended up with a slow, pathetic, two-mile run. Yet my plan was now formed.

When I returned, I knocked on the window of the Jeep. I heard a thud and a groan then a scramble to sit up. My husband sprang out the back door, as if hard sleep hadn't visited him in the night. His eyes were slightly bloodshot, though I smelled no alcohol.

"I guess your case settled early."

"No, shit," I replied.

"Oh, Megan, I am so sorry. I'm just sick about what I've done to you."

"Us, you mean. You don't think I'm the only one who has and will suffer, do you?"

"What…ah…are you gonna do?"

"Think. Until I decide, you are gone."

"I am truly sorry."

"You were mad at me, so you decided to get at me."

"I was so wrong. Won't you believe me?"

He moved toward me. Did he think he could charm me or kiss me and all would be well? When he came close, I stiff armed him, but that just backed me up.

"You better back off or this time you'll be pulling your balls out of your kidneys."

That stopped him. He took a step backwards, as I knew he would.

"Yeah, you better be wary of me, you vile piece of shit," I said. "I've drawn up a divorce decree and a notice of eviction from the firm's office. I'll let you know my timetable."

He started breathing hard. "Divorce?"

"You idiot. Who do you think you're dealing with? Huh? Some wimpy crybaby?"

"Don't you love me?"

"You obviously don't love me."

"But I do."

My head began to throb in anger.

"Then tell me the last time you acted like it? You skulked around here for two weeks pouting like a child then at the first opportunity you screw some Latino whore."

Uncle Bill started to pull into our driveway, backed up, and then drove away.

"But I said I'm sorry."

"Those are just lame words, given your actions, kind of like the vows you took before God in my church."

That made him wince. He watched Bill's truck turn onto the highway then he looked over to the Wilson house.

"Who knows?"

"Harney Street plus Derek and Vonny."

"Your mom?"

I nodded. He sat down hard on the concrete. He rested his elbows on his knees and put his hands on his head. Perhaps he was beginning to understand the scope of his disgrace.

"What'd she say?"

"Nobody has said much. You've shocked the hell out of them—people who thought they knew you. Well, they know you better now."

"Were you...ah... surprised?"

"Yes and no. You'd shown your immaturity before—just not to this extent—that I know of. Maybe this is just the first time you've been caught."

"What? No. I swear I've never...I mean it was only this one time...and I think she was Italian."

That was almost funny. Almost.

"Honestly, Megan. I swear to you that—"

"More words. Now, shut up and listen. This is how things are going to be. First, you're going to pack up and go live somewhere outside of Dexter."

"Wait now. You're telling me where I can live? That's bullshit."

"I have that divorce decree sitting on my dresser upstairs. Should I go get it?"

"No."

"Then shut up. Second, we're going to keep this quiet. We're going to act like there's nothing wrong and your absence in Dexter during the day is due to many clients in Sidney. But don't you even think of coming to the firm's office today. The sight of you makes me want to puke."

I was starting to feel the effect of standing in the sun, so I sat down in the shade from his Jeep.

"Next Monday and Wednesday, we're going to have lunch together at Custer's at noon and act our parts. From now on you will not be in the firm's office in the mornings. You can come in after lunch, but not before. You'll need to work in your Sidney office in the mornings starting immediately."

"Well, hell. Isn't this great. And you think you can—"

"I know I can, you dumbshit. I can end your career in Dexter, Kimball, and every town in five counties. You've nearly doubled your income since you took an office in my firm and benefited from our business and connections. You'd have to go back and see what you can scrape up in Sidney. You've not just defiled our marriage, you've sullied Docket Law"

He stared at me with a slackened jaw, fully aware that I painted an accurate picture.

"Now, if I were you, I'd pack up and leave before Patty gets here with her shotgun."

He surely suspected that was an absurd bluff, for I doubted that Patty had ever touched a gun in her life. I strode into the house. The more he thought about it, the more he'd realize it would be a disaster for him to shame me on my own turf. Though I was proud of my resolve during our discussion, I cried the entire time I showered. He was gone by the time I left for work.

Now I needed to deal with the RT problem. As soon as I entered my office, I set before me the phone number of Robert Foxworthy of the Denver FBI office. I considered how to proceed, jotted down a few notes, closed my office door, and then dialed my cell phone. Surprisingly, I was put straight through to him.

"Yes, I've been expecting your call," he said. "Both Damian and Vonny have called me. And do call me Robert."

I paused. "Ah, yes. Well, then, you know part of the reason I called."

"Part of the reason?"

"Do you know Reginald Martin?"

"Very well."

"You of course know my personal circumstances, of which RT has some knowledge."

"And you were hoping I could oblige you with some dirty laundry on him, to make him keep his mouth shut."

"Exactly. Though I know it would be against your code of conduct. But I also have another concern…he's a dangerous man doing a lousy job as an undercover photojournalist. He doesn't own a stitch of Husker gear and never interviews anyone. Not a soul in town believes his cover, my sources tell me." I didn't add that my sources were my uncle and an arthritic old woman.

"Why do you think he's dangerous?"

"The first time we met, he was trespassing on my property, had already broken into a house we own, and then acted like a complete…so and so. I nearly shot him. And I just—"

"Just what?"

"Just know…ah…feel…that he can't be trusted."

"The fact is, Megan, I know a great deal about you, and not just from Vonny and my cousin. The story about you killing a man with a ditch intrigued me."

"I did have a steak knife and a big dirt clod."

"Yes, very resourceful. Now, the truth is, I don't trust RT either. But, we have nothing on him…at least concerning his present assignment."

"But someone local might discover something…"

"Yes, some person who stays close to the action, so to speak, and has…let's call it special insight."

That shut me up. What did he know or think about me? And how? He waited for me to speak.

"I would need some information to get close to him. He's also dating a local State Patrol officer, Rachel McNeill, whom I've befriended. And he's living on my property."

"Yes, that is all favorable."

"But I need information." I think I heard him smile, but that was probably just my imagination.

"All right, but keep this to yourself. Do not mention anything to Officer McNeill. He's not Mr. Big City, as he claims. He's from a small town in Nevada called Humboldt. Just off Interstate 80. He was FBI here in Denver, till he got booted for poor performance. Later we discovered he was messing with the wife of his boss."

"I can believe that."

"Oh, and he was a teenage truant sent to live at Boys Town for two years."

"*The* Boys Town in Omaha?"

"Uh, huh. Father Flanagan's very own."

"Oh, that's juicy. Anything else?"

"I think that should do it. And you heard none of this from me."

"What about marital status? Rachel says he's divorced."

Silence.

"Oh, I see, you did not just tell me that he is still married and has kids."

"No kids."

"That's good. Some people shouldn't breed."

Robert laughed. "We should meet sometime."

"I think we'd get along quite well. Now, if I find out something, what is the protocol?"

"We may need to meet. How is the security at your house and firm?"

"Both the law firm and my house have security systems and floor bolts and I keep the computer security updated. My housekeeper is there most of the day and I'm there at night...alone now, I will admit."

"Is your husband friends with RT? Might he be a liability?"

"I can make sure he's not."

"All right then. Have you updated the security on your windows?"

"I will do that right away."

"You may be putting yourself in danger...you know that don't you?"

"It's worth it. And I don't just mean for my marriage. We've had a local auto fatality that involved a driver under the influence of meth. I know that unofficially, of course."

"Is that widely known?"

"No, and I'm the attorney for the plaintiff in the case and that's a card I plan to keep close."

"Well, somehow, get the word out about meth in the area."

"That's easily done. Any other drugs involved?" I asked.

"Possibly some pot, which is still illegal in your state. And assuming I know Nebraska, that's not likely to change anytime soon."

"Just as well."

"Megan, take care of yourself."

He gave me his personal cell phone number and told me again to be careful. I pondered the information for several minutes then called Sherman Locksmiths in Sidney.

Chapter 7

THAT evening, I stopped by the Eldritch house. I walked past the black Tundra and into the house. RT was sitting in a lawn chair in the front room talking on the phone. I tossed a copy of the Spencer Tracy-Mickey Rooney movie *Boys Town* into his lap. His face turned red as he ended his call.

"It's just a little gift to make you feel at home," I said.

In a flash, he was out of his chair. I drew my Glock from my back waistband before he could take two steps.

"Now take it easy. Just sit back down."

He paused, his face still red. He retreated to the chair.

"I think maybe we could come to an understanding."

"Oh, I see," he said. "Your football hubby did something nasty, didn't he?"

"Maybe, maybe not. But you'll keep your mouth shut about it. Just as I won't tell Rachel your true marital status."

"Goddamn bitch!"

He started out of his chair then froze when I raised my gun to his face.

"Hey, lighten up. I said I wouldn't tell. Keeping secrets is a specialty of mine. You just make sure you keep your trap shut."

He sat back down, stared at me for a few moments, and then nodded.

I tucked my Glock into the front of my jeans. "Now look, we don't need to be adversaries. I want you to solve this meth problem. Do you know that scummy Platte Motel off Highway 30?"

"Yeah."

"They dug out a storm shelter behind it back in the 1980s. It used to be marked, but that sign is long gone. That would make a hideout or a storage area for God knows what. And there's an old storage shed off Briar Avenue and Tenth Street in Sidney that I know has underground storage. You might check those out."

The Brier Avenue shed was across an alleyway from Sherman Locksmiths. Jack Sherman was to let me know if anyone came looking around, especially someone with RT's description.

"Yeah, I'll check those," he said.

"We've got a couple of upholstered chairs in our basement. I could send those over."

RT looked down at the vinyl chair. "Yeah, this does suck."

I smiled. "And go see Paul Ritter. He owns the hardware store. He likes to mess with electronics. He might have a TV that works, and with a bigger screen than your laptop."

The screen door shut behind me. He'd be curious, so I ducked down, ran around the back of the house, and headed north to the barn. The front door creaked open. I dashed farther north, keeping the barn between the house and me. I slowed, located a rocky ridge Gondor and I had found, and then jumped over it. Peeking over the top, I saw a bright beam of light sweeping southwest toward home. That was one kick-ass flashlight he must have been keeping out of sight. What else was he hiding in there? I supposed I'd need to make another clandestine search of my property. I waited till he went back inside. He'd keep watching, so I stayed north, looping around Big Leo toward home.

Now Monday, it was the one week anniversary of the destruction of my marriage and it sucked. I hadn't seen nor heard from Brian since I cast him out. I executed my plans to punish Brian and silence RT; in a half hour, I would be sitting across from Brian at Custer's attempting to act like all was fine. The numbness had receded, and the raw sting of the wound seared my insides. Last night I cried myself to sleep, but I awoke the next morning livid. I hoped Davey would be working so as to distract Beulah from seeing the big ball of hurt festering and oozing from every pore. With the deaths of my brother and father last summer, I had felt a void—a haunting, aching sense of loss. But this pain felt different—Brian was alive and would be sitting in the booth across the table from me.

Unable to concentrate on work, I left early for the diner. After Beulah led me to the booth, she studied me.

"You look puny," she declared.

I shrugged and said, "It's a Monday...need I say more?"

She cackled. "Heh. It's another hot, dry day that's bakin' the heck outta this land. Your uncle is one of the few around here that hasn't been forced to sell off some of his herd early. Buyin' that Eldritch land was flat out smart. I bet you had a say in that."

"We decided on it together. And Lew refused to sell it to anyone else. It's bizarre if you think about it, since I killed his brother."

"You set Lew free, that's what you done. Oh, hey, I see your hubby on the sidewalk. Looks cooked."

Yeah, he'd be sweating in more than one way. Davey came out of the kitchen with his tub. He stopped at my table and looked at me with his upwards slanting eyebrows and almond-shaped green eyes, waiting and hoping.

"Davey, here is Brian," I said as the asshole slid into the booth across from me. "What will be high for today?"

His face lit up as he said, "One hundred with a heat index of one-oh-five."

"And no rain, I bet," said Brian.

"No, sir. Aunt Beulah says there's enough wind to blow the sweat from one side of your head to the other."

Brian and I smiled and nodded enthusiastically. We both knew we had reached the end of the typical conversation span for Davey. Soon he'd drop his head and retreat to the kitchen.

"Good-bye, Miss Megan, Mr. Brian." With that he moved on down the aisle.

Brian and I stared at each other for a moment then I waved Beulah over to inform her of the news.

She nodded and flashed her silver tooth with a particularly big smile. "Names and titles both. I gotta go tell his pa." She shuffled off.

Even looking over at my husband, the scumbag, didn't dispel the warm fuzzies I felt. We stared down at the menus we had memorized last year.

After a long silence, I said, "People are now coming into the diner and it will look odd if we are not speaking to each other, which causes me no small amount of pain. So I will talk and you will talk and then we can hope to be bothered by someone till we get our food."

"Yes, I know my presence disgusts you. I imagine we'll be eating pretty fast."

"I have no doubt of that. I will say that Patty has announced that her cousin is coming for a visit in November and I hope that no one around here can read lips."

"Is Patty's cousin from the Pine Ridge rez?"

"No, Fremont. She's not a Sioux. She's from that part of Patty's family that is German."

"Really? I can't picture that."

"Patty says she's obnoxious."

Brian chuckled as I gave Carol my order then Brian gave his.

RT and Rachel entered the diner. I motioned toward them. Brian turned to look.

"So what?"

"You won't want to get too friendly with him," I said.

"Who are you to tell me who I can befriend? You can be a real—"

"He's the one who alerted me to your…ah…behavior. A friend sent him a photo."

"What?"

"Time to shut it. Oh, I got an email that said we'd be getting the first of our memorabilia later this week."

We exchanged greetings. They sat down in the table next to us.

"What kind of memorabilia?" asked RT.

"Civil War," I said.

"Nebraska was in the Civil War?"

"The Nebraska Territory sent a high per capita number of troops. They fought and won at the Battle of Shiloh. You still haven't done your homework."

RT scowled at me. What a moron. If he really had a clue, he'd own a closet full of Husker gear by now.

"What kind of stuff are you getting?" asked Rachel.

"For sure a couple of infantry officer caps, two kinds of haversacks, and we're still looking for uniforms from the First Nebraska Infantry," I said.

"And we found a Model 1861 Musket," added Brian, "and a Model 1816 Flintlock Musket."

"And we already have a Sharps Carbine. We've ordered special cases to hold all of it. My dad had an old Colt revolver…that's what got us started."

RT watched Brian and me closely. I think he was surprised that we seemed to be getting along. If he really didn't know the extent of my husband's transgressions, I hoped he doubted his assumptions now. We had been lucky in our timing. Davey stopped by, never looking at RT. He moved on when Carol brought our sandwiches and took RT and Rachel's order. I felt a sense of relief, for now I could eat and leave. I chatted with Rachel a bit then claimed an early afternoon appointment, and then departed, leaving the check to Brian.

That evening I ate supper with my mom. She had been my company in Brian's absence. But tomorrow she'd be leaving for Omaha and Creighton University in Omaha, where she worked. Then I'd be alone.

In the morning, she hugged me long and hard. Wonderful, pure love. Who else can provide that? Not a husband.

"I wish I knew what to tell you," she said.

"You wouldn't have learned anything loving or helpful from my father," I said.

Stalemate. We were two people who closed up when it came to discussing pain. She stroked my cheek and hugged me again. I wanted to disappear into her arms and not come out till all was well, whatever that meant.

"Call me anytime," she said.

As her Nissan headed toward the highway, I fought through the dark cloud engulfing me, eventually finding my way to the garage. I drove with close attention to my speed. Dobbs would love to catch me speeding with his new radar gun. He liked to lurk just off Highway 51 in the mornings. As I passed a rocky ridge, I waved at him as he sat in his patrol car. He sneered at me. I smiled as the dark cloud lifted for a few precious moments.

Chapter 8

THAT morning stunk. I missed my mom. My only bright spot was knowing that I didn't need to fake my way through lunch with Brian. I didn't recognize the name for my first appointment, so I knew it must have been booked while I was in court or simply out of the office. Yet, the name Alana Wyman sounded familiar. She wore skinny jeans and a tight turquoise top that looked like a hand-me-up from a younger, thinner sister. She had short, frizzy red hair, and a thick layer of makeup. I caught the waft of smoke, perfume that smelled like insecticide, and fermenting body odor as she neared the desk. I wished I had an eject button for undesirable trash.

Once she started on her story, I recalled the news report about little Miss Einstein. She had stolen a Trans Am, robbed a bank of several thousand dollars, and then posted it on YouTube.

"Oh, my God, bail was like huge. My grandpa paid it. It's like so effin' stupid. It ain't like I killed someone. Now that's like totally ginormous."

She looked at me, expecting me to comment. That's why she had driven three hours—to hire the attorney that killed someone. I refused to take the bait.

"Miss Wyman, I rarely take criminal cases—"

"But you haveta! I got my rights, too. The state took my little girl from me. They had it comin' and now they want to, like, lock me up."

And she deserved it—not only for the crimes, but also for boasting about her "best day ever" and standing in front of the stolen car on the video, tossing twenty dollar bills in the air then trying to catch them in the breeze. This ditz was an embarrassment to our species.

"Let me give you the phone number for Stan Spurlock here in Dexter. He handles criminal cases. I have no intention of taking on your case."

"Wha? You gotta. You're like the only one who can help me. My pa been sayin' I might as well go to jail 'cause he don't want me back. Now I gotta live with my mom and she's a slob."

Until prison, a thought I kept to myself. Part of me wanted to ask questions as to the mind state of someone so stupid, but I didn't want to encourage her. I handed her Stan Spurlock's card.

"It's time for you to leave. Have a nice day." I walked to the door and opened it.

She slammed her purse down on the carpet. "You bitch! You phony! You ain't nothin'!"

She knocked over my recently purchased National Geographic floor globe. Gus appeared at the door.

"Time to go, miss," he said.

She slapped at my Van Gogh print that hung behind my desk, knocking it on the floor. I picked up the phone and called Dobbs.

When the stupid tart heard the word "police," she turned and scurried to the front door, which was opened by Tom Sedlacek. Melanie rushed to the window with a notepad. Joy, who had started about a month ago, stayed near Glenda. Melanie handed me a piece of note paper with the make, model, and license plate of the car, which I relayed to Dobbs.

Tom closed the front door. With the sound of the latch, I looked from each bewildered face to another then started laughing.

"That's it," I said, "I'm no longer taking appointments from anyone who attacks my globe."

As we ate Glenda's Tuesday cinnamon scones in the lobby, we laughed over the incident. I told my office gang and Tom the name and notoriety of the red-head. We predicted it would soon become the big news at Custer's. This was a dinky town, and the locals reveled over just about anything out of the ordinary. Back in my office, I righted my globe and Tom helped me hang my picture on the wall. He was a big guy and could reach over the cabinets that ran along the back wall.

"You know I got that DUI," he said as we sat down.

"Tom, you know I don't handle that stuff. Go see Stan."

"No, I know. But you see, that was the night of that windstorm. And my truck was sitting out at the back there 'cause Chief Dobbs impounded it. Now it's all dented and scratched. They had a duty to protect my property."

"Are you talking about that old red Chevy?"

"Yeah," he said, scratching his dark beard.

"Ah, heck, Tom, what's a few more scratches on it? What did you expect the police to do? Park it inside the station? And do you even have a garage for it at your house?"

I rubbed my temples. Idiots, it's raining idiots, right here in my office. He was talking again. Oh, what now? I was going to lock my office door as soon as I could get rid of him. Then I heard the name Breeley.

"What did you say?" I was forced to ask.

"I said it was nice of you to hire Joy Breeley and take her case."

"It wasn't charity. We needed the help. She works hard."

"Yeah, I remember she was good in school, not like those Breeley brothers. 'Course it was Dugger and Riley that caused all the trouble."

Was this going somewhere? I needed to work on a new divorce case I received from Cherry County. It was my first case from the Sand Hills. I was looking forward to traveling up there before winter hit. Maybe I'd even get to see the cranes. Brian was always—. Shit, right, no Brian. Why did he screw up my life? Oh, yeah, he's talking about

Douglas "Dugger" Breeley and his younger brother, Riley. Two lazy morons. I wanted to go home.

"Yeah, I guess that's what makes me mad about my truck. Those two got brand new Dodge pickups."

That stirred my attention. "How could they afford new Dodge trucks when the family had to sell off half their herd early?"

"That's what I'm wonderin'...how? And it's like they don't have no more time for me. They go off on trips to God knows where."

"Who are they hanging around with if not you? You guys were always good buddies."

"That's another thing. Sorry...none of this has anything to do with—"

"No, go on."

"Well, it's damn strange with all the trouble they gave Chief Dobbs over the years, now they're chummin' around together. Playin' cards and drinkin' in the Breeley back yard. I don't get it."

I rolled my pen between my palms. It made a clicking noise when it hit my wedding ring.

"Tom, when you got picked up for DUI, was it just booze? And I ask you this with the understanding that anything you tell me is protected by attorney-client privilege."

"But you ain't representin' me."

"Don't worry, you're covered."

"It was just Jack Daniels. I don't mess with any drugs. Couldn't afford it...and I've heard enough stories to be scared of it."

"It is scary stuff and some of it is around here."

"Yeah, I've seen the guy in the black Tundra. He's a cop...easy to tell. Is that why he's here?"

"Yeah. Now listen to me, Tom." I took one of my cards from my center desk drawer. "I want you to tell me if you see anything else strange. It may mean nothing, or it may mean something." I wrote my cell number on the back of the card. "There's something nasty about what meth does to people. It isn't like other drugs. And I don't want to see it ruin this town."

"Meth? Damn. Yeah, I'll tell you."

"Give me a call next time you see Dobbs and the Breeley brothers together."

After Tom left, I sat quietly pondering. Tom was smarter than I gave him credit. He never expected me to take on any case, he needed someone to talk to about something he thought strange, and rightly so. Obviously, he couldn't talk to our police. Did Dobbs have his hands in the meth business? Or was he using his information for blackmail? He had replaced the old pick up he crashed with a new Ford Explorer. This town couldn't afford to pay our two policemen high salaries, so where did that the money come from? I needed to alert my staff to the problem. The more people watching for the unusual, the more likely something would be found.

After Tom left, Joy came in to my office and stood before my desk.

"I-I think maybe it's time to get going on my claim," she said.

"I'll submit your demand by the end of the week. It will take some time to get a response. A claim this large will go back to the home office and through a committee."

She nodded then left. I'd already collected all the documentation and written a rough draft of the demand letter. I'd even asked Brian to calculate potential lost earnings for Jake, which would be a part of the demand proposal. Strangely enough, Joy made more money working for me than Jake ever did as a laborer. I'd even paid a higher premium to make sure her health insurance kicked in right way. Joy allowed me to advise and well, boss her around. I made sure she and her kids went to the dentist the first week she worked for Docket Law. I told her exactly how to dress for the office, and she had complied, with the help of an advance on her wages. I convinced her to sell her old beater and get Jake's Jeep fixed up. Carlos Hernandez billed her $67.50 for a tune-up, and I paid him $780.00 for a list of problems we kept in confidence. I took charge of her, temporarily, and she was grateful for the guidance. Now I intended to do my best to get her well compensated from Troff Construction's liability insurance.

I stayed busy the rest of the day. Once and awhile, my mind wandered to the memory of my mom's hug. I realized I had been spoiled for physical pleasure. Still a newlywed, I possessed plenty of energy for love making with my husband; however, I didn't like thinking about it, for the man disgusted me. Forgiveness was impossible until the sight of him didn't make me want to puke up several small organs. Maybe he even picked up some disease from that skanky bitch. Still, I kept thinking about that hug.

My mom called that evening. We chatted about her drive home and the water rationing in Lincoln and other Nebraska towns. My Uncle Peter, a Methodist minister, was recovering well from his gall bladder surgery.

Then she said, "Hillary didn't divorce Bill Clinton. I don't think anyone would consider her weak."

Did my refusal to let Brian back into my life reflect a fear of weakness? I read about celebrities who took back husbands who beat them or cheated on them; I considered them pathetic and stupid. The fact that our problem had remained a secret kept us in limbo. Had it become public, the shame would have stung badly enough to push me to file for divorce—my ego would have demanded it. My mother understood me, but not completely.

"That's true," I replied. "But I bet she made him pay a steep price. And it wasn't resolved in a week."

Chapter 9

THE buffalo grass turned to lavender and the wind shifted, now blowing from the west and north, bringing the chill of October, and my heart still failed to warm to him. Trust takes a long time to build, but only a few minutes to destroy. He kept his end of the bargain by staying away from me and my home. I began to think of it again as *my* house; Brian became someone who had been a guest. James and Bill often came for supper. Sometimes they would stay around to watch baseball playoff games or football games. My gang still gathered to watch Nebraska football games, but I think we all missed Brian's insider commentary.

Why did he do it? He hadn't denied that he'd been mad at me and wanted to get back at me. He couldn't even refute his immature actions. Was there more to it? Did it emasculate him to live in my family home or to work in the family law firm building? I suppose it didn't help that I began to bill him monthly for the office space. He looked stricken when I told him I had filed to return my legal last name to Docket. That had cut him deeply, as I intended. I even shifted a large chunk of money—the funds from my dad's life insurance policy—to a mutual fund in my name only. I wasn't done punishing him.

As Gondor cantered into the chill wind, I kept us on a northern course, past Miss Gulch, the ditch, the Beast, a tall bluff, and then through the former Eldritch land toward the edge of our property. As we pressed onward, the air became thick with dust. The previous owner of the land, Phil Hexam, attempted to grow wheat for several years, but failed. My father handled the bankruptcy for the family.

The Laramie bank took possession, yet never did anything except evict the family. It was like a Dust Bowl story out of *The Grapes of Wrath*. But the drought of 2012, the single worst year in Nebraska history, persisted, as did the plumes of dust that blew farther south each week.

With the continuing growth of the sporting goods super store, Cabela's, in Sidney, rumors were circulating that a super store, such as Wal-Mart or Target would move into the area. It would create a few jobs for Dexter residents, but kill off the few retail stores we possessed. The notion disturbed and nauseated both me and Bill.

The density of the dust made finding Bill's silver pick up difficult. We located the old gravel road that marked the edge of the former Hexam property then turned east. We were within twenty feet of the truck before we saw it. I tied Gondor to the rear cab door handle then climbed into the front passenger seat. Bill grinned at me as I took off my baseball cap and sunglasses, and then pulled down my bandana off my nose and mouth. I accepted the cup of coffee he offered. I even took a chocolate-frosted doughnut from the bakery box sitting on his dash.

"You look like you're ready to rob a train," he said.

I smiled. "So, what are we going to do about this? This is repulsive when the wind blows from the north."

"Somethin' and soon. Now it's about two miles from our land to the interstate. Most of it is rock hard or grassed over, except for the land Hexam plowed before he got driven off. Don't know what the old fool was thinking…trying to farm out here without irrigation? No way."

"But he's left a big problem. This dust is going to cover us then drift into town. People will be praying for snow just to stop it."

"Snow won't stop it for long," he said. "We're gonna have the same problem over and over."

"Won't it weed over?"

"In time, but now listen. This is what I'm thinking. We buy up this land and seed it with wild grasses. I can get wa-

74   ALONE IN THE WIND

ter trucks out here…the plowed land is only about twenty acres. The water would be thin, but it'll stop the topsoil from coverin' us."

"And by owning this land, we prevent some super store from ever moving in. We're also sitting on a shale basin. They already started fracking in northeastern Colorado. We're next."

"I hadn't thought of that," he said.

"But we're also going to need to buy up some of the land to the west, next to the highway. That's still too close. Hey, where will they get the water?"

"I'm not sure, but I don't ask questions when I don't want to know the answer."

"It better not be from the Raccoon. That creek is just a trickle. It's going to dry up like Miss Gulch. But I agree. I'll contact the bank."

"We'll need to move fast and get the seed down before the land freezes."

We were quiet for a few minutes. Gondor was keeping his head down and out of the wind.

"I should get Gondor back."

"Megan, what're you gonna do about Brian? This is dragging on a long time. Don't you miss him?"

"Sure, but not as much as I thought I would." That was and wasn't a lie. I did miss him, terribly at times, yet I knew I could go on with life without him. "Sometimes when I miss him, it makes me angry. I'm convinced he's still immature and prone to stupidity. Why would I think otherwise?"

"You could try him out."

"I'm not ready for that. If he wants to come back, and I let him, I'm sure he'd be a perfect angel. But for how long? Till the next time he doesn't get his way?"

My uncle wrung his meaty hands, as if the problem was so difficult for him that it was twisting around in his brain. It occurred to me that the discord between Brian and me caused him pain. I wished it wasn't so, but I didn't know how to help him—I couldn't even figure out how to help myself.

Back in my bedroom that evening, I stared into my closet. My clothes had gradually crept into the open half of the closet. The emptiness of his half of the closet made my chest thicken with emotion. A quiet groan rose into my throat as I backed up to my bed and sat down. I felt so alone. In a flash, I was up again, shoving my clothes over to fill the empty part of the closet. I didn't feel any better. The wind hurled itself against my north windows, shaking them and reminding me that Brian was not safe at home. He was probably in his father's house, but he was still out of reach. Rummaging through my desk drawer, I found my Facebook password, but didn't even log on, feeling so far removed from my old friends. I called James to ask if he was watching the AL playoff game. He invited me over to watch it with him and drink hot chocolate. I would've preferred something stronger, but that could wait till later.

That night in bed, I felt mad at everyone. James was good company, but I was angry that Beverly was dead and not there. Why wasn't my mother with me? She had received enough life insurance money from my dad's death to allow her to quit her job. I'm sure the afternoon conversation with Bill convinced him to stay away this evening. And that bastard of a husband—he wasn't here because he was a cheating shithead. Bloody hell, could I ever trust him again? Ah, to hell with everyone. I shoved Brian's pillow off the bed and scooted my body and pillow to the center of the bed. Shit. I wanted a second glass of bourbon, but I didn't want to move from the spot I made warm in the bed. Sweet Jesus, did I really deserve this crappy time of life? No, don't answer that. I'd received more blessings than I was worthy to possess. I flipped over to my other side, maintaining my warm spot in the bed. It was going to be a long night.

The next day, I sat in my booth at Custer's, watching Brian chat with Big Joe McCready. Before I met Brian, I had been guilty of enjoying cookies when I needed and really wanted the meal. With him, I thought I had married the buffet. Did I even still love him? He slid into the booth across from me. It was time to feign conversation. I leaned forward. As I hadn't done that before, he did likewise. When I started a recitation of random phone numbers, it altered his look of expectation. I kept talking, but I had faked him into believing I would say something personal. I stopped rambling when two chairs were pulled out from the table next to us.

"Hey! Hey!" said RT. "Guess what I found in that shed in Sidney? I hefty stash of meth. How about that!"

"Good job," I said, though Jack Sherman had already called me this morning to tell me the police spent hours that morning hovering around the shed. They cordoned off the whole abandoned property and alley with yellow tape.

"Did they catch anyone?" asked Brian.

"Nope. But we're working on it. Forensics is out there now. They'll find the evidence on whoever's been there."

Rachel was smiling adoringly at RT. How sweet. How I wanted to vomit.

"Yeah, I got a search warrant from the judge…ah…Shelton was his name. Says he knows you. Your name got me that warrant. Thanks."

I nodded, but I wanted to shove the pepper shaker down his throat. I already called Robert Foxworthy and told him Jack Sherman had checked the shed on Saturday and it was empty—the leasing company gave him keys to the property so he could check on the building and shed while it was unoccupied. Maybe someone did plan to use the shed to store the drugs, but quite possibly RT had planted the meth to score points. And I was the tip. Shit. My stomach turned over.

Brian continued to talk to RT and Rachel about the break. I acted as if I was following the conversation. Brian had followed my instructions of punishment so well, I wondered if he was even suffering that much. It was nearly two months since the transgression. We ate our meals. RT and Rachel finished eating then said they needed to get back to Sidney. On the way out of the diner, RT bragged about his discovery to anyone who would listen. If he was really in such a hurry, he would have grabbed a burger in Sidney and dashed back to the scene. No, he wanted his opportunity to boast in Dexter. He no longer tried to act like he was undercover. Nobody had believed him anyway, Beulah made sure of that. When I turned my attention back to Brian, he was staring at me.

"I think you're heartless," he said. "Cold and calculating like your father."

I quietly took the blow, studying him. "Obviously, I'm not like your mother. I haven't helped you grow up."

Brian reddened.

"And what is more heartless than premeditated adultery?"

"Is that what you think? That I left to go screw someone? I meant to get plastered. What happened with that woman was not a part of the plan."

I stared at him then out the window. I didn't know whether to believe him.

"Listen, I wanted to show you off. I had married an attorney…I was worthy…and I was a respected accountant. Not the goof-off some of those guys thought I was…probably once was. But there I was…alone…and you weren't there to back me."

"Because I was working. And how dare you blame your behavior on me? Those guys were wrong—you're not a goof-off, you're the ultimate screw-up and a man without character or morals."

He skulked off to the restroom. I paid the bill and returned to the office. He felt enough to try and hurt me. Maybe he was suffering. If our separation wasn't hurting him, then we lacked any chance as a couple. Yet I kept thinking about the look on his face when I leaned toward him. Something was stirring, no forming in me. That big ball of hurt was changing to something else—more like a tumor now, throbbing at times, icy cold at others. He called me calculating, and I suppose I was. Did I have my father's hardness? I possessed resolve—I set my plan in motion—someday I hoped to figure out the next step.

As bad was the week started, our Wednesday lunch was very different. Brian arrived first so he faced most of the diner; the one in that chair had the burden of doing most of the talking. Today, he decided to talk about the baseball playoffs.

"The AL looks wrapped up, but the wild card in the NL is still up for grabs," he said.

I turned at the sound of dishes clanging together. Davey had rushed to our table.

"In the 1950s, Ted Williams had a point four-seven-six on base percentage," he said.

Taken aback, Brian and I looked at each other.

"What was his batting average?" I asked.

"Point three-three-six for the decade."

"What year did he break four hundred?" Brian asked.

"1941. He hit point four-oh-five-seven."

For the first time since July, Brian and I smiled at each other. Off to the side, Beulah came creeping up, but stayed back a few feet.

"It got as high as point four-three-eight in June that year," Davey continued.

Harold and Marva Gush stopped eating and turned in their seats to listen. I didn't want to look around, fearing it would embarrass Davey.

Wanting to keep him talking, I asked, "What team did he play for?"

"The Boston Red Sox."

"Davey," said Brian, "you are very smart."

Davey smiled, but dropped his head into his chest.

"Do you like the Red Sox?" I asked.

"They won't make the playoffs this year. Yankees will."

"Who are the best teams?"

"Texas, San Francisco, St. Louis."

Brian and I nodded with enthusiasm. Beulah winked at me.

"Who was the better player, Ken Griffey, Jr. or Barry Bonds?" asked Brian.

"I don't know." Davey paused for a moment then said, "Ken Griffey Jr. had one hundred forty-seven R-B-Is in 1997."

I felt myself warming with emotion. What a sweet kid. While we were thinking of another question, he suddenly turned away and headed for the kitchen, leaving our empty coffee cups at the edge of the table.

Davey began muttering, "Ken Griffey, Barry Bonds. Ken Griffey, Barry Bonds."

Beulah gave him a kiss on his cheek as he passed by her. She smiled at Brian and me, flashing her silver tooth. I was surprised to see that Rachel was sitting at the table next to us with Carol standing next to her, her order pad and pen frozen at her waist. Carol had been taking our orders at Custer's for at least ten years. At forty-five or so, she had brown hair, colored unnecessarily dark, and a thick layer of foundation on her face that gave her face a pinkish hue. The look of surprise on Carol's face made Beulah laugh. Carol recovered then took Rachel's order. She hurried back to the kitchen, and then returned with a club sandwich for me and a mushroom cheeseburger for Brian.

"I'm sorry, I just couldn't break in on Davey so I got you your favorites," she said.

"No problem, this is fine," Brian said.

We spent the rest of the meal chatting with the people in the adjoining tables about Davey's breakthrough. In private, I agreed to let Brian come back to Custer's the next day. I even called James and Bill.

The next day, both Brian and Bill beat me to the booth. Bill sat in the middle of the booth and Brian scooted over to make room for me. I sat next to him, knowing it would look odd for me not to.

"As soon as the wind's down a bit, we'll start with the seed and water," said my uncle. "Best to put 'em down at the same time."

"That makes sense," I said as I glanced around for Davey. "The paper work won't take long. The bank was pleased to get rid of it."

"Wait, what's this?" asked Brian.

"We bought a chunk of land to the north," I said.

"You bought more waste land and I wasn't even consulted?"

"You weren't available when the decision was made."

Brian raised the menu to cover his face. "And whose fault is that?"

"Yours. You are the one who decided to sabotage our marriage before we were even married six months…like we're some Hollywood couple."

Brian flushed red. Davey came to our table, toting his gray dish tub.

"You sick, Mr. Brian?" Davey asked.

"Just in the soul," I muttered.

"No, I'm fine," said Brian. "So Davey, who had the most hits in the 1990s?"

"Mark Grace," he said as Bill moved over and James sat down in the booth.

I waited to see if Davey would continue with the stat, but he looked distracted when he saw RT and Rachel sit in the table behind him.

"Davey," I said, trying to help him get back on the subject, "do you know who Jackie Robinson is?"

"Second base."

"Do you know why he is important?"

"Second base. Stole bases. All Star."

"Yes. But he was also the first black man to be allowed to play in the major leagues."

He gave me a blank look. "Why?"

"They didn't let African Americans play baseball in the major leagues before him."

"Why?"

How sweetly innocent. "No good reason."

Davey looked at James. "Mr. Wilson is black like Hank Aaron."

"Yes, he is. Mr. Wilson lives next door to me."

I felt Brian's stare, but I kept my eyes on Davey, who looked to be mulling over something. My eyes twitched and felt dry. What was this about?

When he turned and walked away, he started chanting, "No good reason, no good reason."

His mind was occupied, so he passed by tables with dirty dishes, and then disappeared into the kitchen.

I didn't want to fight with Brian, so I turned to RT, who had been watching Davey.

"Strange kid," said RT. "Ow!" he said.

I smiled at Rachel, who had probably just kicked him.

"So, did the lab guys find anything?" I asked.

"Nope. They must have been wearing gloves. They made sure not to touch anything."

"Did you come up with any witnesses?"

"Nobody saw anything."

Of course, nobody would see RT in his black clothes, sneaking around at night.

"Did they find anything in the basement?"

"No. Doesn't look like they even went down there."

"Do you think they've been scared off?" asked Bill.

"Hard to say. We'll be watching for them."

Yeah, our hero, you conniving pile of dung. I would love to ask him in front of so many people, which probably included the occupants of the adjoining booths who were quiet and probably listening, how it was that he washed out

ALONE IN THE WIND

of the FBI. But I refrained. I needed to keep some information close, in case I needed it later.

That night as I lay in bed, in my warm spot, thinking about Brian's smile, my tumor pulsated. Then I recalled Davey's baseball chatter. I doubted that Davey possessed an ounce of malice in his entire being. Brian, who had everything—brains, looks, fame, health, a comfortable living, a good job—was capable of squandering it all with vice and vengeance. My tumor iced-over.

Chapter 10

ON Friday, I drove the Shark into the Ritter driveway, having promised Kayla a ride on Rohan before it got too cold. A black Dodge Ram king cab pickup was parked in front of the house, with its wheels in the Ritter yard, over the curb, smashing the grass. Moron. This wasn't Paul's pickup; he drove an old Ford. I hurried to the front porch, knocked, whipped open the front storm door, and then shoved open the front door. The living room was empty, except for the staleness that turned to stink the farther I went into the house. Magazines and beer cans were strewn about the room; one can was tipped on its side, dripping Bud Light onto the soiled, sticky carpet.

Sheila wandered out into room from the hallway to the bedrooms. Looking either ill or drunk, her hair was a matted blonde-out-of-a-bottle mess, and her T-shirt was rumpled. She smelled of something I couldn't quite identify.

"Where's Kayla?" I asked.

"Downstairs, I think," she said.

"Who else is here?" I was in a state of alarm, but I felt my eye lids twitch. Shit.

"Dugger and Riley."

"You left your daughter alone with the Breeley brothers? You idiot!"

Wishing I had my Glock, I dashed into the kitchen, located a steak knife in a drawer with a sticky handle, and then flung open the door to the basement. I took the steps by twos; meanwhile, Kayla was standing near the base, pressed up against the wall, her face taut. She looked at me with relief.

"You okay?"

She nodded and stepped forward; I think she would have hugged me if I hadn't rushed past her with a knife.

"Well, look who's—"

In a flash, I lept over the coffee table and on top of Dugger. Grabbing his greasy brown hair in my left fist, I pulled his head back so I could press the knife up against his whiskered neck. He gasped then Riley cried out.

"Megan! Don't kill him!"

"No? I thought I might show him how I killed Salt Eldritch. I used a knife then, too."

"Please don't, Megan," said Riley. "What did he do?"

"Oh, I don't have time to list all his wrongs. But today, you both did something you will never do again."

I eased back off Dugger and let go of his hair. I stepped back out of his reach. I saw a trickle of blood flowing down his neck. I was glad to get away from his stink of body odor and smoke.

"You are not to speak to this girl or even look at her. In fact, if I ever see you in the same room with her again, I will take care of you both."

I walked over to Kayla. "Kayla, hon, did either of them touch you? Or even say anything nasty to you?"

She shook her head.

"Now, I want you to go pack up some clothes. We'll go to my house for a slumber party. I don't know how long it will last, so bring some school clothes. Wait for me in your room."

"Okay."

As she ascended the stairs, I turned back to the brothers.

"Now you two listen up. I don't intend to kill either of you...today."

"Heh," said Dugger, "that's good to know. You're a real hot-head."

"Whose truck is outside?"

"Mine, so what?"

"Your family has lost half of your land and most of your herd. Your dad is mortgaged up to his neck, and you have a new Dodge Ram?" I looked over at Riley. "What color is yours?"

"Red."

"Your family has overdue loans with the county bank here and a bank in Denver. They could call in those loans anytime. Your family could lose everything they ever worked for. And I could help persuade those banks."

"The hell you will," said Dugger.

"Oh, I can, if I want. You also owe Docket Law nearly a thousand bucks. Now that account at the firm lists both your names, as well as your folks. You also owe my uncle and me nearly two grand for leasing pasture land. I can slap liens on either of your trucks faster than you can spit."

Now, they were speechless, and staring at me, slack-jawed, like the redneck morons they were.

"I have no idea why you two are in this house and I don't care. But I am that girl's attorney and you will heed my warnings."

Technically, I represented Paul, but they didn't know that. I took out my phone then pretended to be texting, when in fact, I was taking their pictures. I walked around a little to get different views, but acted like I was having trouble seeing the phone's small print, which was partially true due to the twitching of my eyelids. I longed to get outside and breathe the chilly, clean air.

"Now, both of you tell me that you understand what I have told you."

"Yeah," said Riley.

Dugger nodded.

"Now look, I've known you two since we were kids learning to tie our shoes. Remember how we used to play Hide and Seek on Harney Street?"

Dugger nodded.

"Your uncle's dogs always found us first," said Riley.

The three of us smiled. Yes, I knew these two quite well—they were racist, lazy bullies who loved to start fights. I was concerned for Kayla, though I never heard of them giving trouble to nice girls. I was curious why they were hanging around a dumpy, middle-aged woman, but I'd never get an honest answer if I asked.

"I hope you two haven't gotten yourselves into some trouble."

Neither man answered, so I turned and left after I took a good look around the room, a partially-finished basement with a slouching couch and two chairs with worn covers. Upstairs, the furniture was newer, but what had been a nice home was now a stinking pit. Thankfully, they didn't have any pets or the fetid room would have been unbearable. The kitchen wasn't as messy, yet the bottom rack of the dishwasher was pulled out and half empty as if someone, probably Kayla, was unloading dishes before being inter-rupted. I took pictures as I moved through the rooms.

I walked down the hallway and knocked on Kayla's door. I was surprised Sheila's door was closed—I expected a fight. Kayla's room was a stark contrast to the rest of the house, tidy and decorated with white furniture and bright purple accents. When I first started coming over here after I took the case, her room was disheveled. I was pleased she was making the effort, despite the trauma of her parents' divorce saga.

"Did you tell your mom you were leaving?"

Kayla shoved a handful of underwear into the outer pouch of the suitcase. Clearly, she was packing for more than a night.

"Yeah. She didn't seem to care. She just went back to sleep."

I gave her a hug, tightly, like my mom had hugged me. Kayla started to cry. I held onto her as I watched the Breeley brothers climb into the black truck and drive away. She wiped her eyes.

ALONE IN THE WIND

"Don't forget your shampoo and stuff like that. Oh, and make sure you have a key to the house. Don't forget your homework. I need to make a phone call."

I walked out into the hall and called Bo, asking him to take photos of the house. I told him the Breeley brothers had just left and that I was taking Kayla home for a slumber party. He promised to come over as soon as he could. I opened the door to Sheila's bedroom. She was sprawled across the bed on top of the tangled blanket and sheet. The pillows were on the floor. Her breathing was raspy and fitful and oh, did it reek—the Eldritch house on a hot summer day would be preferable. As I shut the door, I realized it was the smell of sex mixed with body odor and smoke. I shuddered and rushed back to Kayla.

I got Kayla into the Shark and headed home, certain I would never let her go back there.

"Oh, I forgot pajamas."

I smiled. "I'll loan you some."

"They'll be too short."

We laughed.

"You were really scary," she said.

"Good. I was trying to be. Do I scare you?"

"No. But I'm glad you scared them. I don't know why they were in our house. I got home from Emily's and they were in the basement. You came like a couple of minutes after I got there. Mom was supposed to be at work."

I was relieved she hadn't seen anything and I didn't need to quiz her on what she saw. Patty helped us haul her stuff upstairs. My trusty friend didn't comment on the two suitcases, the four coats for various seasons, and the stash of personal items Kayla toted in a pillowcase. I put Kayla in the guest room where my mom usually stayed. My father's bedroom, across the hall from my room, was never used. While she was unpacking, I called Paul at the hardware store, told him of the situation, and then I invited him over for supper. Afterward, I told Kayla that Brian and I had argued, so he was staying with his dad in Sidney. This distressed her to the extent that she started to cry. I held her and told her it was just temporary, but that I wanted her to keep this information in confidence.

I helped Kayla unpack and then I went to my bathroom to be alone. Pacing the floor, I felt shaken at what I had seen and what it all meant, but I needed to be strong for Kayla. My next step would involve convincing Paul to push for divorce given Sheila's...behavior. That slattern only needed Paul for one reason—if she was messing with drugs and missing work, she needed someone to bail her out. I called Paul again, this time suggesting he stop by his house and see what was going on for himself. He needed to comprehend the urgency of the situation. Monday morning I planned to put a lien on Dugger's truck, just to make sure he knew I was serious.

I rejoined Kayla in the guest room. She agreed the next thing to do was to watch a movie.

"And eat root beer floats?"

I laughed as we descended the creaking back stairs. "I think we should save that for after supper. By the way, how's Emily doing?"

"She's better. We're like BFFs now. That means best friends forever. You were right. Some of her friends are nice to her, but they've kinda backed off. I told her why you said they'd do that. I think that made her feel better. She likes you. She doesn't like my mom. After today, I don't know if I like her either." She stopped on the stairs. "I was looking for something, and I found a bottle of Scotch whisky in her closet. That was 'bout a month ago. I should've told someone."

"Well, you just told me. Maybe that's why she's acting like she is. Your dad said he would stop by your house before he came here. Oh, and don't tell anyone that I put a knife to Dugger's throat."

"But it was, like, awesome."

I chuckled as we looked over the movies in our DVD collection. I recommended *Young Frankenstein*. She agreed then commented on our extensive John Wayne movie collection.

"I've heard about him," she said.

"You've never seen a John Wayne movie? That's terrible. We'll have to fix that."

Just when Gene Wilder needed to "put the candle back," Paul and Bo arrived. Paul greeted his daughter then Patty came in to watch the movie with Kayla while I went to the living room to talk. Sometimes keeping a distressed girl company was more important than vacuuming drapes.

Out of Kayla's presence, Paul looked stricken while Bo mostly hung his head. They could hardly speak. I told them of my threats to the Breeley brothers. Paul continued to look overwhelmed, but Bo grinned at me.

"Shavers called this afternoon and asked where Sheila was," said Paul, shaking his head.

"Kayla says she found a bottle of Scotch in Sheila's closet," I said. "But that doesn't explain the presence of the Breeley brothers."

I wondered if they had formed the conclusion I had about Sheila and the sordid events before Kayla arrived.

"Paul, your daughter should never go back there. You need to divorce Sheila and take custody of Kayla."

"There's a duplex for rent near my house…both sides," said Bo.

Paul stared out the front window, but nodded. "I should have gone back there long ago."

"Paul, if she's intent on destroying herself, you can't stop her," I said. "Kayla is priority number one for you. At some point, we can try to make sure Sheila is getting the help she needs."

Bo received a call on his phone and departed. I suggested to Paul that we try to have a light-hearted evening. He nodded then walked down the hallway to join Kayla, his footsteps treading heavily on the wood floor.

I stood in front of the living room window. Last year, Salt Eldritch had thrown a copy of *Lonesome Dove* through the window before he tried to shoot me through the study window. I hadn't understood the risk I made in making him an enemy. I seemed to be piling on adversaries this year— RT, Dobbs, the Breeley brothers, and Sheila, who would join them as soon as she realized my hand in pushing for the divorce and Paul's custody of Kayla. So be it—I planned to do everything in my power to protect that girl. Rallying my friends seemed the next step. I called Bill and James to advise them that Kayla was staying with me for a while because of her messy home life. Then I called Brian, my estranged bodyguard, and gave him a more detailed account.

"That poor kid. What did you tell her about us?"

"That we were fighting and you were staying at your dad's."

"I think people know we're apart. Guys keep asking why we stopped going to the Cowpoke."

"I guess I'm not surprised," I said.

"RT followed me from the office Wednesday night," he said. "He's checking up on us. So I drove to my office in Sidney. After forty-five minutes, I got tired of trying to wait him out. So I drove back toward the highway and he followed, but I timed it so that he would get hung up in traffic. I pulled onto a side road and watched him pass by. What a shithead."

After I finished talking to Brian, I thought about how he had never asked if he could move back. Maybe bachelor's life suited him.

Chapter 11

AFTER church on Sunday, Kayla and I met Joy and her daughters at Custer's. We joined Joy at a table in the middle of the room. I identified Davey to Kayla, who had become interested in his story. Kayla stiffened when she saw that Dugger and Riley sat in a booth along the front wall; however, they seemed engrossed in their own conversation, failing to even notice Davey as he walked by. The custom for the brothers was to go scummy during the week then clean up for the weekend—no restaurant allowed them in unless they looked and smelled like they slept in beds not caves. At Custer's, Carol refused to take their order until they placed sufficient money on the table to prove they could pay.

Davey made his customary loop past the booths and around the tables. Muttering something, he ambled past Chief Dobbs, who sat in a table with his wife, Lisa, dressed in their Sunday best. Dobbs jerked to attention at Davey's words.

As Davey approached our table, I heard him say, "Up three eighty-five, dumb Injuns, up three eighty-five."

Davey stopped and looked at me then at the others at the table. He must've thought I was in the wrong place and with strange people, so he hastened by me and entered the kitchen. When Kayla gave me a puzzled look, I shrugged then glanced over at Dobbs, who was glaring at the Breeley brothers. I turned back to my table and made sure not to look around again. What did it mean? It made me angry that Brian wasn't around for me to talk to him about it.

Back home, I sent Kayla to the kitchen to do her homework. She smirked at me, but she did it. Later when she finished, she joined Bill and me in the family room to watch football. I don't think she cared about the NFL, but she seemed to want to be near us. Occasionally, she pulled out her phone to text someone. It stung that it wasn't Brian sitting next to me, but I appreciated their company anyway.

Later in the afternoon, Kayla and I went for a walk among the Seven Dwarfs. The dust cloud no longer clogged the sky to the north. Bill's plan to water and seed the ground worked, though the grasses wouldn't emerge till next spring. A mid-week snow shower gave us enough moisture when it melted to keep the dust down. Eventually, I led Kayla toward Big Leo.

"Have you been running?" I asked.

"Now and then. These last two weeks have been...ah... strange. I'd go home from school and then see that red or that black pickup and I wouldn't go in. So I'd walk over to Emily's. She doesn't make me explain. Friday I only went inside because I knew you were coming."

"How many times have you seen either truck?"

"Mmm...five, no, six times with Friday."

We reached the base of the bluff. "You ready?" I asked.

"Just a sec."

She reached up to push her hair back over her ears then darted up the up the hill. I laughed and followed. We reached the top, panting and laughing. I let her beat me, though I think she knew it. She watched the horses running in a distant pasture, the wind whipping her blonde ponytail against her face until she shoved it inside the back of her coat and pulled up her hood. Meanwhile, I walked over to a spot among some chunks of dirt then pulled out a brown waterproof case. When I extracted a pair of binoculars, Kayla scrambled to my side.

"You keep these up here?"

"Yeah, I like to keep an eye on things." I certainly wasn't going to tell her my main concerns. "We had some dust kicking up in the wind to the north, but it looks clear now."

Shifting my gaze to the northeast, a red Subaru pulled out of the Eldritch yard past the rear of the black Tundra. I directed the binoculars due north to a bluff past the Beast, on the land we now owned. Once I got it in focus, I passed the binoculars to Kayla and guided her line of sight to the bluff.

"See that opening on the east, the right side? What do you think it looks like?"

"A mouth."

I chuckled. "Yeah, an open mouth. I've decided to call it "The Joker," because it looks like it's laughing."

"Maybe it's laughing at us...all the stupid stuff."

I studied her as she lowered the binoculars and bit her lip.

"I think maybe my mom's gone crazy. And she doesn't care about me. She hasn't called all weekend."

"That's because your dad told her she couldn't."

Though that was true, the real reason was that Paul and Bo were keeping watch on her. She had hit some kind of drug-infused binge and hadn't sobered up as of two o'clock when I last called Bo, who said he chased away the Breeley brothers in the morning.

Kayla handed me the binoculars and sat down. I made another scan of the area, looking over toward Highway 51, which connected us to Highway 30 and Interstate 80. Then it hit me—"up three eighty-five" meant traveling north on Highway 385; and "dumb Injuns" probably referred to the Pine Ridge Indian Reservation for the Lakota Sioux, just north of the Nebraska-South Dakota border. Were the Breeley brothers dealing drugs, maybe even meth on the rez?

That evening, I retrieved Jackson Draper's phone number from a drawer in the study while Kayla watched *True Grit* with Patty. Jackson, a Lakota elder, said that the FBI had been inquiring about meth, and yes, he did think meth was in the area. I sent photos of the Breeley brothers to him and Robert Foxworthy.

At Custer's on Monday, Brian and I were given a full account of the life of Jackie Robinson by Davey. He became animated discussing all the accolades and accomplishments, including six consecutive All-Star selections from 1949 to 1954. Just as Davey was about to recite Robinson's career stats, he stepped backwards on RT's foot. RT jumped up from his chair.

"You little shit!" said RT, straining to put his face up close to Davey's. "Watch what you're doing you idiot!"

Davey dropped the tub then ran to the kitchen. Brian was out of the booth before RT could turn around. He grabbed RT under his armpits and shoved him backward to the rear wall where he slammed RT's head up against the wall. The sound of crashing dishes and glassware came from the kitchen. After throwing RT to the ground, Brian rushed past me toward the sound of rage.

"Davey stop!" Blaine, his father, pleaded.

When I saw Davey, he was slamming his head against a metal cupboard in the kitchen. Blaine tried to pull him away, but Davey slapped at Blaine then started biting his own wrist till blood streamed down his hand. Brian pushed me aside then ran up behind Davey and wrapped his arms around Davey from behind. Davey head-butted Brian, catching him just over the ear. Brian slid his grip down to get his head out of the way of Davey's repeated attempts to bash him again—but Brian never let go of his grip around Davey's body and arms.

EJ, the cook, came running out of the storage room with a red foam martial-arts helmet. By then, Davey was kicking wildly, hitting both his dad and Brian's shins.

"Get it on him!" said Blaine.

EJ came from behind Davey and over Brian's body slid the helmet down on Davey's head. Blaine took a kick but yanked on a strap of the helmet, securing it tight on the Velcro.

"We got to take him down," said Blaine.

Brian lifted him up off the ground then tipped him sideways. Blaine and EJ both grabbed a leg. I grabbed Davey's helmet as he kept trying to hit his head against something or somebody. Once on the floor, I pinned Davey's head to the ground to keep him from slamming it against the linoleum. Brian held on as Davey thrashed his legs, compelling EJ to lay across his legs. Davey kept fighting for a few minutes then calmed.

Blaine walked over to a huddled form resting against one of their refrigerators. I hadn't even noticed Beulah till now. She was bleeding from the inner forearm and holding her head. A clump of her long gray hair lay on the ground next to her. Most of her coarse, gray hair hung outside her ponytail holder. Blaine took a white cloth from a nearby cupboard and pressed it against her arm.

"I'm okay," she said. "Go to him."

Blaine knelt next to Davey. "It's all right. Davey is okay. It's okay. You relax."

Blaine nodded to me and I let go of the helmet. I rose then ran out of the kitchen. Big Joe McCready and Tom Sedlacek had RT backed against the wall. Rachel stood near the doors to the kitchen, looking indecisive. I rushed up to RT.

In a loud, clear voice I said to RT, "All right, Mr. FBI wash out. Come see what you've done. Then you can come back and tell everyone about your days at Boys Town as a juvenile delinquent. Oh, and I'm sure people want to hear how you planted that meth in Sidney just to impress us."

RT hissed, staring fire at me.

I looked to Big Joe and Tom and said, "Bring him."

The two big men shoved RT through the doors as Carol followed. Davey was still down.

Beulah was struggling to stand. "I tried to stop him from hurtin' himself. I should know better. Megan, help me."

"Are you sure?"

She nodded then wiped the tears from her eyes, as I helped her to her feet. RT was looking down at Davey as Beulah approached him. I stepped over a pool of blood as I grasped her trembling arms to keep her standing. RT looked at her, but said nothing.

"Get out of my restaurant and don't ever come back," she said.

"I'm sorry. I was—"

"Shut up and get out," I said. "And know this—the last man she kicked out died bloody."

RT left through the swinging doors. Big Joe followed him out then came back with a chair for Beulah.

Blaine shook his head. "He had gone two full years without one of these. You guys can let go."

Brian released his grip and EJ eased off Davey's legs. Davey sat up, looking confused.

Blaine looked over at Rachel, who had slipped into the room. "We don't need you. I don't mean to sound so…but this is family business."

Carol brusquely pushed her way past Rachel. She grabbed two of the plates of food off the counter that had been sitting under heat lamps. Rachel stepped back when Carol turned toward the dining room. "Family business," she said to Rachel.

Rachel looked back at Beulah. "I know first aid and both of you need some."

Beulah nodded.

After everything settled down and the blood was cleaned up, Brian and I returned to our offices. Still riled from the experience, I walked over to his office.

"Damn," I said. "Didn't see that coming."

Brian was holding ice wrapped in a towel against the side of his head.

"That was scary," he said, downing some Advil with cold coffee.

"You did really well," I said. "It would have been a lot worse if you hadn't been there."

Brian just looked at me with his big brown eyes. My tumor throbbed warm. I really was proud of him. This was the man I wanted to hurt, no, that was too mild—I wanted to break him. He was absent at supper when we'd talk and in the evening when we used to cuddle on the sofa. I missed him. Shit. I turned and left for my office, once again angry at him. Soon, he'd be leaving with his brother and father for Colorado for fishing and skiing with friends. And I'd still be alone. My tumor hardened then chilled in my chest.

An hour later, I left for a doctor's appointment in Sidney. My eyes were still twitching and dry. Last week, Patty said my throat looked fat. I hadn't even noticed, but she was right. The physician, Dr. Peabody, dug his fingers into the base of my neck. Then he made me swallow while he jammed his fingers in deeper. He checked my wrists then ran his fingers down my shins. After the results of my blood test came back, he declared that I had an underactive thyroid, but no nodules. He said a little pill every morning a half hour before breakfast would take care of the problem once he determined the right dosage. I picked up the prescription on the way back to work then took the first dose in the parking lot.

I was so relieved that I didn't have an eye problem. I'd never told anyone, but eye issues scared the hell out of me. Surely, there's a name for eye-problem phobia, but I never bothered to check. An under-achieving gland that could be fixed with a little pill seemed less scary. Blessed with good vision, I always wondered how contact lens wearers could stick their fingers in their eyes. Brian wore contacts without any difficulty, but I didn't like seeing him stick his fingers in his eyes. I supposed most people were wimpy about something. More disturbing was the thought of losing my eyesight. My grandmother lost her sight to glaucoma, so the gene was in the family. Still, I had dodged a bullet—I'd take my little pink pill religiously and return to the doctor in a month.

When I returned to the office, Kayla, Emily, and Chelsea were doing their homework in the firm's kitchen and eating Glenda's apple turnovers. After chatting with the girls, I returned a call to Karen Filch, the claims rep handling Joy's wrongful death claim. My demand was of course too high, and Karen's initial offer was predictably low. I felt confident we'd settle it eventually.

On Saturday, I helped move Kayla's things to the furnished rental duplex. Paul had already collected anything of Kayla's that was left at Sheila's house, as it was now called. Kayla approved of her new digs, though she kept adding to a list of things the house lacked, such as a toaster, a vacuum cleaner, a blender, decent flatware and dishes, and serving utensils. She refused to accept anything from her former home, except for the contents of her bedroom. Paul's kitchen stock consisted of old pots, pans, and eating utensils he used when he camped. After Kayla was settled, I went the office to work the rest of the afternoon. By the time I finished a spendthrift trust for a banker in Gering with a wastrel son, it was four o'clock and time for me to undertake a different sort of mission.

Chapter 12

I led Gondor around the eastern edge of Big Leo then took binoculars from the saddle bag. Even though RT's black pickup wasn't visible, I kept Gondor to the south until I could see the entire front of the old house. No vehicles looked to be in hidden in the scraggily copse across the street. I hastened my stallion toward the house then cut north as we approached it to avoid leaving hoof prints nearby.

The barn looked as good as the house looked bad—the house looked ready to collapse if the wind suddenly shifted, whereas the barn sported new wood planks in several places and a fresh coat of red paint. I dismounted Gondor then unlocked the padlock on the new rear door Lew had installed. Inside was relief from the cold west wind, four bales of hay near the center of the barn floor, with several bales stacked against the south wall, and two field mice scurrying out of sight. The flimsy ladders to the second story, which was open in the front and center of the barn, had been replaced by two wooden stairways.

Leaving Gondor to graze on the hay, I walked outside around to the front of the barn. After checking the padlock, which was secure, I looked over the hard dirt ground in front of the barn doors. No tire tracks were visible, yet something about the ground wasn't right. It looked disturbed, as if it had been swept. Walking through the grass, I discovered the ground was etched wherever it lacked the old gravel. The pattern extended all the way to the black top of the pock-marked road; however, the deceiver failed to sweep the dirt that covered the edge of the road.

I studied the tire tracks then dashed along the street to check the tracks in front of the house—they didn't match. Some vehicle other than RT's made a visit then tried hard to conceal the fact. I jogged over to the bushes across the street and broke off a branch, and then I ran back to the barn and yard to sweep away my footprints. I stashed the branch under the front porch and climbed up the north side from a patch of weeds. The porch creaked its complaint as I crossed over to the front door. After I unlocked the door and entered, I realized I left my gun in the saddlebag. Shit.

As I debated whether to go back and get it, I noticed a dead bolt lock had been installed on the door to the basement. What the hell? I stood pondering for a few minutes then went upstairs and did a quick check. Each room had its own draft of varying forces and directions. Plastic still covered three of the windows that were damaged by the tornado that destroyed Bill's house two years ago. I doubted that it was much warmer than outside. It looked like RT avoided the upper level. Back downstairs, I examined the kitchen. He wasn't spending time here either. The fridge still held only beer and Pepsi. A trash can nearly overflowed with beer cans. A coffee pot on the counter with a can of instant coffee next to it were new additions to the room. I then peeked through RT's meager belongings in the front room. He did keep a few shirts and pants in the coat closet. The air mattress was covered by cheap gray sheets and a thick, black comforter.

I found his halogen flashlight in the coat closet then went outside to peer into the basement windows. The room looked to be empty except for some wooden shelves along the south wall that some Eldritch had built. Just after I went back inside, I heard the sound of an approaching vehicle. I quickly placed the flashlight back in the closet. I ducked down and ran for the kitchen. Sure enough, RT had just pulled into the yard. I checked the side door in the kitchen, but realized I couldn't get out without RT seeing me. I did not want to deal with this man, especially now that I had

ALONE IN THE WIND

blabbed that he had been kicked out of the FBI, lived as a truant at Boys Town, and staged a drug find. I dashed to the dining room, yanked open the window, and then stuck my legs through. The truck door slammed. I eased my right hip over the frame. Reaching up, I grabbed the window as I scooted the rest of my body through.

Now hanging from the window ledge by one hand, the front door opened. Straining to hold myself above the ten foot drop where the ground sloped away from the house, I squelched the groans of exertion I wanted to make. I waited in agony until I heard the creak of the front door as it was closing, lowering the window at the same time. I forced down the window just before the front door shut. When I dropped to the ground, the shock of the impact radiated through my legs. Looking down, I discovered that I nearly landed on the edge of the window screen. I wasn't sure if RT had heard me, and I didn't plan to wait and find out. I scrambled around the edge of the house.

The sound of boots clomped across the wood floor and into the front room, no, the dining room. I was caught for sure. Just as I flattened myself against the side of the house, another vehicle pulled into the front yard. The footsteps stopped. I didn't think my heart could bludgeon my chest any harder, but it did. RT crossed the floor away from me. I waited until I heard the front door open then I hobbled to the rear of the barn, which sat several yards farther back from the road than the house. I slipped inside.

Gondor snorted and I tried to quiet him as I pulled the Glock from the saddle bag. I stuck it in the front waistband of my jeans then led Gondor out the back, pausing to peer around the corner. I locked the door then pulled on the reins to make Gondor follow me to the front edge of the barn. I heard voices from the porch. A black Dodge pickup was parked next to RT's Tundra. The pounding of boots on the porch ceased and the door closed. It was time to get the hell out of here.

I mounted Gondor and forced him to walk over ridges and rocky ground to keep us north of the barn and out of sight of the house. Once we crested a hill and descended the slope, we turned west for home, the wind stinging my face, but bringing the sharp, welcoming smell of logs burning in the Wilson fireplace. I sucked in the air, wishing my brain enjoyed the same respite as my lungs. Where was all of this going? I felt the threat, but I didn't understand the danger or foresee who it would involve. I wished my mom or Beverly awaited me at home.

Back at Uncle Bill's barn, I brushed Gondor's coat as he ate out of a bucket of oats. I ignored the two cowhands shoveling out Rohan's stall as I tried to sort out my thoughts. Out of the wind, I still felt the adrenaline surging through me. I wasn't sure whether RT had seen me. The arrival of the Breeley brothers must have been more important at the moment. Maybe he wanted me to get away. And why were they there? If RT figured out they were involved in dealing meth or whatever Sheila was on, then it would be more natural for him to seek them out or even arrest them. Maybe he didn't have sufficient evidence.

Or—

It made sense. But was I off base? I set down my brush and walked over to the two hands, Bud Ritchie and Jack Hoffman, both late twenty-somethings. They tipped their hats to me.

From the time I was a toddler, cowhands in the employment of Bill Docket were instructed not to speak to me unless spoken to; in fact, they weren't even supposed to look at me. Once when I was fourteen, a hand greeted me with something provocative like "good morning." My uncle fired him on the spot. He meant to set an example for every cowboy he hired over the years.

I did my best to stifle a gag from the pungent fumes of manure. I needed to get outside to clear my head of the methane.

"Hi, guys. Have either of you seen a red or a black Dodge pickup over at the old Eldritch place?"

Bud nodded as Jack said, "Both, several times, but just one or the other."

"What about at the barn?"

"Not while we were workin' on it, but yeah, after that."

"If either of you see them again, tell Bill or me."

They nodded, but kept looking at me.

"Yeah, I'm wondering why those two louts would be hanging around a drug cop, too."

That got a grin out of Bud.

"See ya."

They tipped their hats and I returned to Gondor. As I started to brush Gondor's mane, I thought about the dead-bolt on the basement door. Did RT plan to store something down there? Or was he just baiting me into demanding the door be opened to an empty room? He would enjoy thwarting and embarrassing me. I walked back over to Bud and Jack. They stopped shoveling shit long enough to listen to me.

"Next time you go by the Eldritch house and the black Toyota pickup is gone, take a look in the basement windows. Let Bill or me know if you see anything or if the windows get covered up. I think Bill keeps flashlights in one of those cupboards."

Bud nodded. I didn't know if he was laconic or just too chicken to talk to me.

Jack said, "Somethin' fishy might be goin' on."

"Might be or maybe he's just playing a game with us. Hard to know with that guy."

"I hate his guts. I heard about Davey. My sister useta be in the same class with him in Sidney. Went through all their grades together."

"What's your sister doing now?"

"She's in a vocational workshop in Sidney. Likes it real well."

"I'm glad to hear it. I think I've seen her. But about RT, stay away from him. I think he's dangerous…more so that you're mad at him. He likes to provoke people."

"I heard you got a Glock."

I smiled. "A nine millimeter. I gift from my father-in-law. I could get in trouble, but I can't be toting Miss Gulch around."

Bud, in particular, thought that was funny. That pleased me for I didn't really want to be known as some ice queen. In a way, I did feel like a frosty princess. Early winter was colder than normal, but no place was colder than my bed at night with the wind lashing against the house—no making love, no soft baritone, just cold sheets.

Chapter 13

THE phone rang, unnerving me. I'd spent a disturbed evening alone, unable to shake a sense of disquietude. Now this. Who would call me at ten o'clock on a Friday night? Bill, James, and Lew were at the Cowpoke, with Patty and Johnny Two Rivers, whom she had resumed dating. I was alone with Nicholas Nickleby, who was fleeing Dotheboys with Smike for a life at sea. I loved this passage, but it had taken five tries for my brain to focus on one page.

"Brian, what's wrong?"

"How did you know something is wrong?"

"I just do. Where are you?"

"In a jail cell in Fort Collins."

"What the hell for?"

At his response, I plopped down hard on the sofa. The news rendered my brain mushy; I shook my head to think. Incredible. My husband had been arrested for a DUI.

"Where's your dad? I thought you were with him and your brother."

"My dad is so pissed at me for drinking and driving with my brother in the car that he's planning to let me stay here overnight. But Megan, I wasn't drunk."

"It doesn't matter. I'm not letting you spend the night in jail. How much is bail?"

"Five hundred bucks cash."

"Okay, I'll bring it." I paused and he was silent. "Brian, thanks for calling me."

"You're my wife, aren't ya?"

I smiled into the phone. "Absolutely." It was actually smart of him to play to my sense of protectiveness.

I left a message on Bill's home answering machine regarding my whereabouts. Then I headed up Highway 51 to catch the interstate. I stopped at a Kimball ATM to get the extra cash I needed. In a little over two hours, I was in Fort Collins, listening to my GPS, Lucy, for directions to the police station. After waiting for a half hour, Brian was released to me. His face looked strained, just like I'd probably look after spending hours locked up in a cell with undesirables. Just before I reached out to hug him, it struck me. Former Husker football star— DUI. The nightmare was only beginning. But for now I just held him.

"Thanks for coming for me. I'm starved. Can we stop for something to eat?"

"Sure, come on."

In the Shark, Lucy led us to a nearby Village Inn. He ate a burger and three sides. Now that my Brian was safe and I'd eaten scrambled eggs and toast, I began to get drowsy. Brian's narrative was the only thing that kept me from dropping my head into my fruit plate.

"I can't believe your dad would be this cruel. Even my father wouldn't have done something so cold."

"Well, I did have two beers, but with supper. I wasn't drunk. Josh was—that's why I was driving his car. But my dad refused to believe me. He says I was an idiot and could have gotten us both killed. But this redneck deputy had it out for me."

"I believe you. Never once have you lied to me."

He was quiet for a moment then said, "I did what that guy from Scottsbluff did."

"What's that?"

"You told me about it. I refused a field sobriety test and a breathalyzer test. But the idiot cop let me get my hat out of the car. That's when I grabbed Josh's flask of whiskey and shoved it inside my coat. Nobody searched me a second time. So when I was in the police station, sitting on a bench, I started chugging that whiskey, right in front of them. They got really mad. I let them take the blood test after that."

I was quiet for a moment then I burst out laughing. "Good for you. I remember that story now. So they can't prove you were drunk when you were stopped."

"I did run a stop sign...I'll concede that."

He began to look himself again, though he still smelled like he'd spent a month in the brig on a convict ship to Devil's Island.

"You look like you're about to fall out of your chair," he said.

"I am. Can you drive? You know how late this is for me."

A few minutes later, Lucy directed us to the interstate and I conked out. We were nearly home when I awoke. What now? I checked my phone for messages. I read a text from Derek asking if Brian was okay. I bolted upright.

"Did you call Derek before you called me?"

Brian looked over and saw that I held my phone. "Yes, I did. I wasn't sure—"

"That I would rescue you? And that I'd be as cold-hearted as your dad?"

"You've been cold to me for the last two months."

"And in that time, not once have you asked to come back."

"You aren't one to be persuaded. You were dead-set on punishing me."

He drove past the exit for Dexter.

"That's true enough. But how can I be sure that you won't go into another one of your vice and vengeance modes? You were determined to get at me and you succeeded."

"And you've succeeded in humbling me. Are you waiting for me to beg?"

"No," I said.

"Then what?"

"I don't know. Just something that makes me think you've grown up."

"Ah, shit. You keep throwing that at me. You need to be a little more compassionate and a lot less hard. You're the Queen Bee of Dexter. And you act like everyone should be as perfect as you."

"Oh, that's bullshit."

"People have weaknesses…you forget that."

"And is adultery your weakness? Huh? Let me be bloody clear on this—two strikes and you're out. I won't tolerate this again. And you can carve that in stone."

We were quiet as he drove through Sidney. He pulled into his dad's driveway.

"You need to think about what I just said. And don't even think about entering my house without getting a complete blood test. I need to see documentation to prove that sleazy whore didn't give you something nasty."

I got out of the SUV and walked around to the driver's side. The cold wind cut at my face. We stood looking at each other.

"I'm glad you're okay. Do you have your key?"

He nodded. He'd had a rotten day and I hadn't improved it.

"Thank you for rescuing me," he said.

"Yeah." I climbed into the Shark and backed out of the driveway slowly, but I didn't take off until he was safe inside the house.

God above, what a night. Suddenly, achingly awake, I drove home well aware that I wouldn't be sleeping for a while. I tossed my purse on the kitchen table and poured a full glass of bourbon. As I was feeling that first burn, my cell phone rang. I glanced at the clock then took my phone out of my purse. Brian must have timed my drive home.

"Are you getting ready for bed?" he asked.

"No. I'm not ready for sleep," I said, wondering where this conversation was going.

"As soon as I called Derek, I knew it was a mistake. I'm glad he missed the call."

"Vonny would have left you in jail."

He chuckled. I couldn't help but smile. We were quiet for several awkward moments.

"Goodnight," I said.

"Um, goodnight then."

I drank a little more bourbon then dumped it. I spent a fitful night trying to sleep. It didn't get to a consistent deep sleep till nearly dawn, and then I slept till ten.

I dressed then wandered around, ending up in my bathroom. I liked that he wasn't around to bother me when I was trying to shower and dress. He was so damn chatty in the mornings, but I wasn't ready to talk till I'd had my breakfast. I think food must awaken my personality. I walked back into the bedroom. I liked having the closet to myself. I didn't need to worry that my suits were getting squished and wrinkled when I could spread them out. Then I looked at the bed—I wanted him there.

When I went downstairs for breakfast, Patty let me be. Once I finished, I told her about Brian's arrest. She studied me, but didn't say much. Having known me since I was twelve, she knew to wait and watch.

I put on my coat and gloves and trudged out to the Seven Dwarfs. I passed by two of them then I stopped hard. The truth smacked me in the face—I wanted him back. I took shelter on the southeast side of one of the rocky mounds. From a promise I'd made to him a year ago, I carried my cell phone with me. I called his number and he answered right away.

"I want you to come back to me," I said.

"Really? Are you sure?" Then after a pause, he said, "I want to come back."

"Today?"

"Yeah. Where are you?"

"Sleepy, no, this Doc."

"I knew you'd go out there. And I can hear the wind."

"Where are you?"

"Just back from the doctor...er...lab. I got the blood test. I slipped the lab tech guy five hundred bucks to do the test right away and give me a report."

"Hmm. Five hundred...the cost of bail."

"Uh, huh. My dad got home a little while ago. He's tossed me out of the house. I was packing my stuff back into your boxes."

"Where would you have gone?"

"I figured I'd go camp at my Sidney office."

"Come home."

I loved saying that.

"Give me about a half hour. I can't wait to get away from him. He won't listen to a word I say."

"Okay."

I jogged back home, eager to get out of the frigid wind, and excited to make preparations. Actually, there wasn't much to do. I would tell him when he came. I told Patty my plan.

"About time," she said. "Though he deserved everything he got, except for jail, if he really wasn't drunk." She grabbed a rag and the furniture polish out of the mud room.

"Hey, be nice to him, will ya?"

She turned back to me. "If he's in your good graces, he's in mine. Now let me go dust."

Brian paused and scratched his head when I told him my plan to give him my dad's old room as his dressing room.

"And you're kicking me out of the bathroom room, too?"

"One bed."

He smiled at that. We kissed for the first time since July then he grabbed a box and lugged it up the back stairs. I followed with my arms full of hang up clothes.

That afternoon, we went to the family room to watch college football, but we spent most of the time snoozing on the sofa—relieved and relaxed. We went to the Cowpoke for burgers and dancing with Bill, James, and Patty. Lew came and sat with us, without saying a word for the first fifteen minutes. Big Joe McCready squeezed Brian's shoulder and his wife Maggie gave me a wink. Otherwise, nobody bothered us with a reminder that neither of us had been seen there for three months.

Back at home, back in our bedroom, I was sure I wanted to make love, just unsure how it would go. From the first time we made love on the carpet in my father's deceased partner's office till our breach at the end of July, our lovin' had been exciting and smooth. But this was different— Brian was trying too hard and came off as clumsy; I fought the whole time to keep that image of the whore in the towel out of my head—I was distracted and he was insecure. We pulled it off, but lay awake apart from each other for a thousand minutes. I tried to breathe deeply to keep the choke in my throat from becoming a sob. I wished for some peace of mind and Rolaids, for the tumor was now lodged in my stomach; I didn't fall asleep till I heard his steady breathing. Sex was like sleep—you can ruin it by thinking.

At some point in the night, I rolled back toward the center of the bed, to where I had been sleeping. His body was there, warm and hard. It drew me in like a magnet. I nestled my face into his neck and his arms wrapped me up. Tighter and tighter we clenched each other. Our lips came together, too wet, warm, and buzzing to notice sleep breath. I felt as if I had been away and just now came home. Sweet heat. Explosion. When we kissed again I couldn't tell whose tears I felt on my lips. He pulled his head back to wipe his eyes, as I wiped my own. He pulled me back to him. I pressed my head against his neck and we formed a solid, single mass, as one, as God intended. Never did we speak a word—talk was overrated anyway.

Chapter 14

I awoke to my alarm clock and to the feeling that my world had been set right. We were intent on making up for lost time; however, we were forced to get moving or we'd be late for church.

"Your shower or mine?" Brian teased as he strolled into my bathroom. "Ooh, aqua accents now."

"Well, I needed something to distract me while I was alone. If you hadn't come back, I planned to buy an electric blanket. You're warm-blooded, and I'd lost my ability to create enough heat for this big bed."

I followed him into the bathroom, which was essentially white, with an accent color or two I changed every couple of years. Last month, I was struck by a rare blast of impulse—I ordered new towels and rugs even though I had redecorated just before our wedding last February. I suppose I was trying to enliven myself. I thought aqua was the perfect color to contradict the winter that had hit early and the tumor that had iced-over. I liked the aqua, but I wouldn't give it any credit for dissolving the tumor.

After a steamy shower and a quick breakfast, we headed for the Harney Street pew at our little Presbyterian church. Brian didn't normally come to church with me. A Catholic, he attended mass with his dad and brother, at least until this week. We were joined by Bill, James, and Patty. This week, Johnny Two Rivers came along. I supposed he was trying to look respectable to Patty, for this was their second go-around at dating. He'd broken her heart two years ago, so she was taking it slower and with more reserve.

After the service, Johnny asked, "So what's going on at Custer's? Patty said I could come."

"Well, for one thing, Davey is coming back after missing...what two weeks?" said Bill. "Beulah finally convinced him that RT was never going to be there."

"The last few days I've seen him peering out the windows in the kitchen doors, looking for him," I added.

"That's great, he's a good kid," said Johnny. "But Patty says we're gonna be guinea pigs. That's what I'm wonderin' about."

"Beulah says it's a secret," I said as we bundled ourselves in our coats and scarves for the blustery November day. "I guess it's a new dish they're going to start serving. And don't you dare think of stealing it for the Cowpoke."

Johnny laughed as we parted for our cars. As Brian and I arrived at the Shark, he pulled an envelope from under the driver side windshield wiper. A large M was written on the outside. He handed it to me, his face tight with cold and alarm.

The envelope had a black smudge on the lower right corner. I held the envelope up against the light of the sky. The thin, cheap envelope showed a dark powder filled about a third of it.

"Well, it's not ricin or anthrax...that stuff's white," I said. "We should open it in the car so it won't get blown away."

I felt unnerved by it, but we got into the SUV where I opened a crack on one corner then took a sniff then handed it to Brian.

"Gunpowder," I said.

"What the hell?"

I shrugged, not wanting to alarm him. "It's probably some prank. I'll show it to Bo after supper. Don't say anything to anyone. Let's go."

As I slid the envelope into my purse, I kept my head down so Brian couldn't see the anxiety warming my face.

The quick three-block trip wasn't even enough time for the car heater to get going. When we arrived at Custer's, the window shades were down and a big sign read: "Closed for Private Party," written in Beulah's jittery scrawl. In the center of the room, the Shuster gang had lined up all the tables so that there was one long one, covered in white table cloths. Beulah ushered us in then we piled our coats in the empty booths. As the diner was open for breakfast on Sundays, three customers were still in their separate booths along the wall. Lew was sitting in a booth next to Rachel, who was in civilian clothes and sat in a booth adjacent to Eldon Strumple. His son, EJ, was the cook at Custer's. I thought it was shame that none of those people really knew each other; then again, maybe a likable hick, a female state trooper, and a retired Methodist minister didn't have much in common.

Beulah shuffled over to the three booths and insisted the three join our party. Carol took a head count while Blaine and Dane put water pitchers on the table. Barb Shuster, Davey's mom, came out to take drink orders, though Davey had yet to make an appearance. As everyone was settling into their seats, I reached into my purse and touched the edge of the envelope. What did it mean?

Beulah cleared her throat as she stood at the end of the table. "I hope you all like steak," she said to enthusiastic nods and murmurs.

"No vegetarians here," said Bill. He waved to Davey, who was peeking through the kitchen door window.

Davey poked his head out the door. Beulah motioned him to come forward. His head disappeared for a moment, and then he emerged with his tub. I chugged my water so I'd have something for him to put in his tub. Brian did likewise. Davey slunk by a few people to come directly to me. I handed him my glass and he smiled. He took Brian's then Patty's. By the time he walked back to the kitchen with his shoulders back and his head held high, most of us were without water glasses. Barb, Blaine, and Carol soon brought out our drinks, which were mostly coffee and hot tea, given the cold day. Barb walked up behind me and put her hand on my shoulder. She was fifty or so, a bit chunky, with her shoulder-length, graying brown hair pulled back in a barrette.

"Thank you, Megan," she said, sweeping her bangs to the side. "I know how good you and Brian are to my boy." She smiled at Brian.

"My pleasure," I said.

"Ashley will be home at Thanksgiving."

"Oh, I'd like to see her," I said.

Ashley was her daughter, who was a sophomore at the University of Nebraska at Kearney. Beulah told me it took a solid year to get Ashley to go off to college and leave her brother. She'd probably heard about the brawl and Davey's setback.

I glanced over to Rachel and it struck me. Gunpowder. Desruction. It was a warning. Did she know about it? Did she plant it? Wait, I had smelled gunpowder and hay right after I met RT; it had smacked of portent then. But of what?

I allowed myself to be distracted by the meals they served. Oh, my—filet mignon, buttered new potatoes, broccoli covered in seasoned butter sauce, and blueberries in creamy goo.

"Don't forget to breathe," I whispered to Brian, who was downing his steak in record time.

"I can do that later."

EJ, Beulah, Blaine, Barb, and Dane watched from the back wall. I motioned to them. EJ and Beulah came forward.

"Oh, my, this is so good, EJ. The marinade is—"

"Bourbon, yeah," said EJ. "We'll serve a five ounce at lunch and an eight at supper."

"My father would have loved this."

"I'm glad you said that," said Beulah. Then she hesitated. "Um…with you and Bill's permission, we would like to call this meal 'The Frank Docket'…in honor of your father."

The table became quiet. My face warming, I looked across the table at Bill. He smiled.

"We'd be pleased," I said. I really did feel honored and touched.

James lifted his coffee cup and said, "To Frank Docket…the greatest friend this town has ever known."

Cups were raised and clanged together as the chatter at the table reached its highest volume. Davey cowered against the wall behind my chair.

"Davey, I have a big photo of Jackie Robinson at the law firm office," I said. "You should come see it sometime."

"I'll get my coat."

"Oh, um…your aunt said there would be dessert. We could go there a little bit later, okay?"

He nodded and started stacking plates in the tub.

"Hey, Megan, do you like live jazz?" asked Rachel.

"Yeah," I said. "Are you suggesting a trip to Rush Street in Chicago? I don't think I have time today."

She smiled. "No, but could you make it to Sidney over Thanksgiving?"

"Wait. There's a band playing jazz in western Nebraska? I don't believe it. We only know the Husker fight song and twang out in nowhere."

"I'm serious. I know of some guys who play jazz and they'll be home from college over Thanksgiving. I heard them over the summer. I stopped them for speeding on the interstate. The cases in the backseat really were filled with two saxophones and a trumpet."

People began to chat about jazz, who liked it, who didn't. But my mind began to veer then race. Who was threatening me? Was it you, Rachel? Maybe. The Breeley brothers? Nah, they were just two galoots. Dobbs? It seemed too subtle for him. RT was the most likely candidate. He would enjoy scaring me—he was also the most dangerous. A shudder raced up my back.

After a piece of strawberry-rhubarb pie, I became social again. Brian and I drove to the law firm with Barb and Davey in the silver Honda Accord behind us. Davey was only slightly interested in the cases of Civil War memorabilia that now decorated three walls of the office; though he was fascinated by the variety of Union caps we had collected. He did like the colorful portrait of Black Elk, the famous Medicine Man and Holy Man of the Oglala Lakota Sioux, which hung on the wall behind Glenda's receptionist desk. I thought it gave the office a "sense of balance," which Gus called the Docket term for political correctness. Glenda initially objected to the portrait because she heard Black Elk participated in the Battle of Little Big Horn. She smiled and handed me a scone when I told her that Black Elk was christened a Catholic in 1904.

We led Davey to the conference room. As he stood in front of the large Jackie Robinson framed photograph, he reeled off a list of his accomplishments and statistics to no one in particular. Suddenly, he turned to stare at the photo on the opposite wall, as if he was someone who had just entered the room. He scrunched his brow.

"That's Johnny Unitas, a famous football quarterback," I said. Davey started to turn away until I said, "He was my father's favorite football player."

Davey looked back at the photo, and then at me. "Where's your father?"

"He died last year."

"Oh, that's bad."

"For me, yes. Maybe not for him. He's with God now. Do you know God?"

"Mmm. Mom and Dad tell me things, but I don't know…"

"That's okay. God knows you."

Not a master of subtlety, his face brightened. "He does?"

ALONE IN THE WIND

"Sure."

"That's good."

"Very good."

He turned back to the photo. I read that autistics had great difficulty with abstract concepts. I wondered if he would now connect the 1960s football player with a crew cut and a blue jersey to God.

Before leaving, I showed Davey my office. He gave the shelves of law books a cursory glance as he went straight for the Van Gogh print that hung behind my desk.

"Ooooh," he said. "Van-van—"

"Van Gogh," I said, giving it the American pronunciation. "It's called *Starry Night*. Do you like it?"

He nodded several times. Eventually, Barb was forced to lead him away.

"Starry Night, Starry Night, Starry Night," he repeated all the way out to the Honda.

On the way home, Brian asked, "Did you see that in Amsterdam?"

"No, but I made sure I saw it when I was in New York. I love my print, but to see the original...and really see those intense brush strokes...well, the feeling is hard to describe."

He nodded, though I knew he didn't care a bit for art. At least he was humoring me.

"You've been thinking about that envelope," he said.

I nodded. "But I don't know who's behind it. Maybe we'll never know."

His eyes stayed on me—we both knew I'd never let this threat hang over me without delving into its mystery.

Just before supper, Brian came and plopped down on the bed. I was in the process of ordering Davey a megasized book of Van Gogh prints. I clicked on the button to place the order then turned from my laptop to look at him.

"It's hit. Former Husker DUI in Colorado. I'll be in every friggin' newspaper in the state tomorrow. It's on the Scottsbluff evening news."

I sat on his lap and gave him a hug.

"And when you're acquitted, that will be in all those papers and on every station in the state. Tomorrow I'm gonna track down the best Colorado lawyer I can and get things set right."

He wrapped his arms around my lower back so that when he stood up, he lifted me off the ground. Right in the middle of a kiss, the intercom on my house phone beeped.

"Damn," he said. "That will be Patty announcing supper."

"Hey, be thankful. If not for her, you'd be suffering through my cooking."

"I didn't know you could cook at all."

"Steak, tacos, and scrambled eggs. I can clean and iron. I had to fend for myself when I lived in Omaha."

"We wouldn't starve. I can make spaghetti."

"And I'm sure it's good, but let's hope we don't lose her anytime soon."

While Brian answered Patty's call, I dialed Beulah on my cell. I told her about Brian's arrest for DUI, but that he was framed by a redneck Colorado cop and wasn't even drunk.

"You'll be wantin' folks to know the truth," she said. "I'll make sure ever'body at breakfast and lunch knows."

"Thanks. You're always the one I can count on."

I could picture her grinning so broadly that her silver eye tooth flashed.

Chapter 15

THE next morning, I put in a call to the insurance claim rep. I wanted to make sure Joy received her settlement in plenty of time for Christmas shopping. And I planned to recommend paying off her mortgage as part of her spending.

Karen, the claim rep, answered on the second ring. We exchanged pleasantries, for I knew her well—I was usually on her side as defense counsel in automobile cases.

"Now, Karen, it's time to get this claim settled. You don't want this to go before a jury. Don Troff, of Troff Construction, was driving a company vehicle on company time, so the jury will presume the defendant has deep pockets."

"I agree that evidence would get in," she said.

"And you'll be expecting me to take those State Patrol photos and blow them up to ten by six foot shots of a clumsy oaf's attempt to deceive the police. I'll make it crystal clear to the jury that Don Troff not only tried to push wrongdoing onto an innocent family man, but he also sought to defraud his way to making money off his recklessness."

"I'll admit he's not a model citizen."

"And, I'll show all the bloody details of Jake Breeley's death. Karen, I was at the scene shortly after the accident. It was gut-wrenching. I'll make that jury want to puke and punish that scumbag, who was recently convicted of motor vehicle homicide, a felony."

I paused to let that hit its mark.

"Now, Karen, western Nebraska juries are tight with a buck—I'll concede that. But what will they think when they learn your insured was high on meth?"

"Meth? Oh, Lord. Wait…they haven't even released the transcript of that trial. How do you know it was meth?"

"I know one of the investigating officers."

Long pause. Excellent.

"Let me get back to you," she said.

I played my final card, an ace. I predicted we'd settle by the end of the day.

Just as I ended my phone call to Lucas Spencer, the Denver attorney who agreed to represent Brian, I heard a commotion in the lobby. Opening the door, I saw Nick Webster shaking Melanie by the shoulders.

"Huh? Bitch! Why don't you answer?"

Melanie started to duck, but her boyfriend's blow caught her in the side of the head, knocking her to the ground. Nick turned just in time for Brian's left to slam into his jaw. Before he could fall, Brian smashed in his nose. Nick fell to his knees and tottered just long enough to get his left eye bashed in. Brian's chest heaved as he walked over the prostrate man and stomped on his cupped right hand. The sound of cracking turned my stomach.

"Brian, stop!" I yelled.

I got in between Brian and Nick, who had flipped over on his back. Gus rushed up and grabbed Brian's shoulders.

"Enough, Brian," said Gus, who looked at me in a panic.

We both knew we couldn't stop him. I pleaded with Brian as he pulled away from Gus. I got in front of Brian, who heaved a great breath then stepped back. Nick groaned. Glenda rushed to Nick with some rags.

"You sorry vermin," she said. "You're going to ruin this carpet." She pressed a rag to the man's bleeding nose then started wiping up the blood. "I already called the police."

"When you get a chance, call Paul Ritter and tell him we need one of his carpet cleaners," I said.

Joy was tending to Melanie, who didn't look to be bleeding, but probably had a hellacious headache. I checked with Melanie then turned back to Brian. I grabbed his arm and pulled him into my office.

"That was a bit extreme, don't you think?" I asked.

He walked over to my window, but said nothing.

"Brian?"

"I kinda snapped, didn't I?"

"Yeah."

"My sister Danielle got beat up by her boyfriend when I was in college. When I drove home that next weekend, her eye was still swollen and her nose was busted. Josh and I took care of him."

"I don't think I want the details of that."

A car door slammed shut. It was Dobbs—this could be trouble. We met him in the lobby.

Dobbs stood by the front door looking down at Nick, who had been dragged across the floor so that he now bled on the ceramic tile near the double front doors. Melanie was seated in one of the lobby chairs with an ice pack to her head. Fortunately, we didn't have any waiting customers.

"You piece of shit!" Dobbs yelled at Nick. "Hittin' a woman? That's as low as it gets. God dammit! You're a mess."

He walked over to Brian, with Gus on his heels. "That's a hell of a beatin' you put on him, Brian. In fact, I think you went too far."

I stepped up beside Brian. "But, I'm sure you'll do the right thing, Chief. In fact, both Brian and I know it."

Dobbs flashed at look at Brian then glowered at me as his face flushed red. I returned his stare. He was stuck and we both knew it. If he pressed charges against Brian for battery, he knew I'd tell the whole town that he had crashed his pickup in a drunken stupor then claimed the truck had been stolen. He'd be charged with fraud and lose his job. I kept my face as rigid as I could, though it was hard not to smile. Even as the veins in his neck began to bulge and turn purple, he stared at me as his brain fought with his ego. The man hated to be thwarted, and I'd done it again.

Finally, he turned to Gus. "Give me a hand, will ya? I need to take him to the Sidney ER before I lock him up."

Gus helped Nick to his feet. Deputy Bo passed by them and sat down next to Melanie to take her statement.

"Errrrgh!" Nick growled at Brian, as he cradled his hand and stumbled like a drunkard out the door.

Dobbs said as they were going out the door, "You have the right to remain silent. Anything…"

Glenda closed the door against the cold. Brian walked to my office and I followed.

"I do believe you knocked out some teeth," I said. "I'd say three, maybe four broken fingers, a black eye and I think he blacked out for a bit, so maybe, hopefully, a concussion."

Brian looked down. "I nearly got arrested," he said quietly to me.

"You didn't and you won't."

"You're blackmailing the chief of police. That's bloody awesome."

After school, Kayla, Emily, and Chelsea arrived at the kitchen door with their faces stinging from the cold. They dumped their backpacks and accepted the hot chocolate Glenda had ready for them. Kayla and I chatted for a bit. She hadn't heard anything from her mother. Melanie told me I had a call waiting from Tom Sedlacek. I left to take the call, confident Glenda, the Good Witch of the North, would supervise the girls, even with Joy present. She had become the retired schoolmarm turned grandmother for the law firm. Kayla confessed that her dad was a terrible cook, but Glenda brought food over most days after work. Kayla and Joy both confided that Glenda was renting Disney and Pixar movies for them, along with an occasional PG movie.

"Hi, Tom, how are—"

"Megan, listen," Tom cut in. "The Breeley brothers are headed north on Highway 385. I followed them till Gurley then I turned off so they wouldn't think they were being followed. I'm in my buddy's car...they'd know my truck. They're in Riley's red Dodge pickup."

"Okay, Tom. Can you hang on for a moment?"

I pulled my cell phone out of my purse and called Robert Foxworthy and then Jackson Draper, the Pine Ridge rez elder.

"Tom, you still there?"

"Yeah."

"I called the FBI and Pine Ridge. Maybe they'll be able to track them, though they'll either need to stop for the night or maybe stay with their contact on the reservation."

"Okay, good. Hey, I heard Brian beat the crap out of Nick Webster."

"He was protecting Melanie."

"I'm sure he deserved what he got. Hey, you heard from Zach lately?"

"Zach Whitfield? Ah, no. What's up?"

"Something, but with Zane. I'll agree he hasn't been the same since he came back from Afghanistan. Zach has me checking up on him. Mrs. W lets me 'cause she's concerned."

"Did he suffer head trauma over there?"

"Zach says he did, but Zane's denyin' it. He just hangs out in his mother's basement all day playin' video games."

"Well, if you talk to Zach, tell him he can call me. I don't think Mrs. Whitfield wants to see me. She didn't even come to my dad's funeral. He sure supported her when Rick died. I guess she's mad because Zach got fired."

"Yeah, I remember confrontin' you about it."

"It's complicated. Zach might tell you. But the bottom line was that the firm needed an experienced tax guy to replace his dad, not two rookies...me included."

"And now you're the boss."

"Sometimes things work out in weird ways. I'll let you know if anything comes from tracking the Breeleys."

"My dad thinks you should be on the town council."

"Eh, no thanks. They were always trying to snare my dad. Nope, I don't want to be forced into official respectability."

He chuckled. "You'd be great...shake things up."

Life felt shaky enough.

Later in the afternoon, I received a call from Karen. We settled Joy's claim at the amount of my last demand. I called Joy and Brian to my office and relayed the great news. Joy hugged me with a grip stronger than I thought she could possess. Brian held out the tissue box for her as she smiled then sat down in a chair to wipe her eyes.

"It's done," she said.

"I hope it gives you some closure," I said. "But now it's time to think about some things."

"Paying bills."

"Yes, that, but beyond that you need to be making plans. For example, if you can pay off your mortgage without incurring an early pay-off penalty, then you should do that. If there is a penalty, pay it down as far as you can. Also, I would recommend putting the bulk into an annuity and some into an IRA. If you keep a big chunk of money, then everyone you've ever known will be looking for handouts."

"Oh, yeah. Dugger and Riley will be trying to mooch off me."

"Don't even tell your brothers-in-law that you've settled. By the way, they go out of town often. Do you know where they go?"

"No idea. I try to avoid them as much as possible. My brothers have been around quite a bit, so that keeps them away."

"By the way, this settlement is compensation, not income, so you don't pay taxes on it."

"Just the gains from your investments," Brian added.

"It's a lot to deal with. Will you help me?"

"We both will," I said.

"Oh, I can't wait to tell the girls."

Brian looked at his watch. "I could dash over to Shaver's for some ice cream and Bear Lake Beulah root beer."

"Perfect," I said.

Joy smiled and nodded as she drifted out the door, deep in thought.

"Of course, you will help her," he said. "You're like a mother hen."

"She asked for help, didn't she?"

"Yeah, it's just like you need to fix everything."

"I suppose you think I spend too much time with Kayla."

Brian smiled. "You mother her. It suits you and she needs it."

"So, you think motherhood suits me?"

"Oh, yeah. You'll be everything your parents weren't."

"I do want kids…you know that…just not right now."

"No, we don't have time. I need to get the root beer." He smiled. "Good job, counselor. That family deserved it."

He gave me a quick kiss, and then left me standing in the middle of the office deep in thought. Motherhood.

Brian left early the next morning to meet with Luke Spencer, his attorney in Denver, and to attend a hearing at which he would plead not guilty. In his absence, I worked till noon then I met Bill at the Pizza Shoppe, which was our normal Friday lunch spot.

"So what's the buzz around town?"

My uncle knew exactly what I meant.

"Oh, everybody thinks Brian's gettin' the shaft. They love Davey and hate RT. And let's see...oh, there's a rumor that Joy might have settled her death claim."

"Right on all accounts," I said. "Beulah likes Brian, so I knew she'd get the word out that he was getting framed by some redneck cop."

"Lots of people are saying it's because people from Colorado have somethin' against us...probably because they hate Nebraska football."

"Mmm...I don't know about that. Vonny's never said anything. No, I think it's because when they rolled down the windows the cop smelled Josh's whiskey breath and assumed they were both drunk. And yes, I settled Joy's claim on Wednesday, but that's for her to announce."

"Good for her. She seems like a nice gal. Oh, I almost forgot. Bud says to tell you that they've been lookin' and it's still empty. What's empty?"

"The old Eldritch basement. RT put a dead bolt lock on it. But you can see in from the outside windows. I asked Bud and Jack to keep an eye on it."

"What do you think he's doing?"

"Not sure. Maybe just baiting me. I suppose at some point he'll cover the windows. Then he'll expect me to demand a search, only to find empty shelves and field mice hiding from the winter."

"Well, I can send some other hands around, make it seem like they're checkin' the barn for rotting wood or somethin' like that."

"That's good, yeah."

"Beth is coming in tomorrow, isn't she?"

"Around three or so."

He just nodded his head.

The next morning, I slept in till eight, took my little pill for my bum thyroid, and then went to the basement to run on the treadmill and watch the news. Brian went to the gym in Sidney on Saturday mornings. I was happy just to stay home to work out and enjoy a quiet Saturday morning out of the public eye. I'd even brought work home so I didn't need to go into the office. I was excited to see my mother. She'd be staying for the whole week and even promised Patty she'd help with Thanksgiving dinner preparations. I should join them and eventually learn to cook a turkey, but I knew I'd end up watching football that day and eating myself into a state of the full-bellied sleepies. It would be a huge meal that would include James, as well as Derek and Vonny, who'd come home for the holiday.

I worked till two then lost my focus and gave up. I went up once again to make sure her bedroom was in good order. I decided against telling her about the gunpowder—at least for now. From the bedroom window, I watched her pull into the driveway—she must have started early. I hoped she'd be happy to see me. We talked every weekend, so she was up to speed on town and family events. She'd been so happy when I told her Brian and I reconciled that she laughed with joy. I dashed down the front stairs to help her with her luggage. We hugged on the sidewalk, but we were forced inside by the blustery north wind.

"We were coming back from the lake in two cars," she said as she placed a navy sweater in a drawer. "I was in the car dad was driving and Sophie was in the seat with me. We thought we were so smart, getting the car with the air conditioning. What we didn't know was that it was also the car where Peter had put his prizes. Did you know snapping turtles can bite through burlap?"

"Ah, no…guess I never thought about it."

"Well, both of them did and one of them decided to join Sophie and me in the middle seat of our station wagon! Oh, how she shrieked. Peter had to dive over from the front seat and grab it."

I laughed. "Did it bite either of you?"

"It got hold of the toe of Sophie's tennies and wouldn't let go. She just yanked her foot out of it. Oh, I thought I would bust a gut laughing. That snapper held onto that shoe all the way home. My dad made Peter ride in the far back to keep the turtles back there. Sophie, with her one shoe, scampered into the front seat. Have you ever laughed so hard it made your stomach hurt?"

"But you weren't scared?"

"Nah. I just kept kicking at it till it gave up on me and went for Sophie. She's much more squeamish about that stuff. I used to go out fishing with my dad and big brothers. It was either that or stay behind in the camper with mom and Stephanie and embroider."

"I thought Aunt Sophie seemed pretty calm when I met her."

"Oh, she is, except around crawling things that bite."

We laughed together as she shoved her luggage into the bottom of the closet. When she sat down on the bed next to me she held up a pink barrette.

I smiled. "That must be Kayla's."

"How is she doing?"

"On the outside, she's holding it together, mostly for her dad, I think. But I know she's confused and scared…she'd be a fool not to be. We've invited them for Thanksgiving, unless Sheila makes some miraculous recovery."

A knock sounded on the open door. My mom got up and gave Brian a hug. I didn't catch what she said to him.

"I know, I was too," Brian said softly. Then he looked from me to my mom and said, "So, Patty wants to know what we're planning for supper."

"Well, isn't Saturday night your Cowpoke night?" she said. "That's fine with me."

I nodded. Brian smiled and left to tell Patty.

"Uncle Bill will come along. Mom—"

"Beth."

"Fine, Beth. What are you going to do about him?"

She sat back down on the bed and sighed. "I haven't been giving him much attention."

"He's noticed that."

She looked down at her hands in her lap then reached down to pull on her slippers. "You know you've reached middle age when you no longer sit on the floor to put on your shoes."

"If you're going to dump him, you should just do it. I know you're enjoying your freedom. I told him to be patient, but I think that's turning to doubt."

"The truth is...I don't know. I haven't decided what I want to do."

Poor Uncle Bill. His love for my mother probably helped wreck both his marriages.

"So, you'll just continue to string him along." She became quiet and I wished I had avoided the subject. "Well, do him a favor and don't spend the night."

"Are you telling me—"

"I'm just saying waking up next to him will just make it tougher on him. Otherwise, do what you want."

She smirked at me. True, it was bizarre that I was issuing instructions to my mother on dating. But I felt bad for Bill. He was in love with her and I wanted to protect him. My mother didn't seem to need protecting. She was a mystery to me; maybe she always would be, absent from my life for twenty-three years. Perhaps that lost time couldn't be recovered. Things seemed upside down and backwards. Was she Beth or was she my mom?

Chapter 16

BRIAN and my mom were still eating breakfast as I headed south on Highway 51 into town. Suddenly my stomach cart wheeled then my neck and arms tingled. I turned off the radio and scanned the area in every direction. Nobody. Nothing. Then, fifty yards or so before my easterly turn into Dexter, I heard a clink of metal then a rattling sound. The Shark began to fishtail. As I braked, I felt the rough thumping of a flat tire. I turned onto Elm Street and stopped. Still, I saw no one. Damn, I guess I wouldn't be getting an early start on the day. I called Carlos Hernandez for a tow. Though capable of changing a tire, I opted not to risk soiling my winter coat. Carlos arrived in about five minutes. I accepted his offer to drive me the six blocks to work before towing my SUV to his shop.

Yet, I heard nothing from him for an hour. Then his tow truck and a State Patrol cruiser parked in front of the office. What the hell? I summoned Brian from his office then we met Carlos and Officer Merritt in the lobby.

"I think we should go meet in your office," said Officer Merritt as he glanced first at Glenda then at Melanie.

And he was right. Officer Merritt took two plastic bags from his coat pocket and held them in front of me.

Shit.

"These aren't thug slugs, these are bullets from a high-powered rifle," the trooper said. "Someone was shooting at you."

I sat down in one of the client chairs. A lump of confusion and alarm lodged in my throat. Brian placed his hand on my shoulder.

"Once I found that bullet in the tire, I called the State Patrol," said Carlos. "I just couldn't call Dobbs...um...then I started looking real close. The other bullet hit your front bumper."

"I didn't even notice that one," I said.

"No, 'cause it entered from below," Carlos said.

"Wait, how did that happen?" I asked.

"Well, it seems to me that somebody was shooting at your tires," said the officer. "The first shot probably hit the pavement and bounced up, missing the front tire. The second one hit the rear passenger side tire."

"So the shots came from the west," Brian said.

I shook my head. It was all so bizarre. I gave the statement to Officer Merritt then we went to look at the Shark. Carlos said he had to order my tire, but that the spare would work fine for a few days. Brian demanded the gunman be found. Merritt advised that Officers Waters and McNeill had begun a search of the land to the west. Most of the land to the southwest was good pasture land and irrigated cornfields, but along the highway it was rocky ridges and gullies—an ideal location for someone to hide then escape.

On the way back to the firm, Brian and I discussed how we should act. Officer Merritt advised us to tell everyone we knew. That way if someone saw something unusual, they would know to report it. So back at the office, we stunned the staff with the news. Gus turned red in the face. I think he even swore during the boisterous outpourings of Glenda, who needed to be revived with one of her own Danishes.

Soon Beth and Patty were hovering over me as Brian paced my office in front of the window. Uncle Bill arrived with his hunting rifle. Everybody seemed more rattled than me. I spent the morning trying to calm down the crowd in my lobby. I had to clear people out of my office so I could meet with my 10:30 appointment. Beulah even brought us sandwiches when I expressed my refusal to confront the town at lunch.

The day finally ended and Brian drove me home. James arrived for supper with his shotgun. Truly, I was rattled, but I knew someone was just trying to scare me. First with Officer Merritt, and now with my gang, I was forced to acknowledge the gunpowder in the envelope. They were angry that I hadn't told them before. But it was this kind of scene I hoped to avoid. The excited chatter began to gnaw at me till I refused to discuss the matter. I went to the family room after supper and watched *Tootsie*. Bill, Brian, and James spent the evening cleaning their guns at the kitchen table. This demonstration of manliness amused my mom, so I didn't admit that I had placed my Glock in my purse as soon as I came home. The way I saw it, there was nothing to do but go on with life. I knew in my bones it was that snake RT. But I wasn't going to let him scare me into hiding.

Beth and Patty joined me for lunch the next day. Patty told us that her cousin from Fremont, Tammy Ogle, had decided not to come. I assumed my incident had scared her away.

"Oh, that's too bad," said Beth.

"Not really," said Patty. "She's obnoxious. Beth, she'd find a way to insult you…tell you that you look like a terrorist or something. And she's a bint."

I laughed. "A 'bint'? You've been watching Monty Python. Who's she going to prey on around here, Eldon Strumple?"

"Who's that?" Beth asked.

"A retired Methodist minister."

She laughed, but she kept looking over at the kitchen door. Finally, Davey emerged. My mom was eager to see Davey again. He was pleased to see her, "Beth, the Dark Lady," he called her. She hadn't been around him since he moved past weather into baseball. Right away, I knew she had come prepared.

"Davey, tell me about Stan Musial. I heard he was a good player."

As Davey launched into a recitation of his awards and statistics, Blaine motioned to me. I slipped out of the booth and joined him at the back wall.

"So it's 'Stan the Man' today?" the father said with a grin. "You okay?"

"I'm fine."

"Well, I think you're safe here. Both EJ and Dane along with half the diner is packin'. Ah…but what I wanted to talk to you about is a will or trust for Davey. His case-worker mentioned it."

"And probably a guardianship and conservatorship," I added.

"Yeah. Those, too."

"Okay, I'll need some information to get things rolling. Give me your email and I'll send you a list of basic questions. We'll get the guardianship and conservatorship going then we can meet and discuss the trust he'll need. That sound okay to you?"

"Uh, huh, great."

Pleased to be helping Davey, I intended the exchange of emails as a way to stall. I hadn't drafted a trust for a disabled person—this would give me time to consult with John Tremaine, a special counsel for the firm, a Creighton law school professor, and my father's old friend and classmate.

After Blaine wrote down his email, I returned to the table where Davey now praised Mickey Mantle. He rattled off statistics to Beth as if nobody else existed. He kept talking even while Carol was taking our orders. Then in mid-sentence, Smokey Lurch, three tables away, knocked his plastic water glass onto the floor. The noise made Davey jerk. He turned and hurried back to the kitchen.

Patty shrugged—she knew odd, she worked in my house. Alarmed, Beth looked to me for an answer. Although she had raised a child with cerebral palsy, autism was foreign to her.

"I read some autistics are over-sensitive to noise," I said. "Loud, sudden sounds startle them...as if it's painful." I paused to listen for a racket in the kitchen but all seemed calm. "Remember when I told you about RT yelling in Davey's face? Davey's reaction was violent and RT got kicked out of here permanently."

The memory of that day compelled me to slide out of the booth and step into the kitchen. Beulah stood with her hand on Davey's shoulder. He appeared calm, yet was plugging his ears. Blaine and Dane stood together, watching him. EJ stood rigid near the counter. Blaine looked over to me.

"Somebody dropped a water glass."

Davey turned his head to me and unplugged one ear.

"Sometime you can tell us about Babe Ruth."

He unplugged the other ear. I backed out the door.

A half hour later, as we were finishing our meal, Davey emerged from the kitchen with his gray tub. He walked his usual route, collecting a couple of dirty dishes. When he neared the table where Smokey sat, he stopped. He seemed unable to complete his normal route. He walked back to our booth, where he stood in silence. He scooted his feet so he was as close to me as he could get. None of us spoke. Only God knew how badly I wished I could protect this young man. I reached up and lightly placed my hand around his forearm. He leaned his body toward me ever so slightly. I felt my face flush warm—I couldn't prevent that but I wasn't going to cry. Nope, I wasn't. We stayed this way for ninety-nine minutes. Then he gradually drew away and walked back to the kitchen. My mom was grinning at me. I glanced over to the counter where Beulah stood. She looked at me as if she was ready to adopt me right then.

Patty said, "C'mon, fairy godmother. I need to get back to work. This is grocery shoppin' day."

Early on Thanksgiving morning, Beth, Brian, and I took turns on the treadmill in the basement and watched the news. At three o'clock, Derek and Vonny arrived, carrying a folding table and chairs. They were soon followed by Lew then Paul and Kayla, who all looked uncomfortable. My mom got Kayla started on the Fritos and dip we were snacking on. When nobody asked her any questions, she seemed to relax. Paul took me aside.

"Sheila's sister called me," he said. "She picked up Sheila yesterday and took her home to Ogallala. I'm hopin' she'll stay there."

"Yeah, good." I hoped Sheila would shower and detox while she was there.

While Patty, Beth, and Kayla were putting the finishing touches on the meal, Brian, Derek, and Vonny were arranging the seating. When I joined them, I became aware of a great deal of whispering among the three of them; but I made a point to ignore it, as the topic of the gunshots was beginning to annoy me.

With the crowd we had, we were forced to add folding tables to the end of the dining room table and line up the add-on tables so that they veered at a right angle into the foyer. After we set up the tables, we took one last peek at the Detroit game before the feast.

After the meal, I shooed Bill, James, Lew, and Paul to the family room to watch football. The rest of us found ways to help with the clean up. We all needed time to digest the turkey and fixings before we could even attempt dessert.

"I heard about Mr. Baseball," said Derek, a computer whiz who worked in Scottsbluff. "A friend of mine has an autistic brother, but Tyler is real low functioning. He doesn't even speak. He watches Disney movies when he's not at school. He's like a giant toddler with a complicated brain. And he can get violent sometimes. Cute kid. Big brown eyes. He'll just be bouncing back and forth in his chair for an hour then he'll burst out laughing, get up, and just start walking around the house. He's fascinating, tragic, and goofy all at once."

When Brian left the room, Vonny and Derek cornered me.

"So, someone shot at you, but didn't intend to kill you, right?" asked Derek.

"Right," I said. "It was just to frighten me."

"From what?" he asked.

"Oh, somebody I beat in court decided to scare me. Or, well, someone is dealing meth in the area. I think I found a couple of the dupes—the Breeley brothers."

"Those morons?"

"The shots came from across the highway…Dad told us," said Vonny.

"But I don't really think it was them. They're out of town, I think. Somebody purposefully shot out my tire. Those two oafs would've missed and hit me or more likely, hit nothing."

"So somebody could be shooting at you every day," she said.

I hadn't thought of that. "Nah," I said with a shrug, as my hands went clammy.

"But what are you feeling?" she asked.

"Strangely calm. It's not eating at me…like you think it would. I was rattled at first, but now I'm just feeling more and more pissed off."

"But you think RT did it," said Brian as he walked back into the room. "And so does somebody else."

"How's that?" asked Derek.

"Yesterday, somebody slashed two of RT's truck tires…right on Elm Street. Funny thing, Dobbs can't seem to find any witnesses."

Derek and Vonny laughed then turned to me.

"It wasn't me," I said. "I've got witnesses for the whole day. But I wish I knew who did it—I'd like to thank them."

James walked in, peered out the dining room window then walked back across to the living room, his vigilance unnerving me. Then I happened to notice that Kayla was peering around the edge of the doorway from the kitchen, tears forming in her eyes. I pulled her into my arms. She dropped her head onto my shoulder. Derek, Vonny, and Brian retreated from the room.

"I'm scared for you," she said.

"Don't be...I'm not," I said. "It was the act of a coward. It won't be repeated. Now, come show me what's for dessert."

I led her back into the kitchen, where my mom and Patty were quiet, which meant they had been listening. She showed me the row of pumpkin and apples pies, lined up along the counter.

"How come you don't cook?" asked Kayla.

"Well, I can do a few things. When you're older, you should learn. But the thing is, Patty does it so much better. She doesn't draft wills—I do that, because I do it better."

"And these pumpkin pies need a few more minutes to cool," said Patty.

"C'mon, let's go check on your dad. I heard he's a Cowboy's fan."

I led her to the family room where we joined Brian on the sofa. She allowed herself to relax and get interested in the game. I looked toward the TV, but my thoughts were elsewhere. I thought about the people who had come to my home and all the people missing from our lives. For a second Thanksgiving, Bill and I were without my dad, my mom without Scottie. Kayla and Paul were suffering Sheila's absence, and the Wilsons surely missed Beverly. Bill told me Lew lived a tough life with his family, though maybe that was better than being completely alone. We were a house full of hurt.

On Saturday night, we headed to Sidney for jazz at the Blue Note. Brian and I collected Beth, Bill, and Patty in the Shark with James, Vonny, and Derek in the Wilson pickup close behind. Lew, who still lived in the rental on Benson Street, promised to meet us there.

Rachel met us at the door of the Pizza Palace. The Blue Note turned out to be the party room in the back, which had been converted into a one-night jazz stage. We ordered pizza and Brian and I took the opportunity to drink amber ale, which Johnny didn't carry at the Cowpoke. The crowd of twenty or so looked to be a mix of parents and friends of the players, and people just looking for a break from incessant twang. The band consisted of young college-aged males except for a curly-headed whiz-kid on electric guitar who probably wasn't old enough to drive. They played a mix of classic jazz and improv. I was no expert, but I did recognize Dave Brubek's "Take Five." During a break, I told Lew the barn looked great.

"Yeah, I'm glad we got it done and cleared out 'fore the cold. I betcha you thought that stack of hay bales on the floor was strange. I put it there so nobody would walk over the trap door."

"Trap door?"

"Yeah, it's a storm shelter my grandpa built. The first house he built didn't have no basement. One time Salt stepped on it...fell all the way down. Busted his leg clean through."

I nodded and the music started again. A shelter? I wondered who else knew about it. Certainly, the guys who worked on repairing the barn would know. I didn't intend to ask RT—if he didn't know about it, I wasn't planning to tip him off. I studied Rachel, who sat across and down the table. What did she know?

Just before the music started, I checked my phone. I had missed a call from Robert Foxworthy. I excused myself then dashed out to the Shark for privacy. Robert answered right away and went right to the point.

"We arrested Douglas and Riley Breeley on the Pine Ridge rez in South Dakota. We wired and filmed Jackson's nephew buying meth from them. I'd prefer that you not contact Jackson. We think it's best if involved parties remained anonymous and kept a low profile, especially the nephew."

"Well, I can't say I'm surprised. I hope you rewarded Jackson and his nephew adequately."

"It's best to wait a bit on that. And there's actually a number of people to compensate."

"Oh, I'm sure there's plenty of people up there who hate to see drugs and alcohol ruining lives. So, are they talking? Do you know their supplier?"

"No, they clammed up...said they wanted an attorney."

I didn't think they were that smart. I wondered if their parents knew.

"Robert, could RT be the source? I've seen the Breeleys meeting with him. I know that's not evidence."

"He could be, but like you said, we have nothing concrete to pin on him. So far, their phone calls indicate contact, as do email messages that lack anything beyond agreements to meet. Now Megan, I heard about those sucker shots. You be careful."

We concluded our conversation and I returned to the music. Both Brian and Beth knew something was up. I lifted my hand off the table to silence any questions. I gazed at Rachel. Did she know? Was she involved? I was glad I hadn't kept her in my confidence. Did RT know? Where was he?

My last question was soon answered. RT and two muscular guys came in and sat down at a table. Rachel went to sit with them. Brian shouted over the music that RT was with guys from the Sidney fitness center. I slid my hand into my purse then texted Robert, asking him if RT, Rachel, or the Nebraska State Patrol knew about the Breeley arrests. He answered in the negative to all three

ALONE IN THE WIND

questions, and then typed that he wanted to keep it that way for as long as possible.

How bizarre. And why was I even involved?

Chapter 17

SITTING at my desk, I tried to wrap my brain around the details of the Talmadge Industries workers comp case I was handling with Gus, but I couldn't focus. Nothing was sticking, for an increasing sense of unease made the words blurry. Soon, the queasy feeling made my head spin in a maelstrom of portent. My hands left sweaty marks on the cherry wood desk.

In the lobby, all seemed well. Gus was standing in his office talking to a client, who looked to be leaving. Melanie and Joy were at their desks. Glenda was playing cards with Chelsea Breeley at the front desk. Brian's door was open so he didn't have any clients with him. The refrigerator door closed in the kitchen. Emily and Kayla would be doing their homework or messing with their cell phones. Melanie stared at me with her brow scrunched.

When I walked back to the kitchen, Emily was alone.

"Where's Kayla?"

"She left to go check on her mom," said Emily.

"When did she leave?"

"Oh, just a couple of minutes ago."

Now Emily stared at me; maybe she could see the muscles in my neck knotting up. I rushed to Brian's office.

"I need your help."

I dashed back to my office to get my coat and purse. By the time I was at the back door, Brian was already there, zipping up his parka.

Brian started his Jeep Cherokee and then asked, "Where are we going?"

"To Sheila's. Hopefully, we find Kayla along the way."

We caught up with her a block from her house. She said she wouldn't get in the Jeep unless we took her to see her mother. I agreed that we'd drive her to her house, so she climbed into the back seat. The absence of a Breeley pickup didn't calm me in the least. The open garage door and the presence of Paul's truck in the street made the blood pound in my ears, though I didn't know why. I slid my smart phone into my coat pocket.

"Brian, just park here, across the street. Now Kayla, do you know that person pounding on the front door?"

"That's our neighbor, Mrs. Hutch."

"Okay, climb up here in the front seat. No, don't get out, just climb over." I opened the door and stepped out. Once she had moved to the front seat, I said, "Now you two just stay here. I've got my phone. I'll call you."

"I want to see her."

"Kayla, you must stay here for now."

The suddenly obstinate teen glared at me.

"Kayla, trust me."

She huffed but nodded. Brian looked alarmed.

I shut the door and ran up the slushy driveway that hadn't been shoveled after the last light snow. Now closer, I recognized Doreen Hutch, a teacher at the middle school.

"I just came home from school. I was going to get my mail when I saw Sheila come roaring out of the garage like a mad woman."

I ran into the garage and burst through the door into the hallway. The house wasn't much warmer than outside, yet it reeked. Doreen followed me inside. I heard the sound of groaning coming from the bedroom.

Paul lay writhing on the floor; the carpet around him was soaked in blood. I turned to Doreen.

"Call the police and tell them to send an ambulance. And tell them which way Sheila went."

I grabbed a couple of cotton shirts out of a dresser drawer and pressed them to Paul's lower abdomen. His face was contorted in pain. Blood covered his shirt and his open coat.

"D-don't let Kayla see this," he said.

"No, I won't. The ambulance is on its way. You just need to hang on."

Doreen brought some towels from the bathroom. I pressed those to his gut, hoping to keep life from pouring out of him. I told her the phone number for the State Patrol to call. Car doors slammed shut. Soon, both Dobbs and Bo stood over the wounded man as the nurse from the clinic tended to him. A few minutes later, the Sidney ambulance and the State Patrol arrived.

So much blood. I felt the need for sugar and fresh air. I backed up to brace myself against the wall. I needed to clear my head. I looked around the room. It was as trashed as ever. For the first time, I thought about the strange smoky odor. I walked over to Bo.

"Is that pot I smell?"

Bo nodded. "I 'spect so. But there isn't a lot in the air. You'd think you'd need to smoke a ton of it to shoot a man."

"Bo, we need to find her. Pot may not be the only thing she's on."

He gave me a strange, puzzled look then followed me when I went to the bathroom to wash the blood off my hands.

"I think the Breeley brothers have been dealing some-thing, maybe meth, based on what I've heard."

While Bo pondered the situation, I dialed my phone. When Brian didn't answer, I rushed into the hallway then out the garage door, with Bo at my heels. Brian was hang-ing on to Kayla in the middle of the snow-covered front yard; she appeared intent on wrestling her way free.

"Kayla, get in the car," I said. "We need to hurry."

"What?"

"Your dad is going to be taken to the hospital. We'll take you there. Deputy Bo is going to find your mom."

"I want to see him."

"The police won't let you."

Just then the paramedics wheeled Paul out the front door.

"Dad!"

Paul waved at her. "I'm okay. I'll see you in a bit."

"I'm ready to go," Kayla said.

As Bo headed to his cruiser, the three of us ran to the Jeep. I sent a text to Melanie, to which she immediately responded. I pictured her sitting at her desk, staring at her phone from the moment we left.

In the car, Kayla was full of questions, even as the tears streamed down her face.

"Sweetie, all I know it that it looked like your dad got shot. I don't know who did it or why."

"Was it my mom?"

"I don't know, hon. Right now we need to just think about your dad getting better. They'll find your mom and then we'll know what happened."

It was my second long wait at the Sidney hospital in as many years—well, third if I counted my own hospitalization after my battle with Salt Eldritch. Melanie brought a pair of Emily's jeans for Kayla, so she could change out of her pants, which were soggy from her wrestle in the snow. Melanie then offered to call Kayla's grandparents. Otherwise, we sat in the ICU waiting room, where an elderly volunteer was making coffee and a half-assembled jigsaw puzzle was strewn about a table down the row. After Kayla and I returned from the restroom, I gave the volunteer our names, and then I relocated us to the puzzle table.

"C'mon," I said. "Surgery can take awhile."

I began working on the jigsaw. Brian moved to a chair to the side of the table by Kayla to show his enthusiasm for the puzzle. What a great guy.

"I think it's a lighthouse," he said.

Kayla sat motionless for several minutes, her skinny body tense, her shoulders taut. Brian and I kept working.

Finally, she picked up a piece and added it to the shoreline. After a few minutes, a chubby, balding surgeon entered the room, spoke to the volunteer then walked over to us. Kayla popped up from her seat.

"Well, it's not too bad. The bullet had to go through his coat and a glove. I don't know my guns, but it must've been a smaller, less powerful handgun. We were forced to remove his appendix. He'll be here a few days." He looked to Kayla and said, "But don't you worry, your dad will be just fine. You'll be able to see him in about an hour. He's sleeping now."

Kayla collapsed down on the chair. As I sat down next to her, she expelled a long breath of air. I gave her shoulders a squeeze.

"See, he's gonna be fine…and we'll go see him in an hour," said Brian as he checked his watch. "I could go get us some supper. Pizza?"

"Kayla, is that all right with you?" I asked.

"Ah, yeah. Um, I don't like those little fishies."

"Me neither," I said. It was true, though I was ready to do or say anything to help her. "Hamburger and Canadian Bacon?"

She nodded. Brian grabbed his coat and left.

"I need to make some calls. Sit tight." I stood and wandered over to the doorway.

My cell phone vibrated in my hand. It was Bo. Lord, have mercy—Sheila had driven north to the railroad and parked her car on the tracks. She was dead at the scene. He said the State Patrol was planning an autopsy. I gave him a report on Paul.

An elderly man and woman passed by me. They rushed over to Kayla. I called Melanie with a report on Paul. She promised to pass the word on. Then I called Patty to let her in on the story and to advise her of our whereabouts. I kept the news on Sheila to myself. I wanted to wait as long as possible to tell Paul and Kayla. I joined Kayla and the people I assumed to be Paul's parents. I made a quick call to Brian, who arrived later with a ton of pizza and enough salads to feed half the hospital staff.

Once Kayla and her grandparents started eating, I took Brian out in the hall and told him about Sheila.

"Whoa, shit. Kayla has to be told. My God, Megan, how do we do that?"

"We do it tomorrow morning. Let's give Paul a night to stabilize. And the wounding of her father is quite enough for Kayla today. I'm afraid we can't keep it from her too long. Paul's going to get more visitors here and some of them may know. I'm going to ask Kayla if she wants to come home with us."

"What about Paul's family?"

"I suppose I should tell them about Sheila and that Kayla doesn't know. Maybe I can tell her and Paul together. I don't know if that's better or not."

I resisted the urge to turn and look at her. My stomach roiled and I felt a headache coming on. God help us, please.

"Why don't I take Kayla down to the cafeteria to get some juice? She certainly won't need the caffeine from pop. That'll give you a chance to tell the grandparents."

"Good idea," I said. "Bo said he was planning to call Sheila's parents. Brian, how did it come to this?"

He shook his head.

As soon as Brian and Kayla were out of sight, I told the grandparents about Sheila. They were stunned, of course. They agreed with my plans for Kayla. I suggested they call Paul's siblings, so there wouldn't be any discussion around Kayla. Though, the more I thought about it, the more it made sense to get her home and isolated for the night. I made a quick call to Patty.

Kayla and Brian returned while I was on the phone. I ended the call only to meet Kayla's questioning look.

"I was giving my uncle a report on your dad. So, why don't you finish your salad and then we'll go check on your dad. We can go back to my house for the night. Is that okay? I promise we'll come right back here after breakfast."

"Okay, but my uncle is supposed to be coming."

"We'll see him in the morning."

She nodded then went back to her seat and proceeded to drown her salad in Ranch dressing. I looked at the pizza then envisioned the twisted metal and the mangled, bloody body at the accident scene. Toast and Rolaids at home sounded like a better bet.

We were led to Paul's ICU room a few minutes later. Considering that he'd been shot, lost blood, and had surgery, his color didn't look too bad.

Kayla touched the hand of her sleeping father. "It's warm."

Paul's parents said they planned to stay a few hours. That reassured Kayla, so that she agreed to leave.

Back at home, Bill made root beer floats for us. Kayla, emotionally exhausted, fell asleep before she could finish hers. After I lifted her head from the kitchen table, Brian scooped her up and carried her upstairs. I gave her a pair of my pajamas and put her to sleep in our bed. Brian and I sat together, shoulder to shoulder, on my dad's bed, where Brian would sleep, and watched Kayla's slumber from across the hall. We didn't talk much; instead, we sipped the creamy remains of root beer floats and dreaded the morning.

Chapter 18

AT the news, Paul lost the little color he had in his face. Brian caught Kayla before she could crumple to the floor. He picked her up and let her cry into his shoulder for a few minutes before taking her to the side of Paul's bed where she could nestle next to her father.

When Bo appeared in the doorway, Brian and I joined him in the hall.

"Her car was in Park," he said. "I don't understand why she did it."

"I read the come down from meth is really bad," I said. "I think the Breeley brothers were her supplier. But they've been arrested in South Dakota for dealing meth on the Lakota reservation. So she's been without it. She probably tried smoking the pot we smelled at her house."

"How could you know they were arrested? I saw the State Patrol last night and nobody said anything."

"The FBI is trying to keep it quiet, so you should, too."

"The FBI?" Bo studied me. "You're sayin' I shouldn't tell Chief?"

"Yes."

"Why not?"

"I don't know…I just feel that's best. He'll hear soon enough. When he tells you, act surprised."

Bo leaned back against the wall. "You do know something."

"I told you what I know. Anything else is just a guess."

"You sense something, don't you?" Brian said.

"I think RT is involved somehow."

"And Chief?" asked Bo.

"I don't know. I don't have any reason to think he is…but still—" I paused. "Have you ever seen Chief Dobbs and RT together?"

"No."

I left the two men in the hall. Kayla wiggled her way underneath the IV tube to snuggle closer to her father. A nurse walked into the room, but I lifted my hand to silence her. I took her out into the hall to inform her of the tragic circumstances. I asked that she advise the other nurses and the attending physician, and to restrict visitors to family only. She nodded then went into the room to check the IV connection then left for the nurses' station.

"Yes, boss," said Brian with a grin. "She never even asked who you were."

Kayla stayed with her grandparents till Paul was released from the hospital on Wednesday; Kayla and Paul then returned to the duplex with Paul's parents as caretakers. The funeral for Sheila was held on Thursday. At my urging, Kayla started working on missed homework and went back to school on Monday, to regain some degree of normalcy in her life. It made me sick and angry at the tragedy of that family. It was best for the Breeley brothers, and probably for me, that they were out of my reach.

It was tough week for the involved families, but also for the town. Shocking tragedy hit us, as did a herd of FBI agents. The news of the Breeley brothers' arrest forced Tim and Marge Breeley to stay clear of town. I kept my Harney Street gang, and my mom, informed. Beulah even requested an appointment at my office, in an attempt to get the scoop. Everyone felt certain I knew things. I confirmed the likely connection between Sheila Ritter and the Breeley brothers, but went no further.

When Robert Foxworthy came to town, he booked an appointment with me as Robert Baker. Robert was a stocky African American man in his fifties with a square head and a prominent jaw, along with shoulders like a former fullback.

"We're not acting like we're investigating RT...he'd run at the first hint of suspicion. No, we're taking the position that he's part of our team."

"Your obvious FBI team," I said. "Nobody's going to talk to them, even if they think they know something."

"I agree, we haven't made any progress. Nobody knows anything about anything."

"And that may be true, but for one or two people who haven't come forward."

"Do you have any suspicions?"

"Besides RT? Not really. Chief of Police Ray Dobbs is a man who has his hand in everything, but I don't know of any connection between the two."

"The thing is, we can trace them to a seminar in Laramie a year ago. The DEA held a convention on the proper collection and preservation of evidence in drug busts. But we haven't been able to develop anything beyond a possible meeting there."

"So no electronic trail," I said. "Of course, they could go old school and mail letters then destroy them. It's old fashioned, but it would work"

Robert sighed. "Oh, that was tricky the way you slapped liens on the Breeley pickup."

"I'm sure Tim Breeley made it available to you to inspect."

He leaned back in the chair and continued. "There's a piece of the puzzle missing. If RT is the one hiring thugs to carry out his dirty work, where's he getting the meth?"

"Could he be making it? There are plenty of hiding places."

"We think it's getting shipped in. We've found no evidence of any lab or all the toxic crap that results from making it."

"That's what I thought...it's the opposite of what RT said. I'll be honest with you. I've got a strong feeling in my gut that he's the one."

"You're the Woman Who Feels. That's the tag from the rez, isn't it? You knew your father was having a heart attack from two blocks away. Trust me—we've done our homework."

"What else do you know?"

"You mean about your parentage? That's top secret stuff that will stay that way."

"Thank you."

"So far you're our best source of information."

"People come to me. They know they can't trust Dobbs. And they know Officer McNeill is dating RT. I do think something else is going to happen or someone will come forward. But not while your agents are poking around. Oh, there is one thing I know. RT hasn't made friends in town, but he has some buddies at the gym in Sidney."

"Which one?" said Robert as he took out a notepad.

I smiled. "I think there's only one fitness center."

He chuckled. "Well, with the way people have clammed up in our presence, I suppose I'll need to get someone in there...as in undercover. I know just the man. He'll make a legitimate cowhand. Be on the lookout for someone named Joe."

That day, Kayla didn't come by after school, so I drove five blocks to their rental duplex. Rachel was standing near the front door as I pulled up. I parked then dashed into the house, alarming both Rachel and Kayla.

"Why are you bothering this girl?"

"I just want to ask a few questions," Rachel said.

I turned to Kayla and said, "As your attorney, I am advising you not to speak to anyone except in my presence. Only answer the questions I tell you to."

Kayla nodded her head.

"What's going on? I have an investigation to do. What are you hiding?"

"I'm trying to hide this grieving child from heartless people like you."

Rachel glared at me.

"Now, let's sit down and you can ask your questions."

Kayla sat tight against me on the couch.

"Have you ever seen Douglas or Riley Breeley at your house?"

I nodded to Kayla.

"I saw the red or black pickup truck there five times when I was coming home from school…but I didn't go in. Then on the sixth time, I did go in. My mom was asleep in her room and those Breeley men were in our basement watching TV."

"Did you see them?"

I nodded.

"Yes."

"Did they say anything to you?"

I nodded.

"No. I was only there for a couple of minutes."

"Then what?"

"Then I came to pick her up to go horseback riding," I said. "I told the Breeley brothers to never speak to Kayla or to be in the same room with her. Then I took Kayla back to my house where I called her father to inform him of her whereabouts."

"So, that was the only time you actually saw them in your house?"

"That question has been answered. Anything else?"

"What did you do at the Docket house?"

"Irrelevant. End of conversation. Get a warrant for any other questions."

I stood as Rachel did.

"You know I have a job to do," she said.

"Yes. But you'll need to complete your investigation without bothering Kayla. I know that Paul has already been interrogated by Officer Merritt. It's time for you to leave."

Rachel's jaw muscles tightened. She turned and went out the front door. I followed her.

"Rachel, stop." I said from the porch. "You know why I did that don't you?"

"To be a bitch."

"No, think about it. There are lots of people asking lots of questions. She doesn't know to check ID. What if the wrong person starts bothering her? Obviously, those Breeley idiots aren't the ringleaders."

Rachel still looked mad, but nodded.

"Don't you think this poor girl deserves a break? Think what's she going through. She's lucky she didn't lose a father, too."

"All right. I'm done here. And of course, I feel for her. She seems like a nice kid."

"If she tells me anything, I'll let you know. She talks to me."

She nodded and left. I went back in the house, thinking profane thoughts about a cop who was too blind to see she was being deceived. If she ever got a clue, she'd be in mortal danger. I knew in my bones RT was behind the death of two Dexter residents. Who would be ruined next? The dual punch of tragedy and foreboding gave this winter a murky grayness that seemed to pervade each day.

I went in to talk to Paul. The duplex was compact, with two bedrooms, a kitchen, and a living room.

"Sounds like Trooper McNeill won't be coming back," he said.

"That was the plan," I said.

Kayla sat on the foot of Paul's bed, where he lay under an ugly brown-patterned comforter.

"What do you plan to do with the house?" I asked.

"I don't want to go back there—ever," said Kayla. "That's not my house. It's too different. Meth and those Breeley men changed it, made it, like, terrible. They did the same thing to my mom. That meth they gave her made her different. Did you ever see her teeth? That wasn't my mother."

Paul and I stared at her.

"How did you know about the meth?" I asked.

"I've been listening. Sometimes people, even cops, tell you a lot even when they're asking the questions. Then they talk to each other and I think 'cause I'm a kid, I can't hear."

"Ah, hon," said Paul, "she wasn't in her right mind when she did anything lately."

"She killed herself, didn't she?"

Paul's face went limp. My throat muscles contracted.

"She wasn't in her right mind, like you said, Kayla," I managed. "I don't think she knew what she was doing. Meth changed her. Meth shot your dad. Meth made her drive around unable to think clear. Meth killed her."

"It was those Breeley bastards," she said.

Paul gasped. "Kayla, your language."

I shrugged. "That's an accurate description, but maybe something more creative might serve you better."

She scrunched her brow.

"Let's think," I said, hoping this might prove therapeutic. Maybe she'd even laugh or smile—things she recently lost along with her childhood. "Vermin? Maggots? Snakes? Jailbirds?"

"Huh?"

"They've been arrested up in South Dakota. For dealing drugs."

"They have?" said Paul. "I didn't know."

"Lots of people helped the police catch them."

"I bet you helped," said Kayla.

"I did my part. They caught them selling meth on the rez."

"Did people here help?" asked Kayla.

"You bet. And people on the rez helped, too."

Her smile did come.

"I think they're devils."

"There you go. The thing about cuss words is that they lack creativity. But that's a good one. How about insidious worms?"

"Huh?"

"Sneaky and treacherous...dangerous."

"Oh, yeah, right." She smiled.

I'd gotten two smiles out of her.

"Can I tell my dad what you did to scare them?" She leaned in to me and whispered, "You know, with the knife."

"Fine, just keep it to yourselves." I chuckled as I left the room to use the bathroom.

The room declared Glenda at first glance. She replaced Paul's old beige hand towels with new, bright blue ones, an old brown towel with a rubber-backed floor rug also in bright blue, and a thin bar of soap at the sink with lavender-scented antibacterial soap in a pump. Patty had also been here—the grout in the gray tile floor was white again, and the porcelain sink shone like a mirror. I slipped out a hand-sized notebook wedged in between the hand towels and wash cloths on a shelf over the toilet. The first page contained notes written by Kayla: "mirror first then sink, toilet bowl cleaner once a week, use scouring powder with wet brush on tub." It saddened me to think this young girl was now forced to take on her mother's responsibilities; however, I felt certain Patty wouldn't relinquish the work anytime soon. Patty would also assign duties to Paul when he was able. Maybe it would be best if they stayed in this small house for the time being.

When I returned to the bedroom, Paul was still smiling.

"I bet you shocked Dugger good," he said.

"That was the goal," I said. "When I was in grade school, I punched him in the nose for calling Derek Wilson the N-word."

Kayla was smiling adoringly at me. That made me uncomfortable—I was sure to fall off the pedestal at some point.

"He did call me a hot-head or something like that. Actually, I knew just what I was doing and just how to scare them. Now they're sitting in jail cells in orange jumpsuits, sweating their fates. Anyway, we were talking about your house."

"Kayla doesn't want to go back there, I guess I don't either. Maybe we can sell it and buy a house."

"It needs a lot of work before it would be ready to sell. Lew and some of Bill's hands could help. I know Lew is looking for work."

"That's a 1950s house," said Paul. "I bet it has hardwood floors. We could tear up that stinky carpet and stain those floors."

"We gotta paint the kitchen," said Kayla. "I've always hated those icky yellow walls."

I left them deep in discussion over what they could do to revitalize the place. I wondered if after all the work was done if they'd still want to sell.

Back in my office, I listened to my phone messages, one of which was from Tom telling me Zach Whitfield planned to call me. I wondered if I'd ever hear from him again. I'd heard Lindsey, his wife, was pregnant. Sure enough, the phone rang—it was Zach, a former attorney in our office and the son of the late law firm partner of my father's. Zach got booted two years ago, along with Lindsey, the ditz, after I told my father he had to choose between Zach and me. Then we uncovered minor embezzlement on the part of Zach. He eventually found a job at a law firm in Lincoln.

"Hey, Zach. What's up?" I said as I rose to close my office door.

"It's more like what's down," he said. I hadn't heard sadness in his voice since his father's funeral.

"Tom told me you were concerned about Zane."

"Things aren't right with him."

Though I sympathized with him, I failed to see what I could do.

"Like how?"

"It's like he's either a lump or he's in some panic, scaring my mom."

"Does he have head trauma?"

"He says not, but he's lost weight, gets mad at anything, and my mom says he walks around the house at night."

"Shouldn't the army be providing some services?"

"He won't go. Says they'll think he's nuts or weak or both."

"Zach, what am I supposed to do? I mean, I'm sorry, but—"

"I thought maybe you'd go talk to him."

"Why me?"

"Because you know something nobody else around here understands."

"What?" As soon as I asked I knew the answer.

"Killing."

Shit. What do I say to that? I never shared my struggles with anyone outside my family.

"It's not something that's easy to talk about or that I want to talk about."

"Exactly. He knows nobody understands. And he won't talk about it. You know how to make people talk. I've seen you."

"Well, it's a lost cause because your mother would never let me in the house. I expect she hates me for firing you and Lindsey. She didn't even come to my father's funeral. Hell, she didn't even send a card."

"I'm sure she regrets that now."

"Maybe. But I'm not going there to have the door slammed in my face."

"If we could find a way for you to go when she's not there then—"

"I'm not going to go behind her back."

I'd sneaked around that house one summer during high school and lost my virginity to Zach.

"What am I supposed to do?" he asked.

"I don't know. You think on it then call me."

"Okay."

"So, how's Lindsey?"

"As big as a house."

I covered the phone to hide my laughter.

"Okay, I'll call you back. Something has to be done…he's all screwed up," he said.

How do I get myself tangled up in this stuff?

Chapter 19

IT pissed off Zach when I started dating Zane during college. I don't think Kathy Whitfield ever knew Zach and I had a two-week fling, but she knew about Zane and me. The brothers were very different—Zach was cocky, bright, but a little lazy. Zane was driven, competitive, yet compassionate. Zach strutted, Zane charged. Zach was everybody's buddy; Zane was befriended, but feared. Zane only fought once that I know of, and it took four guys to pull him off Jeremy Sempole. Nobody wanted to mess with him. Zane couldn't just eat a bowl of strawberry-cheesecake ice cream—he had to eat the whole half gallon. When he started karate, he was compelled to work at it till he earned a black belt. In football, he played like he was demon-possessed, always tackling with his head. I suppose the military was the most gung-ho occupation he could find.

As a boyfriend, he was kind, but a bit pushy. He wanted all my free time. A year older than Zach and I, he attended the business college at the University of Nebraska at Omaha, so we attended school in the same city, and spent summers together in Dexter. I truly cared for him; we dated for over two years. But I began to feel overwhelmed by his aggressive personality, so I began to push back. I wanted to finish my studies for the day then spend time with someone who could make me laugh, but it was difficult to relax in his company. So I started spending less time with him; soon enough, he began to voice his displeasure. I thought he was ready to break up with me—but my ego spurred me to end it first. I surprised and wounded him. Once hurt, he shut down and wouldn't talk to me. I'm sure his mother was outraged that someone would reject her son. I doubt his pride ever allowed him to talk to his mommy about it; no, Zach would have been the one to tattle; perhaps, he was even pleased that I had dumped big brother, too. How could I possibly help now? Kathy was against me for dumping Zane and firing Zach. And Zane could close off his feelings completely.

Still, it made me sad and it made me wonder. I researched Posttraumatic Stress Disorder, discovering a few of the symptoms I experienced after I killed Salt Eldritch, namely, the flashbacks, recurring nightmares, jumpiness, numbness, and heightened anxiety. During the attack, I kept my head and didn't freeze up; only later was I disturbed by creek beds full of bleeding bodies and heads and rocks spouting blood and shotgun fire waking me in the night. I'd experienced the ultimate power—killing. I hated that such an extreme sense of control had been forced on me. Was Zane feeling any of that?

Then I read something that disturbed me—PTSD lowers one's dopamine level, meth increases it. Would Zane become the next victim? I called Zach back.

"I'll agree to go see Zane on two conditions," I said. "First, you must tell your mom the reason you got fired."

"Damn."

"And that the firm needed a tax guy, not another rookie."

"And you married him," he said.

"A fortunate perk. Anyway, you need to admit to the embezzlement."

"What's the other condition?"

"Zane has to agree to see me."

"All right, I'll work on them. You can't know how it feels to worry about a sibling."

"True," I said, with no intention of telling him that a twin haunted me for twenty-three years. "But I imagine you feel helpless—that's something I can relate to. So call me when you've talked to your mother and Zane."

I wondered if Zach would carry through with his promise to tell his mother about his stupidity. He wasn't a guy who suffered embarrassment easily, and then he'd need Zane's permission to allow me to visit. It all seemed doubtful.

The next day at Custer's, I paused outside to appreciate the colorful Christmas lights adorning the outside windows. Inside, white lights looped down from the ceiling above the booths. As always, I was grateful that the Shusters didn't choose to pipe in music, even Christmas tunes. It allowed me to hear Davey's approach.

"I lost my boot. I lost my boot. I lost my boot."

He paused at the Docket booth long enough to hear our greetings for him, but then passed by as we didn't have any dishes yet. As the Docket booth was one of the first he walked by after leaving the kitchen, I assumed someone from the two tables or the rear booths had lost a boot—bad news for anyone trying to deal with the nine inches of snow on the ground. I resumed my conversation with Gus on the likelihood of the Chicago Bears making the playoffs. Out of professional discretion, we never talked business at lunch—people were either too intent on hearing some gossip or were much too bored with their own conversation for an important sentence to pass between us.

While we were eating, Nick Webster came in close behind his brother, Brett. Nick still looked bad after his beating—his left eye was still purple and black, his nose was covered with first aid tape, and his jaw was fragile, for he drank a shake through a straw and passed notes to his brother whenever he responded to him. After Brett received his burger, a stranger walked in and sat with them in their booth beside the front windows. This waddy received a reprimand from Beulah for sitting down at a table with his cowboy hat on. Now many people wore baseball and seed caps like they were body parts, so she permitted them. But this lanky guy with a buzz cut and a scruffy dark goatee followed Beulah to the wall near the front door where he was instructed to hang his hat on one of the wall pegs. She shuffled back to her position behind the counter, deaf to the hayseed's request for coffee.

Who was he? As a stranger, he attracted the attentions of several people. By now, the FBI had cleared out. He studied the menu intensely, as no local would. Brett pointed out the insert that listed the "Frank Docket" steak. Carol came by with a coffee for the tall stranger then took his order. As soon as she moved, I snapped a photo of him. I wondered about the Websters—could they be the Breeley replacements? I snapped their photos while I pretended to be texting.

Gus noted my photography. "No, I don't recognize him either. If he's FBI, it's a damn good get up. He's even got pliers in his back pocket."

"And wire cutters in the other," I added. "He's older than most of the hands."

Modern cowboys didn't carry guns like in the old westerns. They carried tools in their back pockets for fence repair, and a tool box, not a Winchester, in their pickups. They didn't wear a holster with a gun; they used their zippered inside coat pockets for their cell phones.

Davey emerged from the kitchen with his tub, taking our dirty dishes as he recited the stats for Ty Cobb. When he finished, he moved on down the row as Dobbs and Bo stepped inside the front door. Davey was saying something as he passed by Dobbs, who paused to let him by. Dobbs stared at Davey then glowered at the Websters. Bo looked from Dobbs to the Websters then to me.

I strained to hear what Davey was saying as he continued on his route, the lost boot now forgotten.

"Big red barn. Big red barn. Big red barn."

How could that mean very much? All the barns on our property were red. A dozen or more barns in the area were either red or white, and a few others were stripped of paint.

But Dobb's face was red as he sat down at a table. It did mean something.

Back at the office, I listened to a call on my answering machine from my uncle, asking me to stop by his house at five o'clock. I wondered why he would call me when he knew I'd be at Custer's. He must not have wanted me to take the call in public. He never texted—so that was out—even though I'd shown him how.

I sent the new photos to Robert and asked for a photo of RT. While I was sifting through my bankruptcy files, looking for suspicious disappearance of funds, Robert sent the photo of RT. He then called me.

"The stranger is Joe, our undercover man. He's from the area, so he should fit in."

"Well, he looks like a bona fide cowhand," I said.

"I've been conspiring with your uncle. He hired Joe this morning then made sure he looked the part and knew his job mending fences. We need to keep his cover intact."

"Got it. Now what about the Webster brothers?"

"I don't know if they are connected to RT or to the meth or even to marijuana. Now that pot is legal in several states, it's even harder to track. After work, you're supposed to go give a heads up to Bill's cowhands on keeping their eyes open. Joe will be there, but don't acknowledge him. The hands are to report to Bill or you."

"It will be Bill. They've been trained not to talk to me."

He chuckled. "I get it...the savage cowboys and the pretty niece."

"With a Glock."

He laughed again, gave me Joe's cell phone number, and said goodbye.

I looked at the list of bankruptcy files on my computer screen. I knew a great deal about their lives, but certainly not everything. But I knew so many things about so many people. Over the last couple of years, I had reviewed by father's old files and his files pending at the time of his untimely death. Also, I knew the basics of most of Gus' cases. These files represented people, many of whom had things to hide. Uncle Bill had shared stories about the people of Cheyenne and Kimball Counties. I was privy to most of Beulah's gossip, but she didn't know many of the things I did. No one, not even Gus or Bill, was acquainted with all that I knew about the people of the panhandle. I was the keeper of secrets.

While I was sorting through a nasty divorce from a ranch family near Harrisburg in Banner County, Brian called. He'd spent most of the day in Fort Collins at DUI hearing. I could tell by the excitement in his greeting that he had good news.

"Megan, the judge tossed it! He said there wasn't evidence that I had been drinking. I pled guilty to running the stop sign and paid the fine. I'm clear!"

"Hot damn! That's great. It's time to spread the news."

"Luke said he'd send a bill."

"It will be worth every penny," I said. "When do you expect to get home?"

"I'm on my way, so about five."

"Great. I'm going to start making some calls, including one to the Lincoln Star and another to that Scottsbluff station that broke the news."

As soon as I hung up, I told Gus and the rest of the staff. I was glad the girls hadn't arrived from school yet, for I didn't really want to explain anything about the matter to them. I then called Beth, Patty, Bill, James, Derek, and Vonny. My call to Beulah at home would be especially productive—she'd return to Custer's for the evening meal just so she could tell people, even though she didn't work the supper shift. She loved that people relied on her for news. Melanie brought in a list of news outlets to call, and even offered to make some of the calls. She did a fair amount of work for Brian, for which he supplemented her income from the firm. She was also grateful to him for the rescue from Nick Webster's wrath. Bo was pleased enough to ask me to hold while he told the chief.

Paul Ritter, who was still recuperating at home, was pleased for Brian and the break from his boredom. He said he'd be returning to work next week. He thanked me for recommending Tom Sedlacek for part-time help. Lester and Ruth Sempole could work the books and do most stocking, but they needed a young, strong man to unload and stock many of the heavier goods. I told Paul that Tom had been part of the "team" that brought about the arrest of the Breeley brothers, but to never mention the matter or thank him except in secrecy.

I left work early to change out of my work clothes before I went over to Bill's. As I walked down Harney Street to Bill's house, Bud and Jack were waiting for me in the driveway.

"Where is everyone?" I asked.

"Bill let us stand in the mud room," said Jack. "He's never done that before."

"It's cuzza you, Miss Megan," ventured Bud. "He doesn't want you to freeze."

I smiled. "It's just Megan. C'mon."

"Oh, um, Megan," said Jack, "those basement windows got covered in cardboard just this morning."

I paused then thanked him. What did that mean?

We trudged through a partially-cleared path through the snow to the rear of the house. When Bill built his new house, he added a larger mud room like we had in the big house. Bud hastened to open the door for me in a quaint, clumsy gesture. I gave him a smile. Inside were six other cowhands, including Joe, listening to Bill lecture them on the foolishness of fast money by committing crimes.

"Some stranger or maybe some person that you know might wave some cash in your face and tell you that you can make quick, easy money if you just deliver a package and collect some money. Dugger and Riley Breeley were lazy. They tried to make that easy money. Now they'll be spending a couple of decades in prison. They shamed themselves, their family, and this county."

Bill paused as I passed through the men, who stepped on each other's feet to get out of my way. My uncle continued his lecture. The men wore muddy boots and jeans I assumed covered longies. I wished I was wearing some, of my own, that is. Hardy, raw men in their prime oozed testosterone until I could almost see it floating in the air. Bill mentioned the photo I held in my hand. I passed around a photo of RT. As the men studied the photo, I became aware of a young man who seemed to be edging closer to me. The cowboy wore a waist-length coat that betrayed his hetero enthusiasm. I quickly glanced at his boyish face as his cheeks flushed a bit red. Yet, I had no intention of embarrassing him. I wanted them on my side, so I stressed the need of them to report any activity at the Eldritch house and barn, and any other place where they spotted unusual activity. Still, molecules of manliness bombarded me. I hungered for Brian.

"Who we supposed to tell if we see somethin'?" asked a cowboy behind me I didn't know.

Bud, Jack, and Drew, who was leaning on the washing machine, were the only hands I knew. Bill looked to me for an answer.

"Bill, me, and Deputy Bo," I said.

Dead silence. I assumed the omission of the police chief and the Nebraska State Patrol surprised them.

"What are you sayin' exactly?" asked Drew.

"The fewer, the better," I said. "Based on the information received, we know what to do. We're getting an education we didn't want. We've had two deaths, four wounded families, and three arrests. Meth is addictive and vile in ways even the worst drugs can't match."

The men shifted in their boots. I wanted to go home and not think anymore about it for the evening. I said goodbye and turned for the door. The testosterone parted like the Red Sea. Just as I stepped outside, I heard a voice behind me.

"Ah, ma'am, would like a ride home? It's very cold."

It was Joe. He walked beside me for a few strides—well, three or four of his, several of mine. Now that I'd seen him up close, I could tell he was part Indian. "I know who you are," I said. "I talked to Robert today."

"And I know you."

"Are the Webster brothers involved with the meth?"

"I don't think so...not yet anyway. I saw them talking to RT though. They paid a visit to the Eldritch house."

"So are you convinced RT is the ringleader?" I asked.

"I don't know. Foxworthy says you are."

"I don't really know either, but it makes more sense all the time. Who else would it be? Any stranger stands out. That snake is a liar and he shot out my tire last month while I was driving down the highway...though I confess I didn't see him do it."

"I heard about that."

Once we cleared the sidewalk and turned west toward my house, the cold air hit like a blow to the chest, taking the breath out of me. I had to turn away from the wind to speak.

"Are you staying with Bill?"

"For tonight. I've rented the vacant part of the duplex where the Ritters live."

Alarmed, I asked, "Do they know?"

"Not yet. I haven't even seen the place."

My face was beginning to tighten from the cold, speaking was becoming more difficult. The light mist suddenly changed to sleet. I put up my hood.

"They need to know who you are. I'll call them tonight."

"Well, all right. See ya."

I trod through the snow toward our house. An icy snow hurled itself at me full force, stinging my face. Why don't we have more than a few trees to block this blasted wind? Isn't it enough that our state had turned into a desert? Last year, Nebraska had flooding in the eastern part of the state, now the western half the country was turning to wasteland. As I staggered forward, I bent over to shield my face from the driving ice. Why was the wind fighting me?

Finally, I made it to the house. Once my face thawed and regained movement, I was able to congratulate Brian on the dismissed DUI charge. Still, my body shuddered with foreboding. Something was coming.

Chapter 20

THE next afternoon, Zach called. He told me that he secured the blessing of both his mom and Zane for a visit.

"I could go over on Saturday, about three. But I don't want to see your mother on the premises."

"She said she's sorry. She's mad as hell at me, but you're back in her good graces."

"Oh, joy. Still, I don't want to deal with her. Make sure she's gone."

"All right, I'll work it out."

I planned to avoid inane conversation with that snob. I'd always been polite to her, but I didn't want to chance the possibility of hearing her whine about the disappointing behavior of her sons. She wouldn't mention her likely discontent over the death of her husband, my father's former law partner, but I'm sure she blamed him for not being around to help her.

Later in the week, I met with Blaine and Barb Shuster regarding the necessary legal documents for Davey.

"Now I have the Conservatorship and Guardianship documents prepared. As for his future financial security, we'll want to use a trust, especially since Davey doesn't possess a clear grasp of his money affairs."

"Right," said Barb. "He's absolutely clueless. I mean, he has a shoe box full of coins he likes to stack in little towers."

I wondered if he really understood money. I'd seen customers at Custer's try to tip him. He just added the bill to the tub like it was a dirty napkin.

"Now, before we go over the trust, I want to mention an exercise called a life plan. Are you familiar with it?"

They both shook their heads.

"In a life plan, you set forth in writing what you want for Davey. Assuming you predecease him, this provides a comprehensive plan for Davey, based on his disability, his likes and dislikes, for his future. I've prepared a worksheet for you to start working through some of the areas to address, such as where Davey would live if you both die or become unable to care for him."

At this point, the parents began to look overwhelmed. I summoned Glenda, who brought them coffee and strudel. People don't want to deal with the future or think about death.

"He must have his baseball books and sports channels," said Barb.

"And those things are important to him, so you'll stress them in the life plan. You will also want to include information on his medical care and behavior management—what works, what doesn't—as well as his final arrangements. Remember, you won't be there."

That last comment turned their faces green. I wondered if I needed to call the clinic for oxygen.

"So, you write this all down, and it will give you peace of mind."

Blaine stared blankly at me, while Barb slowly nodded.

"I know...this is heavy stuff. But you'll feel good when all of this is done. People always do."

People do feel better, I knew this to be true, just as I knew the Cubs wouldn't win the World Series this year, Manchester United would never relocate to Poughkeepsie, New York, and the older a banana gets, the more strings it has. These are facts in our world and with our fruit. I felt confident the Shusters would be glad they took these steps.

ALONE IN THE WIND

On Saturday afternoon, I pulled into the driveway of the beige two-story, vinyl-sided Whitfield home. When Zach and Zane were kids, they each had their own room upstairs; however, Zach described Zane as a slob who had taken over the basement of his mother's house. As I walked up driveway, I tried to picture a sloppy Zane, but couldn't. I rang the doorbell and braced myself for disheartenment. What was I supposed to accomplish here?

The man who opened the door wore a wrinkle-free navy long-sleeved polo shirt with jeans. His dark hair looked recently trimmed and his closely-shaven face sported a smile. He swung open the outside storm door, the kind that real houses have but are never seen in movies. The scent of Aqua Velva wafted out to me, as it often did seven years ago. He reached his hand out to me for assistance over the step into the house, as if he was gentry in 1805 England. Had they been wrong about him?

We greeted each other as old friends, but half my brain was dipping into the memories of caring for this man, of making love to this man. If he was broken, I wanted to fix him; I wanted to play Florence Nightingale. Yet that eerie sense of peril, a different sort than the gun-toting RT presented, kept me at arm's length from him. I expected to see some version of a man in decline, but this man looked buff. We chatted about the house and the changes his mother had made over the years. This was the home that would look just right in most middle-class suburbs in America. Like our house, it contained a useless living room and a more comfortable family room. We stopped in the kitchen where I accepted a Bear Lake Beulah root beer.

He led me to the basement, which was more accurately described as a rec room with a bedroom and bathroom. Again, to my surprise, it was also tidy. Where was the shell-shocked slob? He offered me the recliner.

"Oh, that has you written all over it," I said. "I'll just sit on the sofa."

"Your feet won't touch," he said.

"Oh."

That was a problem. He went to the sofa and I sat in the recliner.

"So how goes it, In-Zane?"

He laughed. "Yeah, Derek told me I was nuts to enlist during a war. I guess I was. My mother and brother sure thought I was stupid."

"What do they know about where you've been?"

He studied me for a few minutes. He used to do that, as if he could know my thoughts without letting me talk.

"They've sent you to talk to me."

"Yeah, but they're not here to know what we talk about."

"How's that?"

"Got any ideas on how to stop people around here from dying from meth?"

He looked surprised, as I hoped he would. He never could read my mind and I planned to keep him guessing.

"No, I don't. But I've heard about stuff that's happened. My mom says you're in the middle of everything."

"Oh, so she thinks I'm a busybody."

"Maybe. But she thinks a lot more of you than you think. She's glad you've got your hands on things...she thinks Chief Dobbs is worthless. She chatters all the time...she doesn't think I'm listening, but I am."

"She'd probably like to know that."

He shrugged.

"Does Dobbs come around here?"

"Fat chance. Why the hell don't we get a new police chief?"

I shrugged. "Do you know RT?"

"I've seen him."

"Are you on meth?"

"What? No. Wait a minute now—is somebody telling you that?"

"Do you take any other drugs?"

He huffed and shook his head. "Well, just for acid reflux."

"You and half the world."

"What about you?" he asked.

"Levoxyl."

"What's that for?"

"A bum thyroid. It decided to stop working."

Across the room, the old ping pong table reminded me of his competitiveness. I played to win at table tennis, but I didn't really care if I lost. Zane did. He also tried to compete with me in academics—he always lost. The ping pong table sported a coat of dust. Kathy must be letting him clean the basement. The end tables looked to be dusted, probably as many bachelors do—without moving anything on the table. I nudged a copy of Sports Illustrated that sat on the table next to me. Sure enough, there was the line of dust along the edge.

My surprising approach seemed to make Zane start to relax. For the first time, I saw that his shoulders drooped. Maybe it was the sofa and way he was sitting, but I didn't think so. He was strangely tense and torpid at the same time—as if he was resigned to his situation, yet ready to fight anyone who challenged him about it.

"Do you think anyone is gonna shoot at you again?" he asked.

"Nah. Seems like I'd feel it in my bones if they were."

"How could you know that?"

I shook off the question. It was impossible to explain me. I asked him about his time in the Middle East. He said he spent two tours in Iraq and one in Afghanistan. While he was telling me about serving with a couple of guys from Omaha, I took a book on Tom Osborne from a shelf on the table and let it drop onto the thin carpet of the floor.

Smack!

Zane jerked to a crouch in a flash, his face taut.

"Oops. Sorry about that. So you're reading about Coach Osborne. What's the matter?"

I replaced the book on the shelf. Zane lowered himself back onto the sofa, but his hands were still in tight fists.

"Be more careful!" he barked.

"Zane, do you still have nightmares and flashbacks?"

"What's that to you?"

"I did...for a while after that bastard tried to kill me and Mr. Wilson. He deserved to die and I tried my best to do it. But that didn't help me sleep."

"Do you still have that?" he asked.

"No. It lasted a month or so. I think it helped that it was dark so I never saw him dead and bloody. I fell and knocked myself out anyway. But what you've been through...that has to be difficult for others to understand."

"It is."

"So you've been having these reactions ever since you got back. Did you get them each time you went over?"

"Just when I got home this last time."

"But you're out, right?"

"Yeah. I didn't re-enlist."

"Did you ever get a concussion or hit your head?"

"No. Why do people keep asking me that?"

"Ever think about getting a job?"

He was quiet for several minutes as he twisted his fingers together. His face was tight—I could see him working the muscles of his jaw.

I took a sip of root beer, hoping it would make the situation seem more relaxed. In a flash, he bolted to his feet. I spilled my root beer on my jeans.

"What do you want from me?"

I stood up, now anxious.

"Are you going to hurt me?" I asked.

He stared at me. "How could you think that?" He heaved deep breaths. "Go to work? I'm a disaster! Look at me!"

He strode across the room to the ping pong table and back. Then he suddenly veered over to me. I backed against the wall, fearful of his next impulse. He grabbed me by the shoulders then wrapped his arms around my back, smothering me in a hard, wet Aqua Velvet kiss that pushed my head back. My knees quaked for a moment then I found a way to wiggle my head to the side. He stepped away from me as I sucked air and wiped my sweaty palms on my hips.

"Am I an undesirable mess?" he asked.

"No, you're a stud. But I'm married. You do need to get laid…I'm certain of that…it's just not going to be by me."

He shook his head and even smiled a pinch.

"Are you just going to spend your life here, sitting on your butt watching *Spartacus*?"

"I don't have *Spartacus*."

"Really? Want to borrow it?"

He smiled.

"Come have lunch at Custer's on Monday. I can't tell you who will be there…it varies."

"I don't know. You see how I am."

"Nobody there is going to intentionally startle you."

He scowled at me. "Don't do that again."

"Deal. Listen, people see you as a soldier and therefore, a hero."

I picked up my glass of root beer, took a couple of swigs while he stared at the carpet. Upstairs, he joined me at the front door as I put on my coat.

"It was good to see you," I said. "Remember, noon on Monday."

At home, I found Brian sitting on the sofa with the TV off.

"Oh, no," I said. "Is the cable down?"

He shook his head. Three bottles of Michelob sat on the table in front of him. I couldn't recall the last time I saw him drink during the day—except for that time in Colorado with the bimbo on his knee. In an instant, I knew the problem.

"You're wondering if I did it with my old boyfriend."

He looked down.

"I would never stoop that low."

He winced.

"Can't even speak? Fine."

I left the room. What a wuss. He has no idea how easy his life had been. Yes, people get injured at inopportune times. Yes, parents die. I loved Brian, but he wasn't my everything. Nobody should have that burden. For a time, he made my life miserable. Yet, life was better with him in it. Still, I was responsible for my own well-being and happiness.

Brian spoke as I started up the stairs.

"Do you think he's okay?"

I sighed and leaned against the railing. "No, I think he probably has posttraumatic stress disorder."

"Kind of like what you had?"

"Oh, mine was a short, wimpy version of what he's going through."

"We should invite him over. Don't you think he's lonely?"

"I'm sure he is. I invited him to lunch at Custer's on Monday. Let's see how that goes."

"I can see you're sad. I'm sorry about that."

"You didn't make things better," I said.

"I know. It was stupid of me. You see, I think you could do without me...but I know I couldn't do without you."

That was touching, so I smiled at him, but I needed to get upstairs to freshen up and change. I wondered if I smelled of Aqua Velva.

"We still on for the Cowpoke?" I asked.

"You bet."

Chapter 21

BRIAN, Melanie, and I arrived at Custer's a few minutes early, but Zane was already waiting at the counter. I introduced Zane to Brian and Melanie, who he remembered from school, and then we sat down at our booth. Davey just happened to be on his way out of the kitchen.

Melanie, who was seated next to Zane, said, "Now wait till Davey is introduced to you. Meeting new people is hard for him. Then ask him about...ah...who haven't we covered?"

"Sandy Koufax," whispered Brian.

When Davey stopped by our booth he stared at the stranger. Zane smiled at him as they were introduced to each other. Davey walked on. Zane looked confused.

"Don't worry," said Brian. "He'll be back around."

The diner began to fill, though I paid no heed. What if some loud sound startled Zane? Shit. We could be dealing with both Davey and Zane. The hum of noise increased. Zane looked anxious at times, but he mostly held up. He chuckled when I slid a copy of *Spartacus* across the table to him. He and Brian got on well. He even asked questions about Davey, which he directed mostly to Melanie. In time, he found his chance to query Davey about Sandy Koufax. After he finished his Frank Docket steak, which now drew customers from Kimball, Sidney, and other communities, I invited him to see the law firm.

"I haven't been there since I was in middle school," said Zane.

"You'll find it very different," I said.

And he did. He was awestruck by the sight of Mrs. Purvis, who had taught him in second grade, back when we had an elementary school in town. Nowadays, students went to elementary school in Potter, middle school here in Dexter, and high school in Sidney. He chatted with Joy, whom he had known from school. We peeked in Gus's office, which had been his father's old office. I showed him where the girls did their homework after school. We studied Chelsea's Abraham Lincoln poster, which was propped up on the counter and marked with an "A." I talked about Kayla and her circumstances.

Then I showed him my office. After we walked in, he whirled around to glare at me. I closed the door.

"I'm not stupid, Megan. You wanted me to see Joy and learn about Kayla. Well, I know about the Breeleys and the Ritters. And this was the office of your dead father. You wanted to remind me that others have suffered. I'm not that self-centered. If war is anything, it's the trauma of suffering. I didn't need to see more."

"Oh, I think you did. I think you did need to see past yourself. I know you. I see that you've lost something. You're also stubborn and proud. These people are all in counseling. Why aren't you? Too tough to admit you've got a problem?"

"Do you still think I'm on meth?"

"No, but I bet you drink more Jack Daniels than you should. That's so easy to do. It's there…and it takes the edge off. But how do you know when to stop?"

He folded his arms across his chest and glowered at me.

"You've got PTSD and it isn't going away anytime soon…and you know it."

He took a deep breath and stared at the carpet, quiet for a couple of minutes. I waited.

"I'd like to call Melanie. What do you think?"

"Not yet. She's not ready for another unbalanced, aggressive male."

"Nick Webster, right."

"You've come out of your cage for a day. Are you going back in?"

"Yeah. At least long enough to watch *Spartacus*." He flashed a smile and left.

Florence Nightingale stung with failure. At least he'd smiled.

My two o'clock appointment was Chuck Hadley. His need for legal services now included divorce representation, in addition to his bankruptcy case. He had been a little careless with turning over his records. A little sleuthing on my part led to the conclusion that my client had gambled away his assets, which probably caused his wife of nineteen years to file for divorce. How do people get so screwed up?

We covered the status of his bankruptcy case then I slid a business card over to him.

"What's this?" he asked as he picked up the card.

"Chuck, you have a problem. Are you still gambling?"

His eyebrows rose in surprise.

"What—how did you know?"

"It doesn't matter. You're on your way to losing everything. Answer my question."

"I don't have to."

"You do if you want to keep me as your attorney for the divorce. I can't adequately represent you if you're keeping me in the dark."

He was quiet for a few moments. "There isn't anything to gamble. My wife destroyed our credit cards."

"But you've kept your job, so you have some income. Now, I've seen it happen when people have a problem they don't get treated—they sink to stealing…maybe even embezzlement…then they get caught and they wonder why they're drowning."

I slid another card across the desk to him. "That card lists a hotline for gamblers. Call it. And get some counseling with Carrie. It's not too late, but you need to act."

He looked down from one card to another. "I'm not even Lutheran."

"Now here," I said as I wrote on the back of my business card. "This is my cell phone. Call me. Let me know how you're doing and what you're doing to salvage your life. I want you to come through this."

Today, I felt more like a mother than an attorney. I looked forward to when the girls would arrive. We would talk about their day at school and eat a slice of Glenda's chocolate cake. I needed to remember to check Glenda's invoices for Shaver's, the grocery store, to make sure her food allowance for the firm was covering all her costs. She was so pleased with the social aspect of her job that I suspected she'd work for half her wages.

Zane started calling our house in the evening. He must be tired of his mother's company. It annoyed Brian until he discovered Zane was just as content to talk to him. We invited him to supper on Friday night. Brian taught him how to access movie streaming. I provided him a list of movie suggestions that was heavy on the comedy and non-violent drama. Brian even convinced him to join the basketball league at the Sidney gym. I was pleased that Zane was becoming more social, though he hadn't made any attempt to find a job or get counseling.

Beth arrived for the first half of Creighton's winter break. One evening, Judge Dean Shelton came for dinner; he paid too much attention to Beth for my uncle's liking, which annoyed me on his behalf.

On Thursday, I arranged an early lunch at Custer's with Mom. For a half hour or so, Custer's would be empty and we could talk freely, though quietly.

"Beth, what are you going to do about Bill?"

"I guess I should tell you. There's a man in Omaha, Greg, that I've been seeing for some time."

"You've been two-timing my uncle?"

"That's not quite accurate."

"Do they know about each other?"

"Yes. I told Bill at Thanksgiving."

"That seems like something he would have told me."

She shrugged. "Too proud, maybe."

Or maybe I'd been neglecting my uncle. I let the news of another man sink in. I wanted to ask her questions about him, but my indignation on behalf of Bill kept me quiet. She seemed ready to talk, so I let her.

"I'm just doubtful about committing. Maybe when I'm old I'll want someone to grow gray with. I just don't feel the need to be with someone constantly. For all those years, even when I dated, it was really just Scottie in my heart. Then I lost him...but you fill his void."

I nearly choked on my salad. "I do?"

"Yes, in a different way. I don't need to change your Depends."

I couldn't help but laugh.

"But don't you, um, miss being with somebody?"

"The nice thing about coming from a large family is there's always somebody to do stuff with. But I get your drift. Hon, guys will compromise a great deal to get some nookie. They don't need a wedding band."

We were talking about my mother's sex life—my salad suddenly tasted rancid. I pushed it away.

"But while you're stringing them along, aren't you afraid they'll find someone else?"

"Yeah, that's a concern. But then I might find someone else, too."

"Greener pastures."

"Interesting analogy, cowgirl."

"And with a job and my father's life insurance money, you don't really need a husband for his 401K."

She studied me. I was feeling increasingly defensive on Bill's behalf. Then it struck me that I was hurt—in rejecting a life with Bill, she rejected living down the block from me. I guess holidays and weekend phone calls were all she needed from me.

Davey and his gray tub provided a welcome interruption. It also gave us a chance to eat, though I only made it through half my club sandwich before I gave up, while Davey chattered on about Ernie Banks. I was ready with my inquiry on Albert Pujols if the conversation lagged. But he suddenly stopped talking and walked away. The lunch patrons began to trickle in. Junior Percival and Trent Maxwell sat down in the table next to us, which put our subject to an end. But I felt Beth's eyes on me. She leaned forward so that I was forced to look at her.

"This has nothing to do with you," she whispered.

Though I nodded, felt the warmth in my face.

I looked away just as Rachel and Dobbs sat down at a table near the door. She was a friend I had lost, perhaps unnecessarily. For the first time, I noticed that the two guys I first saw at the Blue Note, the ones from the gym in Sidney, sitting in a booth along the front windows. Davey paused when he first noticed the strangers then he slowly moved forward. The two men leaned in to talk in confidence. Davey quickened his step to get by them.

But Davey's lips started moving. Even Beth turned to see what I was watching. When Davey walked near Dobb's table, both officers turned to look at Davey. Rachel's attention returned to her soup. But Dobbs twisted around in his chair to stare at Davey. He then whipped his head around to glare at the Sidney guys, who didn't notice the chief's purple veins bulging from his neck. I couldn't hear what Davey was saying as he was headed to the kitchen. I grabbed my water glass then hurried over to Davey. I stepped in behind him so as not to stop his chant.

"Underhay. Underhay. Underhay."

What did that mean? He turned around so I set my glass in his tub and said, "Thank you, Davey."

He nodded and resumed his trek to the kitchen.

Back at the booth, my mom gazed at me, but knew not to ask any questions. On our way out, we stopped to chat with Big Joe and Maggie McCready, and then Dobbs and Rachel. I gave nothing away, yet Dobbs struggled with his composure, clearing his throat twice in a short conversation. Rachel ignored me as she told Beth that the jazz band would be back at the Blue Note over Christmas vacation.

Outside, the cold west wind stung our faces and stole our breaths. Instead of getting into her car, Beth waited for me to unlock the Shark for her.

"What did he say?" she asked once we closed the doors.

"Underhay."

"What does that mean? Is it a name?"

"I don't know. Maybe he didn't catch all of what he heard."

"Chief Dobbs looked ready to bust," she said.

What did it mean? Under the hay, maybe? I shook my head, but I couldn't shake the uneasiness that clung to me the rest of the day. None of my gang—Patty, Bill, Brian, and James—came up with any other ideas, though my anxiety unnerved them. I stayed up late staring into the family room fire. Brian gave up on me and went to bed. I drank a second bourbon, which alarmed my mom. She seemed dead set on keeping me company, though I said nothing.

Finally, near midnight, she asked, "Are you feeling something?"

"Yes," I said. "But I can't get a hold of it."

"Maybe it's too far off."

I nodded. Clearly, she wouldn't go to bed until I did, so I headed upstairs. I thought about sitting in the "dressing room" as we now called it, but it would be cold. The wind had shifted and now blew from the north, right at our windows. Only one place could give me the warmth I needed, and he was the broad-shouldered silhouette in the bed.

When I was ready, I wiggled in close to him, careful not to awaken him. I caught the wonderful blast of warmth then tucked the comforter in tight to me on the other side. I stared out the window for ninety hours before sleep found me.

Chapter 22

I slept through my morning workout. When Brian woke me, I didn't feel as disturbed as I did last night. If I could just get through the day, I'd have the weekend to sort through the nebulous images that agitated me as I tried to sleep last night. Patty even came over early to make us a big breakfast with eggs and bacon. Bacon! Ever since my dad died of a heart attack she'd stopped serving fatty meat. I had alarmed her. Perhaps rightly so—I had never felt that queasy, haunting feeling without something bad happening.

At work, nothing seemed amiss; yet as the morning progressed, I started to feel that sense of disquietude percolating again. By ten, I was sick to my stomach. I chewed on Rolaids the rest of the morning. I tried reading my computer screen, but the words were fuzzy. By noon, they were floating off the monitor. When I told Brian to go to lunch without me, he refused. He paced across the lobby. Glenda brought in a plate of double chocolate cookies and a bottle of Tums. I kept my head down, trying to ignore the fact that the entire office was milling around the lobby, whispering to each other.

In time, a plate of toast appeared, even though we didn't have a toaster in the office. Then my mom brought in a club sandwich from Custer's. I ate some of the toast and sandwich. James sat in his truck in the street across from the office. I would have laughed at the absurdity of it all, if the sense of peril had eased its grip on me. At two or so, I started to feel lightheaded from shallow breathing. Then a ripping headache came on. I took some Advil then started pacing across my office, something I'd never done before. Now and then, a head would peek around the edge of the door. I was destroying the productivity of the office. I even spotted Joy and Gus out in the lobby. What had they been told? Brian or my mom would occasionally step inside my office and look at me. How I longed for release from this troubling chokehold.

A little after three, I was still pacing. Then it hit. I jerked so hard I smashed my shoulder on the bookshelf. I grabbed my purse and coat. I whipped the door back and ran out of my office. I heard gasps.

"Should I call the police?" asked Melanie.

"I don't know where or what."

Brian only had one arm in his coat sleeve when he opened the backdoor for me. We zipped up our coats as we jumped into the Shark. Brian sped out of the parking lot.

"Where do I go?" he asked.

"Just go…um…east!"

He careened down Benson Street past the sane drivers on the road. I thought my chest would burst open as hard as my heart was pounding.

"South!"

He turned down the next street. What had been nebulous was forming into something more focused.

"Death." I felt death.

"Death?" he said.

Had I said it out loud?

"There! Shavers!"

The Shark roared into the parking lot. I gasped and pointed. Brian steered toward a silver Honda where a woman knelt over a body on the ground.

"No!" I cried.

Brian slammed on the brakes as I flung the car door open.

Barb Shuster was weeping over the body of the open-eyed Davey.

He lay on his back with one leg twisted awkwardly to the side, and both arms bent and pulled in tight to his chest.

I grabbed his wrist, seeking a pulse. Please, God! Brian unzipped his coat then started CPR. James knelt beside me as he called the police. Dobbs was present in minutes. He shook his head. Brian pumped a few more times then stopped. His wrist grew colder in my hand, or was that me?

God in heaven, no. This couldn't be. How does a healthy young man just die? My head swam, my lungs contracted and I gasped for air. Brian and I looked at each other, both of us in a spasm of disbelief. I shook my head to clear it. I must think. But first I pushed hard on Davey's eyelids to close them. His face looked strained, unnatural in death.

I whispered to James, "Call the State Patrol...discreetly."

He nodded and moved away through the forming crowd. Two women bent over Barb, who was still kneeling in the parking lot slush.

"Barb, can you tell me what happened?" I asked.

"Everything was fine. Then in the car he started convulsing. I ran to his side of the car and pulled him out so he wouldn't hit his head. Then just like that...he-he was gone. So fast. So fast. How could it be?" She broke into sobs.

Chief Dobbs said, "Barb, Davey was an epileptic, wasn't he?"

"Yes, but he was on meds. His last seizure was eleven years ago."

I stood up and looked around at the crowd. "Did anybody see anything?"

Four voices agreed Davey seemed fine in the store. Bo arrived. He looked at Davey for a few moments, swallowed hard, and then started pushing the crowd back. Brian came over and gave me a hug. I dropped my head into his chest. Despite my hours of foreboding, this shocked the hell out of me. This was wrong, just wrong, in some way, but I didn't know why.

The doctor on rotation at the clinic came and talked with Dobbs as he examined Davey.

A State Patrol cruiser pulled into the lot. Dobb's face turned red.

"Who called them?"

He looked at me, but he knew I had not been on the phone. Nobody said anything. Rachel and Officer Waters came to the scene. Gus, Melanie, and Beth stood off to the side, looking incredulous. I saw Zane standing on the sidewalk holding two plastic bags full of groceries.

Rachel pulled me away from the bystanders. "Of course, you're here."

"Do you know what a cold, heartless bitch you are?" I asked.

She fumed and started to say something, but Brian pulled me aside. I broke away from him and went back to Davey. His face seemed to turn whiter by the minute. He looked cold, as if his winter coat and gloves did him no good. I grasped his wrist again. My father's hand went cold when I held it. Now Davey was cold, as cold as the icy slush he lay in. Cold and gone. Why do the innocent die?

Barb grabbed my shoulder.

"Will you tell them? Will you go to Custer's? I must stay with him."

I nodded. God help me.

Brian parked right in front of Custer's, five feet from the fire hydrant. Who cared? I stopped Brian outside the door.

"They'll want to close. Will you help Carol do that? Then meet me in the back. Okay?"

He hugged me. Don't cry. Don't cry. Later I can, but not now. My guts churned at full speed as we entered the diner. Brian went behind the counter and told Carol, who gasped. Just as I reached the kitchen doors, Brian announced to the three booths that held patrons the diner was closing.

Beulah was standing by the sink, fixing a salad. She looked over her shoulder at me. I guess I wasn't wearing my best poker face for she whirled around and walked toward me.

"What? What has happened?"

"Davey," I managed. I took a breath. "He's dead."

I caught her before she could collapse. She heaved silent sobs as I wrapped my arms around her torso. I would have cried with her if I wasn't straining to hold her up. She was thin, with a thicker middle, but five or six inches taller than me. I began to sweat from my physical and emotional exertion. When my body started to shake from the effort, I lowered us to the floor. I reached out to keep her head from dropping to the floor.

She took a deep, tremulous breath. "How?"

I shook my head.

The office door opened. Dane rushed over to us.

"You need to get Blaine," I said.

"He left a few minutes ago for home," he said.

EJ emerged from the freezer with a large cardboard box.

"Davey is dead. Dane, you must go find your brother."

Dane stared at me. "But...how?"

"I don't know. Barb was with him at Shavers. He got into the car and something hit him, a seizure maybe, and he was dead about as soon as she could pull him out of the car."

"Wait," said Beulah, who was wiping her eyes as she struggled to sit up.

Brian kneeled down to help prop her up.

"What?" I asked.

"I remember those seizures he useta have. They took a long time then he just fell asleep. Are you sure—?"

"That Dr. Reynolds from the clinic was there. Brian tried to give him CPR, but he was...gone."

"My God," said Dane. "Where are they?"

"I saw the Sidney ambulance entering the parking lot," said Brian. "They'd be at the Sidney hospital."

Brian helped Beulah to her feet.

"C'mon," she said to Dane. "We gotta go find Blaine and get to that hospital."

Chapter 23

I wanted to go home, cry in my mom's arms, and eat, so I did just that. Bill and James joined us for supper. Afterward, I just needed to move, so I paced up and down the hallway past the study. Something gnawed at me. I went into the study and logged into my laptop to research seizures. Then I paced some more. From time to time, Bill or Brian or Patty would step out from the family room to check on me. My mom took a seat on the front stairs to keep me in sight. James brought over brandy "for the shock." And a couple of swigs did seem to calm me. But still, I paced. Then I stopped in the middle of the hall, whipped out my cell, and called Zane, who agreed to come over; in fact, for someone who'd been playing the recluse, he seemed eager for company.

A little while later, he was sitting in the family room recliner eating apple pie. Bill predicted an event, so he brought in chairs from the dining room.

"It's been botherin' me, and I don't know why…and I can't say what either," Zane said.

"Okay," I said. "Let's just take it step by step. Did you see Barb and Davey in the grocery store?"

I handed Brian a notebook and a pen. He started writing.

"Yeah. I got there just after they did. They always go there on Friday afternoon, like I do. A regimen, I guess."

"Were you near them?"

"Yeah, like a lot of people, we start in the produce section and then head to the bakery in the back. I only needed a few things, but I kinda tagged along 'cuz he's interesting to watch. I don't mean...that came out wrong. It's sad...but—"

"We understand. Where did they go after the bakery?"

"Um, next is the canned goods, and then the snacks and pop. Well, I went to buy some of Beulah's root beer while they were in the meat section at the back of the store. That's when I saw Dobbs. He was carrying a basket and he put a liter of Coke in it. I never liked him so I turned away to go to the next aisle for some Wheaties. Then Barb and Davey came near and they stopped to talk about what kind of Chex to buy."

"Where was Dobbs?"

"Still in the other aisle. But I was on the end of the aisle, and I happened to look up and see that RT guy in the security mirror they have in each corner."

"Where was he?"

"Well, I've been thinkin' on that. He was walking slowly by the shampoo, but he kept looking at the corner security mirror. He didn't seem to be looking at the stuff in the aisle."

"Wait, now was he looking in the same mirror as you?"

"No, the other mirror on that side."

I paused to think. "So you were near the front of the store and RT was walking toward the back of the store."

"Right."

"Okay, then what?"

"Um, Barb and Davey separated. Davey was looking at something near the end of the row, but I can't seem to recall what's down there."

"Near the back are the cereal bars, jelly, and oatmeal," said Patty.

I nodded to her. "So Barb came toward you."

"Yes. I said hello. And we said something about the weather. Then I heard Davey make a noise."

My mom, who was sitting next to me, grasped my hand and squeezed it tight.

"What kind of noise?" I asked.

"Well, two noises really. Sort of a gasp then 'Ow.'"

"Who was near him?"

"Nobody."

"Nobody?"

"Right. But he was holding his stomach, or just to the right...ah, his left."

"Was his coat open or closed?"

"Unzipped."

"Where was RT?"

"I don't know. I followed Barb who went to Davey."

I tried to picture the scene. Too bad I didn't spend more time there.

"Dobbs got to him first."

"What? What happened?"

"Well, he said, 'Musta got stung. Here's a wasp.' Then Dobbs bent down with his handkerchief to pick up something off the floor."

"Did you see it?"

"No, but I didn't look down till Dobbs reached down...and I was still a ways back."

"How far from Davey were you when Dobbs appeared?"

"Still, um, fifteen to sixteen feet away...about at the Cheerios."

Patty nodded. Brian, who sat in one of the dining room chairs, continued writing furiously.

"And how far ahead was Barb?"

"A body length from me."

"So, she was nine or ten feet from Davey. What did Dobbs do then?"

"He turned and left. I went to the end of the aisle and looked around, but no one was near. Then I saw in the mirror that Dobbs was at the cashier."

"Did you see RT again?"

"No."

"The entrance has a chime," said Patty.

"Oh, did you hear the chime after Davey was…um…after he exclaimed?"

"Yeah, a few times."

I thought for a few moments. "What aisle number is the shampoo?"

Zane shrugged. I looked over to Patty.

"Seven," said Patty. "And Zane and Davey would have been in aisle five."

"How long did you and Barb talk?" I asked.

"Mmm. Fifteen…maybe twenty seconds. The weather hasn't varied much."

Patty cleared her throat.

"Yes?" I said.

"They keep it so warm in the store, when it's so cold outside. I often take off my coat."

"And when Davey was found in the parking lot his coat was—?"

I pointed to James.

"His coat was zipped closed, all the way up," said James.

I looked over to Brian, who nodded. He understood to write down the speaker.

"Zane, did you see Davey react after he exclaimed and held his abdomen?"

"He turned around in a circle like he was looking around."

"What do you think he was looking for?"

"I don't know. He looked down when Dobbs bent down, but he just looked so confused…and agitated."

I leaned to whisper instructions to Bill, who left the room.

"What happened next?"

"Barb put her arm around Davey and she led him back to the shopping cart. I followed them. They went directly to the checkout lanes. I asked if she needed help. She thanked me, but said no."

"How did Davey seem then?"

"Well, he seemed to walk slow, but he always does. Otherwise, I didn't really see anything. I thought everything was okay. I just wish...I should have stayed with them. But I went back for a few more things."

"Did you see them leave?"

"Yeah. I saw them going out the doors."

Patty waved her hand. I nodded to her.

"Did a sacker take the cart out?" she asked.

"No. Barb was pushing that herself."

I gave Patty a nod.

"I didn't see them again till there was some commotion inside and people started running out the doors...then I saw Davey on the ground."

"Can you think of anything else to add? Take your time."

Bill returned and stood at the doorway.

Zane shook his head.

"Now please list all the people you remember seeing inside the grocery store including staff."

I joined Bill, who backed into the hallway.

"They're on their way."

"Good. And Bo?"

"Yep."

I listened to Zane's recollection. When he finished, I said, "Now, please read over the notes and make sure it's accurate. Tell Brian if you think of anything else."

Patty and James were watching me closely. I was right and I was going to prove it. Zane told Brian it was all correct. Brian brought the notes to me.

"Great job, babe," I said to him.

"You're welcome, Perry Mason." Then he leaned in to me. "Damn, that started to make my hands sweat. You're thinking something happened."

"We need proof," I said. "Now will you ask Zane if he'll stay a bit longer? And maybe James might pour another round of brandy."

Brian nodded and went back into the room. The door-bell rang. Bill opened the door to Melanie and Gus. They arrived so promptly—it was as if they expected to be summoned. I took Gus and Melanie to my study. While they read over the notes, I called Beulah.

"Hello, Megan, hon. God Almighty. I just can't believe this."

"I know. I keep hoping it was just a nightmare, but I can't seem to wake up. Are you still at the hospital?"

"Yeah, yeah. Gotta wake up, all of us. Barb said you were right there. Did you come from your office?"

"Yes."

"Who called you?"

"No one."

"You knew. Now you're givin' me the creeps."

"Beulah, I need to talk to Barb. Is she with you?"

"Eh-heh. What're you thinkin?"

"We need an autopsy."

Gus jerked his head up to stare at me. Melanie didn't seem surprised.

"God above, why?" asked Beulah.

"It's not an uncommon request."

"A'right, hang on."

"Yes?" said Barb.

"Barb, I think we should get an autopsy. Davey was on several medications, right?"

"Yes."

"What are they?"

I wrote down Prozac, Risperidone, Seroquel, and Valproic Acid/Depakote.

"Fine. Now I think an autopsy is important. You or Blaine can request it."

"Okay. We will. Should you be our attorney for something?"

"Yes."

"Okay." She took a long, quivering breath.

ALONE IN THE WIND

"Barb, this is so terrible. But can I ask you a couple of questions?"

"Yeah. No, he hadn't been sick today."

"Good, you're ahead of me. And he took all his meds like normal, at the normal times, right?"

"Yes, we're very good about that."

"I know you are."

I told her Zane's account of the time at Shaver's. She agreed with his assessment, but added two names to the list of people present.

"Oh, and Earl Ferdy was choppin' meat. He might have seen something or somebody else."

"Very good. I know you don't want to think about this right now, but Davey had seizures when he was younger, right?"

"Yeah. So we were told he needed to get an MRI and an EEG so they would know what kind of anti-seizure medication to give him."

"What were those seizures like?"

"Um, sometimes his body would go stiff and he'd fall over. Or his left wrist would bend tight and his left side would jerk. He often drooled or even threw up. Oh, and his eyes rolled back in his head. His skin turned gray. He never knew what was happenin' and he never remembered the seizure."

"Is this what happened when he was in the car?"

She sobbed a few breaths. I felt tears stinging my eyes.

"No, it wasn't like that at all."

I tried to steady my breathing as I waited for her to continue.

"He just...um...spazed out. He jerked back and forth and tried to speak."

"Wait. He tried to talk to you?"

"He tried to say my name. He said 'Maaa' and then he kinda choked and grabbed at his throat. His face was blazin' red. That's when I jumped out of the car. I couldn't do anythin' to keep him from knockin' around in his seat."

"How long did he keep it up?"

"By the time I got him out of the car and to the ground, he was done movin'. He was gone, Megan. Gone. What happened?"

I took a couple of deep breaths. "That's why we need the autopsy. That will tell us a lot."

"We'll get it. Am I supposed to talk to the police or do you need to be with me?"

"No, it's okay to tell them what happened. Oh, wait. Don't talk to Chief Dobbs."

"Why not?"

"Because he was a witness to your presence in the grocery store. That takes him out of his role as an investigator. Deputy Bo is on his way here, so I'll fill him in."

"Okay. Megan, what should I do now?"

"Go home. Get out of that hospital. Try to sleep. The autopsy might delay the funeral, so don't set the date, but you can make other arrangements."

After I hung up the phone, three quick sobs jolted my body. I turned away from Gus and Melanie to wipe my eyes. Brian brought in a glass of brandy. We ran out of sifters long ago and were using wine and whiskey glasses. I sent Brian to bring in Zane. He signed the notes, which now became a document. Melanie notarized it.

"I'll go to the hospital," said Gus.

"Gus, I think a vial should be sent to the Nebraska Medical Center for analysis," I said. "Oh, and they should check for an injection site."

"I agree," he said.

Bill brought in Bo, who looked somber. I made four copies of Zane's affidavit. I gave the original to Gus to lock up in the firm's safe, and then he left. I locked a copy in my desk and gave the other two copies to Bo.

"Bo, this is going to sound bossy, but here goes. Give one of those copies to the State Patrol, Officers Waters or Merritt, but not McNeill. Do not let Dobbs see this. Keep this at home. He is a witness and should not be investigating this. Got that? And make sure they know RT was also present and is dating McNeill, so neither of them should be involved in the investigation. Let the State Patrol do their investigation, but request that you be kept informed. Tell them I represent the Shusters—in what capacity I don't know yet. There will be an autopsy."

"Dang," Bo said. "But why?"

"I think RT blames Davey for repeating something that led to the arrest of the Breeley brothers. RT didn't want to risk whatever Davey might say if questioned by the police. And he should be very afraid of what those two oafs will say once they've been in jail for a while."

"He thinks Dugger and Riley will squeal on him, right?" asked Bo.

I nodded. "RT's probably making plans for his escape as we talk." I took a deep breath. "I need some pie."

As I returned to the family room with Brian, I suddenly felt exhausted. I wanted everyone to go away. My brain and heart needed to rest. When I entered the room, Paul and Kayla had arrived and were enjoying Patty's apple pie. Johnny Two Rivers stood by the fireplace with a brandy, while James stood near the threshold talking on his cell phone to either Derek or Vonny.

Kayla ambushed me right off.

"Megan, what do you think happened?"

"I don't know. There needs to be an investigation."

"What do you feel?" asked Patty.

Now I was stuck, but I couldn't say the m-word. I looked over at Beth, who looked traumatized.

"Foul play, yes."

Collective gasps sucked the air out of the room.

I trudged up the stairs and collapsed face-forward onto my bed.

Chapter 24

I hoped putting on my pajamas would help, but my mind was too troubled to sleep. So, I pulled a chair in front of the gas fireplace then lit it. I wrapped myself in a blanket from my armoire and settled into my chair. My body ached with exhaustion and my soul wailed in grief—God in heaven, how could you let this happen?

My mom set a tray on my lap. I gulped down the apple pie. I would need to brush again, but that was okay. She pulled an end table next to my chair and placed a glass of bourbon on it.

"James offered to go get more brandy, but Bill told him that was ridiculous when we had so much bourbon here."

"Is the house still overflowing?"

"It's worse. Carlos Hernandez and Big Joe arrived. Carlos brought a vat of vanilla ice cream and a case of root beer. This was the last piece of pie."

"What's the mood?"

"Somber. Sugar is the only thing keeping people from a mass sobbing. Though it perked them up when you became the topic."

"Me?"

"Oh, hon. Everybody now knows you spent the day waiting for something bad to happen then left the building and drove right to Davey. Patty called Jackson. Is that the elder on the reservation?"

"Yeah."

"She said she'd called him earlier. They're holding some sort of vigil right now for the 'death of the innocent' and friend of the Woman Who Feels."

"I didn't think anyone would remember that."

"Oh, they do and more," said Brian as he approached.

He gave me a kiss square on the lips even though I had just taken a bite.

"Joe McCready said the 'Pocket Docket is a marvel.'"

"I'm gonna be pissed if someone calls me the 'Shelf Elf.'"

"Too late. Kayla brought that up. Those were the only smiles I'd seen all night."

I nodded then resumed staring into the fire. "I should have foreseen it." Did I say that out loud?

"How?" asked my mom.

"Davey must have overheard something. You know how he repeats things. Most of it doesn't make sense. But remember yesterday he picked up 'underhay'? I should've known it would get him in trouble at some point."

"Oh, you're wrong, Megan. There's no way you could have protected him from something so vague."

"Your mom is right. Ah, Beth, I mean."

But it must have meant something to prompt such drastic action. I tried to think back on other things Davey said. He'd mentioned a big red barn. That made Dobbs mad. As I sat thinking, I became aware that Brian and my mom had both spoken. But I was in my own thoughts now. How did they do it? I ran through Zane's account. Had I asked everything important? Damn, I didn't remember to thank him. I realized my mom had left. At some point, she returned and I heard Brian in the room. What was the only way they could do it? RT made impulsive mistakes, but he might be smart if he had enough time to plan. Either Dobbs or Rachel or both told RT the things Davey said. RT decided his stupid minions couldn't be trusted to keep their mouths shut. So RT got rid of the messenger—he killed the mockingbird.

The term "underhay" probably meant under the bales of hay in the big red Eldritch barn under the trap door. RT probably planned it and dictated the scheme to Dobbs, who was tied up either in the dealing of the meth or in blackmailing RT. If RT was discovered, then he'd finger Dobbs. So RT knew Davey would have his coat open in the warm store. He could inject him and Dobbs could cover it with the claim of a sting by a wasp he found on the store linoleum. A wasp this time of year? It was certainly warm enough inside the store, but I'd never seen one inside in December. RT would need a poison so toxic that he needed only to prick Davey with it. RT would take the syringe with him, crush it, and scatter bits and pieces along the roadside of several desolate acres of snow.

I looked around the room. The chair my mom sat in was pushed back to the corner. Brian lay sprawled on the bed. He must have tried to wait up for me. The wall clock put the time well past midnight. That was late for the early risers of the big house. I awakened Brian and convinced him to get under the covers, and that I'd be there soon. Instead, I went back to my chair once he fell asleep again. I pictured RT's face—rage stirred in my chest and made my head throb. I should've killed that bastard when I first met him. Davey would still be alive. Suddenly, overheated, I jumped up from my chair, my chest heaving.

Staring into the fire, I saw Davey's face, his eyes sparkling with excitement when he first recited the batting statistics for Ted Williams and when he first saw the Van Gogh in my office. Atop the armoire sat a gift wrapped in red foil paper with shiny silver Christmas trees. I wished I had given it to him when I ordered it instead of waiting for Christmas. I thought I had time. I pulled my chair to the armoire and pulled down the book, ripping the wrapping paper off. Brian snorted then turned over. The first page I opened to was a self-portrait of Van Gogh with his head wrapped in a bandage. Davey's face flashed into the portrait, his ear bloody.

The fire then showed me the corpse in the parking lot. That boy now lay in a vault in the Sidney morgue, with a tag on his toe. Silent sobs shook me till I dropped to my knees. God, how could you let this happen? I cried then I climbed back into the chair and wrapped the blanket around myself. I began to think again.

What was the next step? How could anyone prove RT did it? The State Patrol would interview possible witnesses, but RT probably made sure no one saw him. Dobbs would be so tangled up in the meth business and the murder plot, he could never extricate himself. And did I even trust the State Patrol with my suspicions? If Rachel caught wind of it, she would tip-off her lover. I didn't know her role, but she was compromised and if not involved, at least a willing dupe.

The State Patrol might even dismiss my ideas and claim they didn't have sufficient evidence for a search of our property—even with my permission. And the information could be leaked and RT warned. He probably had an escape plan—money in a bank in Nuevo Laredo or Nogales or some such place. One hint of trouble and he'd be gone. Dobbs wasn't smart enough to have scored enough money to flee. No, he'd help RT escape to save his own skin. And Dobbs would be watching Bo closely to get a read on the situation. Maybe Dobbs even knew Bo was here tonight. Bo was smart enough to lie and say that the gathering was just a sort of vigil for Davey that even a young girl attended. No, I couldn't risk arousing suspicions against RT until I knew the autopsy results and I had a plan.

I slept till ten the next morning. Patty made me scrambled eggs and toast.

"Thanks, Patty, for staying so late. I bet it took forever to clean up."

"Oh, some stayed and helped."

Brian came in with some papers and sat at the table.

"I've been doing some research. But you need to finish before we discuss it. Where's your fruit?"

Patty handed me a banana then sat down at the table.

"Go ahead. I'm almost done."

"Okay, so this is the deal," he said. "You don't always have convulsions with seizures and you don't need a seizure to have a convulsion. Here's a list of drugs that can cause seizures. I don't even know what most of that stuff is. But these are anti-seizure drugs—valproic acid or Depakote as it's often called, and phenytoin. Given in really high doses they do the opposite and cause seizures. But Barb said it didn't look like Davey was having a seizure like he'd had before."

"Right," I said, studying the list. "So this says cocaine and lithium can result in…wait—amphetamines?" I did stop eating my banana.

"Take a look at this, but eat your banana first."

I growled with my mouth full. He handed me another printout.

Methamphetamine. Shit.

"Yeah, see," he said as he pointed to a paragraph. "Meth can cause convulsions and death."

"It would take an extreme dose, in fact, a highly concentrated dose," I said. "RT didn't have time to inject…he only had time to stab and disappear."

I dropped my banana onto the table. Patty and Brian both looked sick. I wondered where RT was now. Maybe he'd already fled, but that would create the presumption of guilt. I pulled my cell phone out of my back pocket and dialed Bo.

"Bo, do you know where RT is?"

Meanwhile, the house phone rang and Brian answered it in the family room.

"Bo says RT's truck is at the Eldritch house," I said.

"I get it," said Patty. "That's why you didn't evict RT when he upset Davey—you wanted to keep an eye on him."

"Right, though he mostly sleeps at Rachel's apartment. Brian, who called?"

"Bill. He says Jack saw Dobb's cruiser and RT's truck together up on that gravel road by the old Hexam place yesterday morning."

"That's when they planned the murder, I betcha," said Patty.

"I need to call Robert Foxworthy," I said.

"Who's that?" asked Patty.

"Denver FBI. By the way, where's Beth?"

"Over seeing Beulah," said Brian.

I nodded as I dialed Robert's cell phone. I told him my suspicions then I asked what he knew about Rachel and the Webster brothers.

After I hung up I said, "He says it's possible, but proof is a problem. At least he knows. He even asked for a copy of Zane's statement."

Brian said, "It makes me sick to think RT and Dobbs could get away with this."

Heat rose from my guts to my throat where it stuck like tar. As I tried to swallow, I felt that queasy sense of danger grow. Where would it end?

Patty and Beth cooked and baked while Brian and I stewed. We climbed into the Shark and delivered the food to Barb and Blaine. They looked shell-shocked—it was bad enough to lose a child, but then to add the possibility of murder was gut-wrenching. Barb held up till Kayla, the motherless, brought over some chocolate chip cookies. That sent Barb to her room to cry.

"Did I do wrong?" asked Kayla, whose eyes were forming with tears.

"No, sweetie," I said. "You did powerful."

I hugged her tightly.

On Thursday, Bo called to tell me preliminary tests confirmed poisoning, though additional tests were necessary to determine the toxin that caused the death. The lab analysis was made complicated by the presence of Davey's daily autism medications. He said the State Patrol had released the body to the family.

Davey's funeral was held on Friday. It drew people from Sidney, Potter, Kimball, Dix, Colton, Lorenzo, and

Brownson—the communities drawn to Custer's for the Frank Docket steak. Everybody knew Davey, even if he had never spoken to them. They had enjoyed the steak and the wealth of baseball knowledge you could pick up if you listened. And nothing hits people quite as hard as the death of youth.

After the funeral, my heartache turned to fury. I knew where I needed to go. Brian protested, but I just gave him a look that made the former linebacker back out of the way. Dressed in snow gear, I trudged through the whiteness, over Rufus and to the Seven Dwarfs. The wind had blown the snow off the tops of the rocky crests and Big Leo. The day wasn't as cold as most, so I stood facing the wind. I waited, I wanted, but I heard nothing. Had RT blotted out Davey's spirit, his voice? Perhaps I really didn't hear the dead. But what about Beverly? Maybe she was closer to me than Davey ever could have been. But I couldn't hear her calming voice today—anger deafened me to her goodness. I turned my cold-hardened face away from the north wind, sadly aware the joy of the Christmas season felt trounced by misery.

I meant to travel to Omaha with my mom and Brian to spend time with my Simon relatives for a few days over vacation. I'd been to their gatherings twice before. Those people were much too intent on telling stories, laughing, eating, and enjoying each other's company. I couldn't possibly deal with that much happiness. No, this was a time to think, and mourn, and fume.

And the only way to mitigate my anger was to take action—so I formed a plan.

Chapter 25

MY plan required brute force, so I called Bud and Jack to set a meeting time for the next day, Saturday. I told them to bring whatever tools necessary to bust down the basement door in the old Eldritch house. They knew about the trap door in the barn and affirmed that it was not locked, but it was heavy. If we found something, then we'd call the State Patrol. The presence of Jack and Bud would also make violence less likely. I intended to bring my Glock, which required me to rip open a seam in my coat pocket so the pistol could be concealed.

The only hitch in my plan was my eagerness to move on it. I was supposed to meet Bud and Jack at eight, but at twenty till I left the house in the Shark, alarm rippling through my intestines. Brian was still in bed and Patty hadn't arrived for the day. I parked across the street from the house on the snow-packed shoulder. As expected, RT's black Tundra was parked in the yard. I brought the car door to the frame then pushed it closed to minimize the sound. I started for the house as I scanned the area. I halted when I saw that the barn door was ajar. I walked through the powdery snow in my snow boots without a sound, as prickles radiated down my spine and into my arms.

I drew the barn door back far enough to poke my head inside. The stack of four rectangular bales of hay were toppled aside and the trap door was open. I backed away from the door and called the police. Dobbs would answer as Bo's shift didn't start till noon. I told him I thought I'd come across a trespasser at the old barn then I asked him to come out.

I stepped inside the barn and shoved both hands in my front pockets as if I was cold. It was wicked cold, but my heat was beginning to rise. When I heard creaking on the ladder, my heart began to race, pulsing malice. RT didn't see me right away because he didn't even pause to look around. Once again, he was much too relaxed in my presence. His black winter coat was unzipped. His handgun was shoved into his front waistband.

"Well, if it isn't Annie Oakley," he said when he spotted me as he climbed out and stood on the dirt ground.

"How cute," I said. "I know why you haven't caught the source of the meth—because it's you."

"Ha! You're cracked."

"You were dealing death even before you killed Davey."

He reached for his gun, but I was faster, I was ready. By the time he grasped the gun handle, I was aiming with both hands and firing. I squeezed hard—the first shots went into his chest then as he fell backward, the next bullets ripped into his throat then his face. The recoil moved from my hand to my chest, and then to my guts with a crash.

After the shock of the gunfire, an eerie silence ensued. My breath came out in quick, frozen blasts. I stayed in a trance for several seconds then looked around. Nothing was stirring, not even a mouse. My brain began to work again. *The Godfather*. Drop the gun. I stood and waited. Annie Oakley didn't need cowboys or police to rescue her—but they could affirm her story.

I don't think it was long before a vehicle pulled up. One door slammed shut—Dobbs. Despite my lack of familiarity with criminal activity, I knew just what to do. He entered then gasped when he saw RT. He looked over at me then down at my gun on the ground.

I walked over to RT's body. His wick-away shirt was no match for the blood saturating it. His hand was clenched tight on the gun handle. With my gloved hand, I flipped off the safety and put his finger on the trigger. Dobbs took several steps forward. His gun remained in the holster. Again, someone too relaxed in my presence. I positioned my hand over RT's ungloved hand then knelt behind RT's right shoulder and lifted the gun level with my hips. Dobbs was only about a dozen feet away. This was no time for a worthless monologue. Steadying the gun with both hands, I fired several times into his chest then twice into those bulging purple neck veins.

Blood gurgled down his chest. He collapsed straight down onto his knees then fell backward. I walked over to Dobbs, where I waited for about a minute. My hands sweated inside my leather gloves and my heart battered the wall of my chest, forcing me to gasp for big gulps of cold air. Two doors slammed shut. Within seconds, Bud and Jack stood in the open doorway, jaws slack, mouths open.

"Call the police...ah...the State Patrol. RT just killed the police."

It took Jack a few moments, but he dialed his cell phone.

Bud stepped forward as Jack summoned the State Patrol.

"My God," said Bud.

I hardly expected him to say more.

"They're dead," I said.

Even in the frigid barn, a creepy heat swept over me.

"Jack, will you call my uncle and my house?"

Jack nodded.

Officers Waters and Merritt arrived within a few minutes—or maybe more—I was losing my grip on time. After Officer Waters stopped in the doorway, he told Bud and Jack to go stand in the corner. Officer Merritt hastened to the bodies. Officer Waters walked a wide path around the scene to get to me. I knew just what to do. I reached out for his forearm to brace myself, thereby casting me as the lone survivor of the trauma. I wasn't feeling weak, but I let him think so. He placed his hand on my shoulder to steady me.

"What happened, Mrs. Culhane?"

"I called Chief Dobbs because I found that someone had trespassed here. When the Chief arrived, RT was coming up out of that hole. The Chief accused RT of trespassing and said he was going to find out what was down in there." I looked over to the pit, as did Officer Waters. "Then RT shot him and I pulled out my gun and shot RT because I thought he was going to shoot me. He-he pointed his gun at me. Can I sit down?"

Officer Waters backed me up several steps and lowered me to the ground.

"Then Bud and Jack came. They work for my uncle, Bill Docket."

"Mrs. Culhane, didn't you think you'd be confronting Agent Martin by coming here?" asked Officer Waters.

"I thought he'd still be at Rachel's."

Trooper Merritt looked over at us as he knelt over Dobbs. Waters twisted his lips, but said nothing.

Car doors slamming. Sirens wailing. I sat in the cold dirt, astonished—partly because I just shot two men, but also that I had done it with such cool resolve. Yet I made sure I looked like a person in quiet distress by staring blankly at the body of Dobbs. Another State Patrol officer came and interviewed me in more detail. I answered him and the next officer to talk to me with consistency, even stating RT fired from his knees to account for the low angle of his shots. I told them honestly why I had come there and the plans I made with Bud and Jack. No one heard any shots, so no one could refute my story. My footprints in the dirt matched my story, I'd been careful about that. Measurements were made and photographs were taken. They even inspected my boots.

I looked over at the body of RT, his legs sprawled out, his left shoulder against a bale of hay. I thought of Jake and Sheila and Davey. I didn't feel sorry I had done it. But what was I to say about Dobbs? Maybe nothing. I didn't know if any evidence regarding meth dealing existed against him.

Dobbs helped kill Davey; now he was dead, too. His wife, Lisa, seemed a nice lady, always ready to volunteer for funerals and community projects. Suspicions would be whispered behind her back, but I didn't want her punished. I looked once more at the bloody mess of him. I think my first shot to RT's chest must have killed him quickly, for he didn't seem as much of a mess. Dobbs gruesomely bled for at least a few moments before he died. Still, I marveled that I had done it and with kick-ass shooting.

Once I finished my statement to the officer, Brian, Bill, Beth, and Patty surrounded me. Brian knelt behind me then wrapped his arms around my shoulders. He asked me why I didn't wake him to come with me, but I shook my head in response. Now was not the time to talk.

Of course, the news of a shootout spread lightning fast through our town. They allowed Gus in when he said he was my attorney. Gus said I had a "legion" of supporters on the grounds, but the authorities wouldn't let anyone else in. Rachel wailed in shock when she saw RT, but that stupid dupe failed to move my heart. Officer Merritt kept her away from me. In time, she was even asked to leave. Our confrontation would come later.

I sent Patty to gather my supporters and bring them to the big house with the assurance that I would be there eventually. My mother refused to leave me, even when I suggested she get out of the cold. Brian went to talk to Officer Waters. They returned to me.

"They're allowing you to go sit in your car to get warm," said Brian.

"I'll warn you, ma'am, there's a bunch of reporters out there," said Officer Waters.

"Then why don't you let her go home?" asked Bill, heatedly.

"It will be soon. I promise."

"Officer Waters, I've seen officers go down into the pit," I said. "What did they find?"

"We need to do a complete investigation. But let me say it looks like your hunch was correct. Oh, and the basement in the house was empty." He gave me a smile.

I nodded and he walked away. The adrenaline that had been heating my body over the last hour or so began to subside. I shivered with cold and the knowledge that I had killed two men. RT had reached for his gun. Would he have shot me? I didn't know, but I had provoked him. I wanted him to grab his gun so that I could kill him. My decision to kill Dobbs came fast and easy. I shuddered with a queasy sense of my own evil.

A few minutes later, Officer Merritt came to escort us out. When I stood up, I felt light-headed. Brian offered, but I refused to let him carry me. Bill called over to Bud and Jack. My little group was escorted to the far wall, skirting the involved area. Bud and Jack fell in behind like they were the trailing cowboys on a cattle drive. The bright sun and snow that lit the day attacked my eyes when I neared the doors. I straightened, resolved to walk with dignity to the car, whatever these people thought of me. They probably wondered if I'd be killing someone every year.

When we passed through the doors, a murmur rose in the crowd. Cameras began clicking, though I looked straight forward. James, Big Joe, Johnny, and Carlos were at our side, pushing reporters and photographers back. Just before I reached the Shark, I looked up and spotted an airplane. This was an isolated area in a desolate part of a fly-over state. A hell of a lot can happen in nowhere.

Chapter 26

THE mood at my house was markedly different than it was after Davey died. The Saturday morning revelers toasted me with orange juice and coffee for surviving a gunfight. I was pressed with so many questions that I was forced to take center stage.

"Yes, to answer your questions, I do think RT was the source of the meth in the area. And yes, I believe he killed Davey. He would have killed me this morning, but he was too slow."

That remark resulted in cheers and spilled coffee.

"I cannot say anything else about what happened this morning. Now, some of you have been asking about Chief Dobbs. All I can say is that I don't know of any evidence to link him to dealing meth or any other drugs. As for Davey's death, well, I don't know if he had a part in it. Like others who have suffered this last year, I see no reason to treat Lisa Dobbs with anything but sympathy and kindness."

People nodded and murmured assent.

"Uncle Bill, where are Bud and Jack? They stood by me. They should be here."

James made his way to me through the crowd that now covered most of the main floor.

"Officer McNeill just drove up," he said.

"Will you tell her that I will talk to her another time? She's just come to pick a fight with me. She is not one of the investigating officers, even if she is in uniform."

He nodded and left.

"Now, if you'll excuse me, I need another breakfast."

"Is anyone else around here in this meth business?" asked Carlos.

"No. I don't think anyone else from Dexter is involved."

I wished I could say no one was using meth, but I didn't know that. Hands patted me on the back as I made my way to the kitchen. In the hall, I came face to face with Kathy Whitfield and Zane.

"Oh, Megan! I'm so glad you're okay. Bless you." She hugged me. "I know things haven't been right with us." She paused with expectation, her eyes soft.

I thought I might be encountering a sincere moment with this woman, so I said, "We shall be good friends again. You must come over for cards. Remember how we used to play when I was young?"

"Oh, yes."

She'd never come, but we'd made our peace.

"Your son is a hero. Without his awareness, we never would have known RT killed Davey."

He gave me a smile.

"Is that for sure?" she asked.

"Oh, I doubt it will ever be proven. What's the point?"

"True."

"But RT's meth killed Jake Breeley and Sheila Ritter."

She slowly nodded.

"Now come have some coffee." I ushered both of them into the kitchen.

I received a call from Robert Foxworthy. He said he wouldn't keep me, but that he heard the news. When he asked how I was, I responded: "Numb."

I then went in search of chocolate. Though I didn't see her, I recognized Glenda's cake pans. After my successful search, I was attacked by a skinny blonde. Kayla hugged me so tightly around the neck I had to stop chewing or I would have choked on my brownie. Kathy had wandered off, so I introduced her to Zane.

"Wow, a real soldier. I've just seen pictures."

"Touch him, he's real," I said as I gave him a wink.

Wasn't I wonderful? Rescuing widows from scandal. Healing wounded friendships. Impressing teenagers. Pronouncing judgments. Killing killers. So marvelous. So righteous. So ready to puke up my black heart.

Later when the house quieted down, I stared out the back window at Rufus and Big Leo yearning to escape to my hills.

"Don't even think about it," said Bill. "You'd freeze to death."

"I'll take the Shark," I said.

"Who's going with you?" he asked.

Brian, James, Beth, and Patty all gave me looks of distrust.

"I'm just going to drive up on the old Hexam road."

"Yeah, but who's going with you?" asked Brian.

"No one," I said, now perturbed. "I don't want to talk. I just want to breathe."

"Fine," said my mom. "But take my car. People know the Shark." She rose. "And don't go without a thermos of Earl Grey."

My mommy said it was okay. My mommy was making me tea. My mommy decided I needed space. However, I intended to take the Shark—that's the vehicle I knew and trusted. I didn't plan on driving near any humans. Ten minutes later, I was driving north on Highway 51, looking for an elusive dirt road covered in snow. Eventually, I turned onto some tire tracks and headed east. I could have found it easier if I'd headed north on the Eldritch road, but I wasn't going to drive by that barn. It only took my uncle a couple of minutes to find where I'd turned. He parked his pickup fifty feet behind me. I couldn't help but smile. I pulled out my cell phone.

"Did I even find the road?" I asked him.

"I don't know," he said. "Maybe in the spring we ought to mark it and put down some gravel."

"How soon do you think they'll let us demolish that crappy old house?"

"I can ask. We can tear down that barn, if you want."

"Nah. Seems a waste when Lew and your guys worked so hard to fix it. Okay, signing off."

"Don't fall asleep."

"I don't think that's happening. Bye."

In movies, people just hang up, they don't say goodbye. When they get disrupted while reading, they never put a bookmark in their book before they close it. I killed two men today. I used bookmarks. I suppose I did the town a favor. My father was a hard man, but he never would have done this—his brains and the law were his weapons. Would any of it happen if Brian's dad hadn't bought us those guns? I'd even learned gun safety and practiced at the range. I wanted to be a responsible gun owner. I let it make me overconfident, reckless, and daring.

What the hell had I done? I killed two men—they were dead, families would cry over it, Rachel and Lisa Dobbs were already sobbing. RT was somebody's son. And I did it. What a hypocrite—I was a lawyer yet I didn't let the police and the rules of our society work. Those laws were created to protect against people like me. The death of Davey was so clever and so far-fetched that it would be incredibly difficult to prove RT did it. They could prove the poison and the death, but not the act since no one saw him do it. His conniving deed cost him and Dobbs their chances for trials—it cost them their lives at the hands of a self-righteous vigilante.

RT might have shot me once I accused him—I'll never know. But I didn't need to accuse him; I could have stayed outside and called the State Patrol. But Dobbs—no way around it—that was cold-blooded murder. I didn't just kill, I murdered. I gasped for breath then rolled down the window to suck in the cold air.

Murder.

I detested Dobbs, even as a kid. I watched him bully Derek, James, and Carlos along with his sons. I even kicked Dobbs in the knee once when I was nine. Strange thing about him, he never bothered the wives or daughters. I guess even that old redneck had his code of conduct.

I hated RT since the moment I first met him last April. Did either of them deserve to die? It had been avoidable. People were calling it the "Shootout." Really, it was a slaughter. Neither man expected it from me. I knew I could kill to defend myself or someone else. Did I know I could murder? I let the anger over the death of Davey overcome me. I was guilty. Should I confess to the police? Would it give me peace? No, but it would certainly result in prison. A degree of justification existed in my actions, yet that didn't absolve me before God.

What did God think of me? Did He always know I possessed a black heart, one that could murder? Did He know my soul was filled with malice, hatred, lies, and vengeance? I told Davey that God knew him. God certainly knew me. How terrifying.

I wondered if any of my friends and family suspected what truly happened. I think Brian felt hurt that I went off without him. But I was going someplace potentially dangerous and I didn't want him to get hurt. He couldn't have done what I did, and I didn't know if he could have been ready to defend himself. Then his death would have been on my hands, too. Then again, maybe nothing would have happened, maybe Brian's presence would have held me in check.

Had I acted on impulse or was it all really done with premeditation? I went to that barn with hatred, indignation, and a gun. When I drove to the Eldritch house, did I do so with the intent of killing RT? No. Did I quickly assess the situation? Yes. I called Dobbs to set up a confrontation. Did I plan to kill Dobbs when I called him? No. What if I'd only killed RT? Dobbs would show up and I would say I shot RT in self-defense. But my position would be weaker. And he'd still be police chief, one with suspicion. Would he try to blackmail me? That's probably what he'd done with RT.

The truth remained—I saw my chance and I took it with quick, calculated determination. Now, two men had tags on their toes at the Sidney morgue.

I rolled up the window. My tea was cold. I was cold. My soul was certainly a cold chunk of evil. My vengeful heart still wished those men dead. I deserved God's condemnation and punishment.

I gazed north to the bluff with the cleft on the east side that looked like an open mouth. The Shark rested on high ground that extended most of the two hundred yards north. I turned on the ignition and yanked the wheel northward. I followed the wind-blown high ground over two inches of hard-packed snow covering drought-hardened ground. I was surprised how fast I could go. What a damn fine vehicle. I was even able to drive through deeper snow to get to the base of the bluff. I bet the designers of this vehicle never anticipated this use. I climbed down out of the SUV and charged toward the rocky protrusion. I grabbed the rocks and the occasional squat conifer and scrambled up the side, over the crunchy cold snow. It took only ten minutes or so to climb to the rocky wall, which lacked snow, but was fifteen feet straight up before I could get to the Joker's mouth.

I found hand and footholds easily enough. My uncle yelled at me, but I didn't intend to stop. I hoisted myself up the last rocky juts, and then swept the snow off the jaw line of the mouth. I scrambled into the mouth and discovered I could sit upright. At first, I waited for the Joker to laugh at the pathetic human who invaded him. But all was quiet. It was a frigid day, but I didn't feel it. Bill stopped yelling, for he was busy trying to negotiate the first several feet of the base. I wondered if anyone had ever climbed this bluff. Perhaps some Northern Cheyenne or Lakota had once taken a fancy to the strange gaping form. Below me, Bill wasn't making any progress. He started yelling again. The wind took away his words.

I waited. If God decided to punish me, here I was, alone in my guilt. Alone in the wind.

Chapter 27

B UT nothing happened. So after a while, I climbed down. I helped Bill back down the twenty feet of the bluff he had managed. His face looked wind-blown and red, his lips were chapped and his jeans were covered in snow. I needed to get him home.

"Are you gonna tell me what you were doing up there?" he asked, panting.

"Maybe someday."

We drove home. He was mad at me. I shrugged off everyone's inquires and climbed the back stairs to change my clothes. I looked down at the sweatshirt and jeans on the floor as I changed. I killed two men in those clothes. I laid the jeans over the edge of my hamper to dry. Brian stood by the bed watching me.

"I'm hungry," I said.

I went down to the kitchen. I ate two containers of yo-gurt and poured a half glass of bourbon. Patty huffed then made me a sandwich. My mom sat down at the kitchen ta-ble and gazed at me. Bill came back from his house in dry clothes. He was still mad. James came over, followed by Derek and Vonny. They had been summoned—Megan was in a crisis—again.

Yes, eternal damnation was serious. God decided to let me live. I didn't know what came next. People talked and asked each other questions when I didn't answer—though I did once. I stated the name of the bluff was the Joker—they needed to be clear on that. More talking. I kept eating and drinking as I slipped into numbness. I got up to pour more bourbon. Their stares felt like laser beams trying to bore into my head for answers. I could tell Brian thought about grabbing the bottle, but I snatched it quickly. I didn't pour but a couple of ounces. How long would I stay this way? Somebody mentioned the Cowpoke; after all, it was Saturday.

"I don't want to see anyone," I said. People would try to talk to me. They would stare.

Vonny and my mom went into the hallway. I was numb, but my hearing was fine, when I wanted it to be.

"Do you think she's in shock?" Vonny whispered.

I didn't hear my mom's response. She probably nodded. She was right, I guess. When I finished my sandwich and bourbon, I got up, which seemed to alarm everyone. I walked into the family room, took *David Copperfield* off the shelf, and started to read. He was born. I was dead, or something close to it. God didn't strike me down, so I'd just read till I knew what would happen to me next. I skipped David's abuse. Someone turned on a football game. They all sat around in the family room, Brian on one side of me, my mom on the other. Everyone else sat in other chairs. Deputy Bo arrived, stood quietly against the wall, refused a chair, and stared at me or the floor then left after an hour or so.

In time, Brian and Derek hoisted me off the sofa. My mom marked my spot in the book. They led me to the dining room and gave me food. I ate it, though I can't think now what it was, for soon I was busy reading again. Later, I was hoisted from the sofa again. My mom took me to my room and supervised my preparations for sleep. I then crawled into bed as directed. Brian joined me and my mom left.

Faces, they had been lacking. They were there, but I wasn't looking at them. Brian wrapped me in his arms. That felt good. I nestled into him, but never saw his face. No faces. Faces had worry or wonder. I wanted to go beyond those things. Brian tried to talk to me. I shook my head. I stayed in his arms, but turned so that I faced away from him. In time, he slept. I didn't. Damn, what was that commandment? I could only think of nine.

I slowly wiggled out of Brian's grasp, pulled on my socks, and then tip-toed down the front stairs. I located a copy of the King James Version in the study. I took it up to the dressing room, turned on a lamp then wrapped myself in my dad's old bedspread. I cuddled up in the chair and found Exodus chapter 18, no, 20. *Thou shalt have no other gods before me.* I was okay on that one. *Thou shalt not make unto thee any graven image....* Oops. This was the one I forgot. So obvious. *Thou shalt not take the name of the LORD thy god in vain.* RT and Dobbs both used it. Now, I was pretty careful on this one; though, I'd say or think all sorts of vulgar words. I tried not to use the F-word, but it still popped out on occasion. And I tried not to misrepresent God for personal gain. *Remember the sabbath day, to keep it holy.* I wonder why that wasn't capitalized. I did go to church most Sundays, but I spent more time in the afternoon thinking about football and the tight pants the players wore than I did thinking about God. Guilty there. *Honour thy father and mother.* I hadn't been nice to anyone today. Hmm. This was a mix of honor and memories of getting a raw deal in life. I would never understand why they separated me from Scott, but I had accepted it and forgiven them. I even let Beulah name a steak after my dad. I had taken away my mother's true identity, but she ratified that.

Thou shalt not commit adultery. In our small community, that seemed everywhere I turned. Drugs made Shcila a whore. RT and Rachel probably broke this commandment as often as they could. And even Brian had been guilty. My Brian. *Thou shalt not steal.* Mmmm. I couldn't think how this applied. *Thou shalt not bear false witness against thy neighbour.* Right, British English. Well, that liar Don Troff certainly blew this one, claiming his sober passenger was the driver. How despicable. Wait. I blackmailed Dobbs to keep him in line and later to keep Brian out of trouble.

Hmm. I didn't actually bear false witness, but I withheld the truth to gain power over someone. Well, if this commandment didn't cover that, it was still a sin. I was beyond pathetic.

Thou shalt not covet thy neighbour's house...nor anything that is thy neighbour's. Nah. My dad deeded me the biggest house in the area, which he inherited from his father, a successful banker. My robust law practice, which I owed to my dad, brought me all the material possessions I needed. And I wasn't coveting anybody's husband or wife. Nope, not that one, not several of them. But I had skipped one. One I never even needed to open the Bible or any state's criminal code to know.

Thou shalt not kill. Oh, sweet Jesus! Help me. I was a vile sinner in thought and deed—twice over. Well, three times if I counted Salt Eldritch, but that really was him or me in a fight to death. With RT, I provoked him to put his hand on his gun; I was ready and faster and determined to blast that bastard to hell. With Dobbs, it was simple revenge. Where was it that God said "Vengeance is mine"? Probably in Psalms. Lord Almighty, I avenged Davey's death, but at a terrible cost to me. Dante ought to draw a circle just for me. I needed to feel my due pain so I looked in the concordance. Oh, Deuteronomy 32:35: "To me belongeth vengeance." God, not me. "Vengeance is mine" was the stronger, more modern prose, but both began to reverberate in my head. We humans were supposed to make some laws—the Bible doesn't say thou shalt not proceed past a stop sign without coming to a full stop. We were supposed to make the world more orderly. But I ventured far beyond the duty of a citizen. Vengeance—I took it, I swiped it from God. It wasn't just that I played judge and jury—I set myself before God.

My self-accusation began to claw at my chest. First, the sin burned then an inferno of guilt raged in my heart and mind and soul. Was I to burn in hell right now? I threw off the blanket and fell to the ground. I was lost.

ALONE IN THE WIND

I heard my mom's voice and a gentle nudge.

"Oh," I uttered with great articulation.

The devil hadn't taken me. Why, I didn't know. But my mom was trying to get me to my feet. It was still dark. I shivered without a blanket. Why did the room smell of gunpowder and hay? I could even taste it on my lips. Hay had been present in the barn, but no gunpowder. Was I going crazy?

"Do you want to talk?" she asked.

"Sometime, but right now I don't think I'd make much sense."

She put the Bible in an empty dresser drawer then escorted me back to my room. It was nearly four in the morning.

"Now please promise me you'll not go anywhere."

I pointed to the lump in the bed. "I'm going where it's warm. I'll see you in the morning."

But I did leave. After I got warm and relaxed, I blissfully slipped into sleep when I took a wrong turn. I went to a cold barn where men had bloody chests and gaping holes in their heads and necks. Dobbs—his neck just kept spouting blood. Those purple veins were filled with gallons of blood that gurgled. Annie Oakley. She was there. She was looking at a man whose fancy, gray wick-away-sweat shirt burst open with a blast of blood. Now I was covered in it. I wanted to wake up, but was I asleep? I was bound to the gory scene before me. Men kept bleeding even after they died or maybe was it me that was bleeding somewhere deep where no one could see it. Where was I to fasten the tourniquet? When blasts came out of my hands, I jerked upright.

"What? Megan, are you all right?"

I looked down at my hands, though I couldn't see them in the dark. But I had felt the jump of my Glock in my hand, no, in both of them. Brian turned on the bedside lamp. I looked down to see where I was bleeding, for I could feel its stickiness, but I couldn't see it. It was staying inside me.

"Megan, it's okay. You're home. You're fine."

So he thought. If I'm fine, why am I bleeding? When will it stop?

"Yeah." I lay back onto my pillow. It had already turned cold. "I'm okay. Goodnight."

I pulled the comforter up to my neck and shut my eyes. He sat up and looked at me for several minutes. He wanted to help me. But I deserved this torture. In time, I drifted off to sleep, comforted by his warm shoulder against mine.

But then I saw them, so many dead bodies. Sheila torn to bits by a train. Jake Breeley with the back of his head bashed in. Davey with his arms in tight to his body, lying in a pile of mushy snow, with his mother sobbing over him. RT against that bale of hay, holes and blood. Dobbs falling backwards into the dirt, holes and blood. So many dead bodies. So many images I'd never forget. Why wasn't I dead?

Then I saw Davey again, but he had Scott's face. What? Scott lay in the slushy parking lot, while Davey sat in my brother's wheelchair. Then I went to the railroad tracks where Sheila's body lay tangled in a bloody, grotesque mass. But it now had Kayla's face. My heart throbbed so loud it should have awakened the town, but it didn't. Kayla. Scott—my Totty.

Just before dawn, I jolted awake, the sound of my Glock echoing in my head. I must have slept for a little while in peace. Brian wrapped me up in his arms. I burrowed under him. It's something petite women can do to muscular, former linebackers who can hold themselves up for quite awhile and not squish a little badger. I nestled in under him, hungry for his warmth. Soon though, I wanted heat and flesh against flesh. Then I'd want all my stud could give me. And my darling wanted to comfort me, so a quickie wouldn't do. Nope. He loved me up good and I slept hard.

ALONE IN THE WIND

When I opened my eyes this time, I was still naked under the comforter, but it was nearly ten. I hadn't planned on going to church anyway. I wasn't worthy to enter the house of God, nor did I want to go where people would stare at me.

Killer. I would be that forever.

I sat up then realized I had just flashed my mom, who was sitting in the chair in the corner.

"Oops. Sorry."

"Don't be. I haven't seen you since you were a tot. You've changed."

"More than you know."

After lunch, the whole gang assembled once again in the family room. Derek and Vonny needed to leave for their homes, but like the others, they waited. Right at the start of the fourth quarter of the Broncos game, I turned off the TV. All eyes were on me.

"I made a choice. One I have to live with. There was a point in time when I could have backed off...not entered the barn when I saw that RT was down in the shelter. I could have just called the State Patrol. But I didn't. Now two men are dead."

Silence. Under their scrutiny, my arm pits started to go clammy. I had no intention of making a full confession—I hoped no one would start asking for details.

Finally, James said, "You did what you thought you needed to do. I can't fault you for that."

"No, but God can," I replied.

"You killed the man who killed Davey...and Dobbs helped him," said Bill. "God knows exactly what they did."

"And it sounds like it was gonna be hard to prove what they did," said Patty. "Jackson says you were God's instrument of justice."

I didn't say anything. Others murmured assent. But I didn't deserve their good opinion—I'd been too angry, too calculating, too willful. But if they wanted to think that, then maybe I'd be spared their doubts. I'd made a sort of confession. Perhaps now they understood my peculiar behavior.

Somebody suggested root beer floats. I lifted the remote and turned the game back on, fully aware that most eyes were still on me. Players in blue and orange collided with those in red and white. Yet my black heart kept beating. Even with the burden of my guilt, I was selfish, concerned only with my own soul—I lacked any remorse for RT or Dobbs. I doubted that I could ever truly mourn their deaths.

Later in the afternoon, I began to get nervous about going to work. I had a strange sense that people could see my guilt, especially if they stared hard. I thought I saw Joy, Glenda, Melanie, and Gus here yesterday. They probably thought I was okay. Then I remembered I had a hearing on Tuesday in Sidney. Strangers staring. I broke out in a sweat. I went to the hallway to pace. Brian waited for me in the foyer.

"Just thinking about going to work," I said.

"Maybe you're not ready. Stay home. I heard the funeral for Chief Dobbs is on Wednesday. After that, you can decide. You were planning to take vacation for Christmas next week. I think things would be pretty slow."

I didn't say anything, but I did keep pacing. He left. After a few minutes, my smart phone rang. The Caller ID indicated it was Gus. I wondered if Brian called him.

"Megan, you should just stay home for a while," said Gus.

"I have a hearing on Tuesday," I said.

"Yeah, Docket is on the docket."

That was lame, but Gus was a good guy. I'd hired him based on my dad's endorsement; my dad had rarely been wrong about people.

"Look, I'll handle it," he said. "You weren't even going to contest the motion."

"True. Okay, I take Monday and Tuesday and go from there."

"That's settled then. Oh, Glenda wants to put up a bigger Christmas tree in the lobby."

"That's fine."

"Well, I'll see you then. Take care. Call if you need anything. Bye."

I suddenly felt relieved. I could hide out here for now. Wandering off my route, I stopped next to the Christmas tree and stared out the window. The sunlight made the snow sparkle. The wind had blown away the snow down to the grass in our front yard, but it drifted three feet high along the front of the house. The sidewalk leading to the house where Brian had shoveled looked like a luge tunnel.

A year and a half ago, Salt Eldritch shot through this window then chased me into the darkness. I did some fast thinking then, just as I did yesterday. I recalled Salt's silhouette in the darkness and remembered feeling for a pulse in his cold wrist. But I hadn't been forced to sit and look at my deed like I did yesterday. Could I ever erase from my memory the sound of those shots? Or the sight of those bloody bodies?

I started pacing again. I walked by the copier and lifted some pages from the bin. I must have printed something and forgotten about it. I took a look at the first page. It was Davey's trust. I had printed it out to proofread. I crumpled the pages in my hands and plopped down hard on the carpet to sob. Truly, I was a pathetic mess—unable to control my grief and my guilt.

I went upstairs to my room and put on a Christmas album. Luciano Pavarotti sang "O Holy Night" and I wept. This had always been my dad's favorite. It made me cry last Christmas after his death; I hadn't progressed. Or did every emotion just feel amplified? It struck me that I was still grieving, not just over Davey, but also for my dad and Scott. Maybe Davey was a high functioning version of Scott. That possibility left my mouth ajar.

"What, hon?"

Someone else was here. I called Kayla "hon." I was "hon," too. My mom came around the bed toward me. I didn't remember sitting down, but I had. She knelt in front of me.

"You're still grieving. You got that on top of that gunfight yesterday."

"I know that now."

She wrapped her warm hands over mine.

"It's time for supper."

"We just had lunch."

She smiled.

Didn't we? I looked at the clock. It was six. I was lost, time was lost, too.

"It's going to take time to get over this," she said.

"Do I get over it?"

"You learn to cope. Time helps."

She stood and tugged on my hands. I followed her like a sheep, or maybe a little girl.

In the kitchen, people were milling about, getting in Patty's way.

"I thought I'd have a cup of tea," said my mom. "Would you like one?"

I nodded. Vonny gave me smile as she passed by me. She wanted to see what I did next. They were all waiting on me. I stood in the middle of the kitchen; people moved around me. My mom handed me a cup of Earl Grey. I sniffed the Chinese black tea's aroma of bergamot, letting it fill my nostrils.

Slam!

I jerked. The sharpness stabbed inside my head. I had dropped the tea cup. It lay shattered on the floor. Hot liquid was splattered on my socks and slippers. It had just been a cabinet door. The sound hadn't been loud. Did I make it loud? I looked down at the cup. The others in the room stopped moving and talking. They were looking at me. I didn't want their eyes on me. One or two people were talking to me. I hurried through the hall and up the back stairs to my room. I knew what they were thinking.

She's disturbed. She's weak.

Chapter 28

SUNDAY night haunted me as much as Saturday night, except that I no longer felt the gun in my hand. I also stayed in bed. No matter what image or memory disturbed me, getting out of bed meant getting cold. Gunfire woke me nearly every hour. Gunpowder and hay stung my nostrils. Near morning, my nightmares took on a distorted, yet sharp quality, as if I was in a barn Salvador Dali would have created. I moved away from Brian to avoid waking him, but I still did; then I needed to calm him so he could sleep. The floor creaked several times in the hall. My mom wasn't sleeping well either. We all slept in till nine. Brian went to work and I stayed home with Mom and Patty. Unfamiliar cars and trucks were parked on the street in front of our house. Patty caught me peeking through the dining room blinds at them.

"They're reporters," she said. "They were here all yesterday. Bill drives by now and then to chase them away, but they come back."

"Well, at least they're not coming to the door," I said.

My mom smiled. "Barnaby would never allow that."

Sure enough, I saw James' dog run by the front of the house and back again, tethered to the porch railing.

"Traddles is tied up in back. Bill thinks he's more likely to bite someone."

While we were watching, a big Ford van pulled up. Three men got out. Two approached the dog with their hands out, trying to be friendly. A third man skirted around to the west to walk through the front yard. He got halfway up the yard then looked west and made a mad dash back to the street. Soon, James walked toward the van with a shotgun. The other two men ran back to the vehicle with Barnaby barking at their heels. The four other cars left, too. We laughed, but it made me feel disquieted. I walked away from the windows and didn't go back again, though I asked Patty to invite James in.

He was muttering under his breath, but stopped when he saw me. He set the shotgun behind him as if he thought the sight might disturb me.

"They'll be back," he said.

Later Bill made all his cowhands park their pickups alongside both sides of the road. One car parked in the middle of the street. As soon as the scumbag reporter left his car, Bo dashed from his own pickup and wrote him a ticket.

I really didn't know what to do with myself. I never just sat at home. I went to the study and called Melanie to discuss my rescheduled appointments. I didn't like missing work, but I didn't want to deal with people. I spent most of the day reading *David Copperfield*. At three-thirty, Paul brought Kayla over. When she arrived, we decided to watch a movie. Kayla suggested a western, but that made my hands sweat. My mom suggested *The Sting*. The sight of an occasional gun made me cringe. Kayla was mesmerized by Robert Redford and Paul Newman, neither of whom she'd seen before. A shirtless Redford made her jaw drop. My mom and I glanced at her and exchanged grins.

We all went to bed early, bracing for another eventful night. I downed a hefty portion of bourbon to help me fall asleep faster. Brian suggested keeping the fireplace on so that it would be a little lighter in the room. At first, it did comfort me, yet later I started seeing the faces of Davey, Sheila, and Jake in it. Soon, no one was dying by gunfire, everyone was burning. Whatever groan or wail I made woke Brian. I tried turning away from the fire, and that seemed to work, for it kept the room lighter and when I woke, I was immediately aware that I wasn't in a burning barn. The hallway continued to creak on occasion. Once I got up to go to the bathroom, which alarmed Brian so much that he stayed awake till I returned. I looked out the drapes and saw that not only was our front light on, but the Wilson house was well lit. Our Christmas tree lights shone out the living room window onto the snow. Shouldn't those be turned off? I was throwing my family and my friends out of whack.

I awakened at nine again, feeling like I'd been through a battle. I didn't have any external contusions, but I felt roughed up. Robert called a little while later.

"How are you doing?" he asked.

"Like someone's hiding all my marbles from me," I said.

"I'm not surprised. I killed a man in a drug bust seven years ago. Seven years and four months ago. I still think about it. It was on a Thursday. Anyway, the Breeley brothers heard about RT's demise. Now we can't get them to shut up. Riley coughed up two more names, a guy in Sterling we'd been watching and a florist in North Platte. She wasn't even on our radar."

How bizarre. My horrible deeds were reaping benefits. Could things get anymore screwed up?

"Oh, and those two guys in Sidney, Chris and Alex, RT's gym buddies…Joe nabbed them. That blew his cover, of course. Funny thing, he keeps saying he wants to stay."

"Well, we still have users around. But that's probably Bo's problem."

"Yeah, but you're down one police chief."

Tuesday evening, I started to get nervous about the funeral for Dobbs the next day. Thinking about it made my stomach roil. I'd be attending the funeral of a man I murdered. It would be so—oh, I hate to use a word everybody and their bleeping cousin overused to the extreme—but it was going to be surreal. Come to think of it, it was going to be fucking surreal. And every person in America who overused those words owed me a letter of apology.

Lots of bourbon, David in the blacking factory, Bill and James and Beth and Brian all trying to help me, but I couldn't be helped. Brian brought home some dark chocolate Melanie said would help so I ate a ton of that then I ate a ton of Rolaids then I drank some more bourbon then I was in bed staring at the fire. Blood gurgled out of Dobb's neck all night long. Gun blast, gurgle. Then again.

Brian woke me at eight, I looked and felt like hell. Advil, shower, lots of eggs, lots of toast. Then I was walking up the steps of the Methodist church. I'm glad it wasn't my church, not that I saw much difference between Methodists and Presbyterians, except that our basement was beige and theirs was mint green, and we had a baritone who could give you goose bumps when he sang "Ava Maria." I just never wanted to come back here, not after agonizing through Davey's funeral. But I was in a pew with Brian at my side. And people were looking at me and I stood when they stood and sat when they sat and I never heard a word.

In the narthex, I stood with my back to the exiting crowd. The despicable fraud was unable to look people in the eye. Panic made my hands shake.

I looked at Brian and said, "Get me out of here."

But it was too late. Lisa Dobbs rushed up to me and hugged me.

"Oh, Megan, I'm so sorry you had to see it and…it's just so terrible," she said, her good heart ready to burst.

What could I say? I murdered your son of a bitch husband? No, that wouldn't do. Bill and Beth stood nearby, unable to help me. I couldn't just hide in her hug. We were front and center, and the people around us became quiet. But like a good attorney, I found the right thing to say.

"We both need time to heal and we need God's comfort."

It was true. But I didn't deserve comfort—I deserved punishment, though right now I hoped for a chance to escape home to that chocolate. I caught a glimpse of Zane, who wore his Army dress uniform. I hadn't realized he'd made the rank of lieutenant. He did look impressive. Melanie thought so; I saw her edging through the crowd to get near him.

Mrs. Dobbs finally released me then somebody started talking to her, so I edged away. Bill offered to stay and represent the family. Soon, I led Brian and Beth toward a side door. We'd kept our coats, so we hurried around the side of the building toward the parking lot. By the time I'd finished taking deep breaths to rouse myself, we were home. Home. Could I stay here and never leave again like Miss Havisham?

Patty soon arrived. I asked my mom to call James. Neither he nor Carlos could muster the hypocrisy to attend the funeral of a man who had bullied them for decades. Brian ate a quick sandwich then headed for work. Beulah called to ask if she could come over. I nodded yes to Patty, who relayed my answer.

A half hour later, she was shuffling down our hallway to the kitchen. I was still eating chocolate. She stood over me in a moment of speechlessness I'd never seen. She grabbed my shoulders then tried to pull me up. I stood and looked up at her. She hugged me hard then put me back down in my chair and pointed to the chocolate. Mom and Patty loitered in a state of amusement. James stood against the wall, in content anticipation.

"We've all heard about your interrogatin' Zane," she said. "Heh! 'Course we couldn't be goin' to the funeral of the bastard who helped kill our Davey. I bet they shipped the body of that killer back to wherever he's from."

She shuffled over to Beth. "You ought to be proud of your kin. Can't know the courage it took to defend herself and beat that bastard to the draw. Made Blaine and Barb mighty proud. Killin' that killer. Saved the state a ton of money not puttin' him in jail. Yeah, heard all about it. Might not have beaten him in court, no eyewitnesses and all. But Megan, hon, you gave out justice as well as you ever could in court. Yeah, my girl." She squeezed my shoulder.

"Won't you sit down and have a cup of coffee?" asked Beth.

Beulah smiled at my mom. "I think I will."

I slid a chocolate bar over to her and said, "It's supposed to cure shell-shock. It's not really working, but I like the effort."

She cackled then sipped her coffee.

"Shell-shock. Yep. You do look different. Kinda puny. I guess a gunfight would do that. And you almost died from what I hear. But you listen to me, young lady. You got to take care of yourself. You take on too much. You been takin' care of Joy and her girls and been watchin' over that sweet Kayla and her pa. Before that you helped Lew. And there's whisperings about how old man Breeley made good money selling Riley's truck that somehow became his. Those are mysteries, but I bet you had a hand in all of it. In fact, I can see on your face the truth."

"What else can you see on my face?"

"Weariness. Load of it. Not sleepin' well. Know what I think you should do?"

"What?"

"Go back to work. That's what we're doin' tomorrow. Gonna reopen Custer's. EJ ordered a ton of that good tenderloin. You get back to normal. Get some days in before Christmas. Come then, you're gonna be missin' your dad. And I know you cared for Davey. You got that stuff, too. Go back and be an attorney. You done your hero work. Now Dexter needs your law work."

She sipped her coffee and accepted a hunk of chocolate from me.

"Mmmm. That's good. Well, best be goin'. Gotta get ready for tomorrow. Be packed all day with people wantin' to talk."

I rose with her. "I'll be there. I don't want you giving my booth away."

"Oh, pshaw!"

She sashayed out the door into the hall, all the while giving us her Queen Elizabeth wave. We laughed. I followed her and helped her down the front steps.

"Thank you," I said.

She nodded, climbed into her Chrysler, and coasted away.

I sat down in the living room, gazed at the Christmas tree, inhaled the pungent Norway spruce scent, and thought about Beulah's advice. I lay back on the decorative pillows in the corner of the sofa and stared at the colorful lights for a few minutes until I was staring at the insides of my eyelids. The doorbell woke me. I looked at the table clock. I'd slept for three blissfully blank hours. A State Patrol cruiser was parked in the driveway. It was Rachel. I went to the door and waved Patty away. She scurried down the hall to the kitchen. I might as well get this over with.

I opened the door and led her into the living room. She stood glaring at me, even after I invited her to sit down. So I stayed on my feet, too.

"I want to talk to you about the events of Saturday morning," she said. "No way did RT try to kill you. And even if he had, you couldn't beat his fire."

"Is that so? Well, I have no intention of discussing that day with you. The case is closed. And you're in no position to doubt me."

"What the hell does that mean?"

"It means you're either stupid or corrupt. I'll give you the benefit of the doubt and just say stupid."

She took a step toward me as her face flushed red.

"Oh, back off."

"I didn't care that RT was married. That was ending."

"And I suppose you don't care that committing adultery with a murderer and major drug dealer won't affect your career."

"He didn't murder anyone."

"He poisoned Davey Shuster with the help of Chief Dobbs. But you were too blind to see what was right before your eyes. And he had at least four minions right under your nose."

"Four? You're crazy."

"Besides the Breeley brothers, which even a kid figured out, those Sidney oafs from the gym, Alex and Chris, were operating while you were screwing. You're a cheat and a sap. You must have withheld a lot of suspicious activity to keep Waters and Merritt in the dark. And you're busy trying to pick a fight with me? You need to pull your own ass out of the fire."

"Where are you getting all this shit?"

"Does it worry you that I was more in the loop than you? You weren't even allowed to investigate the shooting. It's strange, don't you think, that neither of you knew about the undercover FBI in the area? You're pathetic. And you're also a liar."

She grabbed my blazer.

"What are you going to do, shoot me? 'Sweetheart, you don't have it in you.' Remember that line? Well, I killed that murdering son of a bitch."

I yanked her hand off my collar.

"Go home to your husband. Yeah, I discovered that lie, too. Both you and RT always underestimated me. I did my homework, neither of you did."

We glared at each other for a few moments.

"Now, get the hell out of my house."

She whirled around and stomped to the front door. Soon, her cruiser roared down the street. I thoroughly enjoyed that encounter—I'd regained my fight. I put on my coat and I went into the kitchen. I could tell from the grins on their faces that they had been listening.

"Where are you going?" asked my mom.

"To the office."

Chapter 29

NIGHTS continued to be hell, but it was good to get back to work. On Thursday, my appointments resumed. If a client said anything, it was supportive. I'd thank them then proceed with business. The whole gang met for lunch at Custer's. Carol helped us add a table to the booth. We even invited Bo to dine with us.

"Hey, Bo, are you going to run for sheriff?" asked Bill.

"Naw. Don't like all that paperwork. No, we'll find somebody. State Patrol is helpin' me for now." He leaned toward me. "I need some time to forget that scene at the railroad tracks. Officer Merritt threw up. But don't tell anyone."

I nodded. I wasn't the only one in shock.

Back at the office, Glenda handed a message to Brian from his dad. I followed him into his office after I praised her for the beautiful Christmas tree in the lobby.

"It's time, Brian," I said. "You've punished him long enough. And Christmas is nearly here. Don't forget, that Glock your dad bought me saved my life."

I was bending the truth, but I thought it would accomplish a good result.

"Yeah, okay. I'll call him tonight."

When I got back to my office, I found a big welcome back poster the girls made. It included some photos Kayla had taken with her phone. She and Emily must have let Chelsea pick the colors—pink and lavender—colors I favored only on chocolate-covered Easter eggs.

After supper, my mom led me to the living room. I guess it was becoming our new semi-private conference room.

"I need to ask your permission before I do anything," she began, "but I'm thinking of quitting my job and staying around here."

I was stunned.

"Why?" I asked.

"You're going through a difficult time and I'd like to stay and help if I can."

"Well…ah…I'd love to have you stay. You steady me. Do you want to stay in the house with us?"

"Well, I'm afraid that might be overdoing it, but yes, for now. Brian told me he likes that I'm around—especially because he's always worried you'll bolt."

"But what about your job?"

"No offense, but I think you need me more than Creighton does."

I nodded. "I am a mess."

"This will also give me some time to figure out about Bill and me."

She reached over and grabbed my hand. Her hands were always warm. How did she do that? Was it a Mediterranean thing?

"This is the first time I think you've ever really needed me."

"Sometimes a girl needs her mom."

She smiled. It was always warm, too.

On Friday, I invited Zane over to supper. I planned to ask him if he wanted to come with our gang to the Cowpoke on Saturday night, but for now, I just wanted to talk. After supper, I took him up to the fourth bedroom, which was mostly a storage room with a day bed, so that our conversation would be private.

We sat on the day bed, with Zane on one end and me in the corner, with my knees pulled up to my chest. For a while, we stared into our bourbons.

Then I said, "Do you still hear gunfire?"

"Nah. But man o man, I did for a long time. Night-mares are better, too."

"Now you've been home for several months, right?"

"Yeah, but I didn't have problems right away…too numb, I guess. Well, I was jumpy…really hyped. But other stuff started later when it started to feel raw."

"You know that you have posttraumatic stress disorder."

"What's your point?"

"Why do they call it a disorder? I mean, it seems perfectly natural to see horrible stuff and be affected by it."

He shrugged. "I didn't get it till the last deployment."

"Why was that different? Just because there was more?"

"Why are you so concerned about me?"

"Because I need you to get better."

"Why? I haven't heard from you in—"

"Because I care. And I need to know that I can get better."

He looked at me for a long time. I looked down. I didn't like anybody's scrutiny.

"I got it again," I said. "But this time it's fifty times worse. Even without the anxiety and the nightmares and the frailty of everything, there's this shadow hanging over me. Do you have that?"

"It's more like I'm drowning in something…because of something."

"Something specific?" I asked.

"Yeah."

"But you don't want to talk about it because it's so horrible."

He nodded.

"I've been thinking I got three things," I said.

"Three?"

"You've got two."

"Do I?"

"Yeah, your combat…ah, thing…and grief over your dad's death."

"That's what you've got."

"I have one more—choice. I made a choice to do something when I didn't have to and two men died."

"Wasn't that RT going to shoot you? The papers all say he had the gun in his hand that shot Dobbs."

"I do think he would have shot me. But I provoked the situation. I could have backed off, but didn't."

"You always were…willful, strong."

"Well, I had to be with you. You were a bulldozer ready to squash anyone you thought weak. I had to get out. I couldn't relax around you."

His eyebrows rose and his eyes got big. I just hurt him.

"Well, now I'm a lump. A jittery lump. Not anyone I know."

"Sometimes I feel so alone, so lost," I said. "If I blow away, I don't know if I'll find my way back."

He was quiet, not drinking, just thinking or maybe remembering. I couldn't and wouldn't say anything more about what I did.

"I shot a kid."

I gasped then regretted it. I just didn't see that coming. So I said, "But it was on accident."

He looked at me. "Yeah."

I nodded.

"I was chasing down some bastard who'd been playing sniper. We finally flushed him, got him on the run. I sprayed him. We'd been so angry that he killed Jason and Lex. Then I saw that one of my bullets went through a window. I knocked and went in. Then I saw him—he was just so small. Our medic worked on him, but we lost him. I still see his face—so surprised, so startled when he looked at me and then down at his chest."

"But it was an accident."

"Oh, God. I killed him just the same. His sister said he was seven. I still see all their faces—mom, dad, sister, grandmother. He was just trying to watch TV."

Zane began to sob. I grabbed his glass and handed him a box of tissues. I didn't know what else to do. He wiped his eyes.

"I've never told anybody that part. I mean, my squad knew. That stuff happened sometimes, even when you tried to prevent it. But it still rips at your guts. I-I didn't need to fire that many shots. But that sniper made us all angry."

He reached for his drink. We both took large swigs.

"It's four," I said.

"How's that?"

"Grief, trauma, guilt, and anger."

"Why were you angry?"

"Because of RT, Jake Breeley, Sheila Ritter, and Davey Shuster all died. And I was convinced his murder of Davey could never be proved. I bet he was getting ready to run."

He nodded.

"But you have one thing I don't—remorse," I said.

"We've got a lot."

I nodded. "But I'm in this hole and I don't know how to get out."

"I know what your pastor would say."

"Yeah, I know," I said, "but I'm too chicken to ask and too undeserving for God's mercy."

I swilled the rest of my bourbon.

"Got any idea why I smell gunpowder during my nightmares?" I asked. "I smelled it the first day I met RT, but I've only seen it in movies." I was rambling. "I bet there hasn't been gunpowder around here since the Union Pacific railroad was blasting its way through the west. When was that—mid-1800s?"

Zane stared at me, wide-eyed, his jaw slack.

He cleared his throat and said, "Ah, yeah. Something like that. The Golden Spike…connected the east to the west in Utah. Never been good at dates."

He thought I'd lost it. Maybe I had. Wait, was I the gunpowder? A keg ready to ignite? I just needed the detonator—which RT's murder of Davey supplied. Truly, I had exploded. Zane's voice brought me back.

"I called that Lutheran services place. They sounded nice. They've worked with vets before."

"Good. You should go."

He studied me as he always did. "I'll make a deal with you. I'll go if you go."

"Me?"

"You're screwed up aren't ya? Nightmares and smelling gunpowder."

"And hay."

"There ya go. Don't you want to get straightened out or at least find ways to sleep at night?"

I thought for a few moments then said, "Here's a condition for you. Get a job. It's the only place to feel normal. You have a business degree. Brian's dad works at Cabela's. Maybe he can get you on."

He sat in quiet contemplation for a few minutes.

"Come on," I said. "We deserve root beer floats. By the way, bourbon, or even your Jack Daniels is pretty good over vanilla ice cream. And you still need to get laid. If you want to make it with Melanie, put that uniform on again. Just make sure all the buttons are sewn on tight."

He was still laughing as we started down the stairs.

I was screwed up, but I'd been smart enough to do my Christmas shopping early. I got Uncle Bill a pair of cowboy boots—custom fitted for his wide feet. I investigated my mom's closet and discovered she favored Donna Karan and Ralph Lauren, so I got her a nice sweater, as well as a fancy tablet. Brian's present certainly wasn't a trip to Colorado—he seemed to get into trouble there—but I did book a summer vacation to Chicago and Wrigley Field. I thought about a winter trip to someplace warm, but I selfishly decided to stay home so I could work, my one good anchor to normalcy. For Kayla and Paul, and with Paul's approval, I arranged the delivery of a black and white Husky mix puppy. Kayla named him "Boo" for his black coat.

But I received the best present of all—an enclosed structure we dubbed the "Fort." It turned out to be Kayla's idea that Paul designed and he, Bill, James, and Lew built in the old Eldritch barn—a place they knew I wouldn't go. With careful planning, they constructed my own little club house that sat right on top of Big Leo. Without disturbing the natural geography of the bluff, they inserted this wood and glass hut between and anchored by two rocky outcroppings. It could seat four, and included an asphalt-shingled roof, padded benches, windows with a vista in every direction, and a vented coal stove that would keep me warm whenever I felt the desire to escape. The location also gave people in the big house a view of the fort—and its inhabitants—from our upper story windows. The bench seats lifted to store coal, a first aid kit, a lantern, and the binoculars I'd left on the bluff from my last surveillance of RT.

Gazing at it from my bedroom window, I felt like a kid with a new tree house. It was installed a couple of days before Christmas, just before a blustery snow hit that kept us all inside. Derek and Vonny acted as excited as I was, but we'd need to wait for the weather to clear. As pleased as I was, I stubbornly refused to let any vehicle drive across my wild land to deliver me to my gift. I'd wait. The only time in my knowledge that vehicles had driven on the rough land was when police and an ambulance needed to rescue me from Miss Gulch after I killed Salt Eldritch. Even then, the trucks drove east from the highway and never neared Big Leo.

Christmas Eve day brought me to a crisis. I'd been stewing over whether to confess the full account of the

Shootout. Should I tell someone the complete truth? It wouldn't be any therapist I would see after the New Year. I'd go a few times just as encouragement to Zane, but I didn't see how they could really help me when I didn't plan to disclose the truth. I was concerned that telling Brian would make him afraid of me. I could tell my mom, but was it fair to burden anyone with the truth? Nebraska didn't have husband-wife immunity, but we did have parent-child immunity, which meant she couldn't be forced to testify against me. Then again, that would require the disclosure of her true identity and that admission would lead to a whole new set of problems and inquiries.

Still, I needed to do something to stop my descent. My black heart pushed me over the edge—at times I could stop my plummet by going to work or by spending time with Brian or my mom or by giving a young girl a puppy—but every day I plunged back into the darkness.

Maybe this was a secret I needed to keep to myself. I protected the information of so many people—I was the secret keeper. And anyone I told would point out what I already knew. I acted alone; I needed to face the consequences alone.

So that afternoon, I donned my snow pants, boots, and my heaviest winter coat then trudged out to Big Leo to see my new present, the Fort. Beverly whispered to me and I thanked her. Shrouded in a black mist of evil, one I couldn't escape on my own, I climbed the bluff to bare my soul and beg forgiveness. I went to meet with God.

ALONE IN THE WIND

About the Author

JUDY Bruce is a resident of Omaha, Nebraska, USA, where she lives with her husband and two children. She has a law degree from Creighton University. Judy is the author of *Voices in the Wind* and *Death Steppe: A World War II Novel.* She maintains a website at judybruce.com and a blog at heyjoood.com.